Titanic: Legacy of Betrayal

By

Kathleen E. Kovach
&
Paula Moldenhauer

Edited by
Marjorie Vawter
www.shevetwritingservices.com

Content Review by
Lynnette Horner

Cover Credit:
The Creative Pixel
thecreativepixel.com

Titanic: Legacy of Betrayal
www.titaniclegacyofbetrayal.com
ISBN-13: 978-1477445808
ISBN-10: 1477445803
Copyright © April 2012 by PK Publishing, Ltd

Scripture quotations are taken from the King James Version of the Bible.

Dedication

This novel is dedicated to the brave men and women of the *RMS Titanic*. The tragic deaths of over 1,500 men, women, and children on April 15, 1912, are matched only by the painful memories of those who survived. Our historical protagonist, Olive Stanford, is not meant to represent the worthy and honorable people who experienced this tragedy. Human nature is complicated, and our story illustrates both the heroic and the selfish within us all.

The story you are about to read is fictitious.

Thomas Keaton, Olive Stanford, and Charles Malcolm Stanford III are figments of our imaginations, as are the characters in the contemporary parts of this novel. Every effort has been made, however, to accurately portray the real people and settings of this historical story. In some instances exact quotes have been used, taken from the accounts of survivors. In others, the events portrayed lean heavily upon documentation. So as not to interrupt the fictional narrative, there is no reference within the story itself to these instances. However, historical notes placed at the end of this story give proper credit, greater historical understanding, and links to historical sites for readers interested in learning more.

Prologue

We both knew I would get what I wanted, no matter how unconventional. An incredulous flicker passed through Mr. Williams's controlled features. The slightest rise of my left eyebrow squelched his resistance. With a deposit of cash, a signature, and a shake of the lawyer's hand, the deed was done.

I left his office leaning hard upon my favorite cane, the one topped with the silver bird whose wings stretch forth.

I, too, make ready for flight.

Faithful Earl, watching from a parking place across the way, brought the Studebaker around. His gray, pressed uniform honored my status, and an unusual sensation beat in my chest. I thought it gratitude, but perhaps it was merely pride. Earl may be the only person in the world I truly like. With great ceremony he opened the door and settled me into the automobile. Then he offered his customary stiff bow and returned to the driver's seat. He didn't even flinch when directed to Cunard Pier—good man. Together we've avoided West Twelfth or Fifteenth streets, and most certainly the docks, since that day thirteen years ago this month.

I detest April.

Perhaps others in their twilight years have made peace with the twists and turns of their earthly existence. But not I. There are events I would pretend never happened, but it is hard to fool one's self. Earl would be surprised to know what goads me to the pier this day. Perhaps he would be disappointed in me—or maybe all these years he has known me as I really am and has not been fooled by the facade.

Either way, we will share in the grief of this place.

As Earl directs the automobile down West Twelfth, the sun pours through my window, making the car too warm with mocking cheerfulness. Would that the sky was dismal and dripping tears as it had the last time Earl drove me down this blasted avenue! Memory of his trembling hands upon the steering wheel shortens my breathing.

Tragedy began long before I planted a determined step upon that glorious, doomed ship. It was upon her we thought to hide, and hide we did.

Earl glances in the rearview mirror, worry and pain clouding his typically clear eyes.

"Drive on!" I punctuate my directive with a stab of my cane upon the floor. He drives forward, and a slip of Atlantic becomes visible out the window.

A single funeral verse haunts me. "There is a way that seemeth right unto a man, but the end thereof are the ways of death." If there is a Maker, He taunted me that day, depositing the verse deep into the recesses of my mind.

I've never had a moment's peace from it.

The automobile slows. Earl parks and awaits my next command.

"The door, Earl. I intend to stand a moment in solitude."

He nods and comes quickly to my aid. Beneath his driving gloves I sense tenderness as he helps me from the automobile. Or maybe I simply conjure kindness into his touch, so hungry is my wretched soul.

Slow, measured steps take me closer to the Atlantic.

Some say the ocean is beautiful. They speak of its sparkling waters. But as I gaze upon it today, it is dirty, dark, and menacing. More is concealed underneath icy waters than I dared hope possible. Yes, it was a calamity. Even now the cries of the unfortunate haunt my dreams whether awake or in repose. But the sinking of the *Titanic* was also our ticket to freedom.

Or so I thought.

Now I wonder if those who perished are the lucky who found liberty. My choices that dark, frigid night turned the lock on my lonely cell. There are only two men I've truly loved. One of them was gone long before I'd even heard of the *RMS Titanic*. And I lost the other that fated voyage.

Thirteen years fade as I remember stepping from the *Carpathia*.

I had moved down the gangplank stoic in my resolve not to give way to emotion, not to kiss the solid ground beneath my feet. I played my part to the end. The reporters rushed forward, snapping pictures of the *Carpathia* and her strange stock. Seven hundred and five of us, along with two little dogs, faced the crowd. There was the occasional quiet weeper, but most of us were resolute. We had braved the ravenous waters, and we would brave this hungry, swirling mass of humanity.

Those starved for lost loved ones were harder to face with such resolute control, but one look into the eyes of those who panted for the sensational, and our backs stiffened. Our collective grief was sure to line the already padded pockets of Mr. William Randolph Hearst and the sons of Joseph Pulitzer. As it turned out, Mr. Hearst's paper offered more of the ridiculous.

The cry of a gull brings me back to the present. The solitary tear tracing my cheek pays tribute to the heroic, dead and alive. Resisting the urge to wipe it away, I give myself to its eulogy, feeling the cool of its wet descent as the sea breeze whispers against my skin.

The hated clutching seizes my throat. My knees threaten to give way as the weakness claims me.

Earl rushes to my side, his own grief, shining wet in his eyes, adding insult to my own. "Is it your heart, again, Miss Olive?" Always the faithful servant.

I lean harder upon my cane. Shortness of breath prevents response. He stands with me, propping me up, until the episode passes. Nausea predictably follows as I cling to Earl's offered arm and take the few grueling steps to the Studebaker. He settles me in, pulling a light wrap from the front and tucking it around my lap and legs. Head against the back of the automobile seat, I am determined to finish my endeavors tonight. Mr. Williams will arrive in the morning to complete the tasks I assigned to him. The treasurers must be delivered safely to await their future.

Yes. All will be in final preparation this night. Perhaps some small grace will be afforded me on the other side because of this act.

And if there is any mercy left on this earth, I will not be asked to live through another anniversary of the sinking of *RMS Titanic*.

Chapter 1

April 2012, Portland
Ember

Contrary to popular belief, Friday the thirteenth would be Ember's lucky day. Putting her impeccable Saturn in park, she turned off the ignition and gazed with satisfaction at the "sale pending" sign in front of the grand old estate. No one thought she could turn this baby over with the failing economy, but she had.

The jangle of her cell phone brought her to the present, and Ember modulated the got-it-all-under-control voice that had helped her become the top sales associate at Wright Realtors. "Ember here."

"Good afternoon. Diana Warling."

Ember hated the way her stomach flipped at the sound of Diana's voice. "Diana! I hope everything is in order to finalize my loan on the sixteenth."

"I've scheduled our appointment for four o'clock."

Ember exhaled before replying. "Perfect."

"I feel it my duty to remind you that with the downturn in the economy, First National is more cautious than ever when it comes to small business loans. It was only the promise of your pending commission on the Dowling Estate that secured the proper signatures for your loan. Should something go awry—"

"I appreciate your concern, Diana. The estate will close as planned, April thirteenth." And, after all the years of kissing up to the boss, working insane hours, and smiling when she felt like spitting, she would march into Dean's office with a sweet little resignation letter.

"I look forward to seeing you on Monday, then, Ms. Jones."

Ember fought the urge to correct Diana as she hung up. Was it that hard to say her full name—Keaton-Jones?

Ember stepped out of her car and breathed in the sweet aroma of peach blossoms wafting toward her from the thick grove to the left of the mansion. She would not allow unfounded worry to ruin this perfect day. The warm sun settled upon her shoulders, and she took great pleasure in the clack of her heels upon the long, circular driveway.

Almost free.

Ember fought the girlish inclination to kick off her shoes and run across the lush green grass as she visualized the signage already on order, "E. E. KEATON-JONES AND ASSOCIATES: FINDING THE HOME OF YOUR DREAMS." She imagined it hanging above the bright green-and-white awning of the adorable cottage turned office.

Ember adjusted her silky burnt orange collar and surveyed the manicured lawn with its flowering trees, dual fountains, and gorgeous landscaping. While she had no need for this opulence herself, she enjoyed brushing up against it, especially when placing property into good hands. Selling a home wasn't only about commission, even though this one would bring twice the payoff of any previous sale. Her job was all about matching the perfect home with the perfect owner. And she'd done it this time. Julia Gyle belonged here like a dolphin belonged in the sparkling Pacific, only a few hours to the west.

She watched the black Jaguar glide down the drive toward her and imagined the parties Julia would throw—and the grandchildren who would play hide-and-seek in the peach and apple groves and splash in the fountain, making the mansion a home. Ember's phone rang as Julia stepped from the Jag. She frowned at the unfamiliar number and silenced it. The warmth in Julia's handshake was genuine, and the woman's bright eyes shone as she looked beyond Ember toward the stately house.

Ember smiled. "Ready for one last tour before she's all yours?"

* * * *

She should probably have returned the call she missed, but she needed a few moments to celebrate. Indulging in the rare luxury of taking off early, Ember checked the temperature in her sunken tub—the feature that had convinced her to buy the sprawling condominium on the top floor. She added a few more drops of pomegranate bubble bath and placed the goblet containing spritzer with lime on the beige tile. After pulling her thick auburn hair into a messy bun, she allowed the fluffy white towel to slip from her body and stepped into the hot, soapy water. The afternoon sun streaming from the upper window painted rainbow colors upon the iridescent bubbles.

It was strange the way expectation rolled through her in clashing waves of joy and fear. She couldn't wait to call all her own shots—but hated it that one sale could make or break the whole thing.

Such was life.

A couple more sips from her spritzer, and Ember leaned against the back of the tub and closed her eyes. No more worries. Tonight was for celebration. If only she could share the moment with Grammy Nora . . .

Her cell phone rang. Ignoring it, Ember sank deeper into the water, letting time pass unwatched. When the bath grew tepid, she climbed out and wrapped herself again in the fluffy towel. Then she plopped on her bed and dialed voice mail. Frowning, she grabbed paper from the nightstand and doodled the name of the company the caller represented: Williams, Williams, and Smythe. The second call was from the same person. She took a deep breath and returned it.

"James Williams here."

"Mr. Williams, this is Ember Keaton-Jones."

"Ms. Keaton-Jones, I'm grateful to speak with you. As my message indicated I'm with Williams, Williams, and Smythe, a law firm in New York City. I've been trying to contact Beverly Keaton-Jones on a matter of utmost importance. Our research indicates she is your mother."

What kind of trouble had Beverly gotten into this time? "May I ask the nature of your business?"

"It is somewhat confidential—and quite time sensitive. Do you know how to reach her?"

"My mother travels extensively."

"We tracked her to Rome, but not beyond. Does she carry a phone?"

"She prefers to check in at her convenience." And rarely with her only daughter—or her mother for that matter. Ember bit her lip as tears stung her eyes.

"Our records indicate that your mother never married, and you are her only child."

"Yes." Lucky me.

"Since we're unable to contact her, I'm authorized to speak with you. I'm representing the wishes of the late Olive Stanford. Her instructions are explicit. I'd like to take the red-eye to Portland and meet with you first thing in the morning to discharge my duties. As I mentioned, the matter is urgent."

"Who is Olive Stanford?"

"I presumed the name might mean something to you."

"It doesn't."

"Further discussion would jeopardize the appropriate carrying out of our client's wishes. I'm to meet with you personally, Ms. Keaton-Jones. I can only tell you that our business has something to do with Mrs. Stanford's dealings with Thomas Keaton. Is there a convenient place to meet with you eight o'clock tomorrow?"

The blood drained from her face. Thomas Keaton. Grammy's grandfather, who had disappeared after surviving the sinking of the *Titanic*. Foggy family history spoken about in hushed, disapproving tones taunted her. "There's a Starbucks close to my home."

After finalizing their plans, Ember hung up the phone and shuffled to the kitchen. She poured herself a glass of filtered water only to leave it, untouched, on the countertop while she trudged to the living room to turn on the evening news. She curled up on the couch but soon realized that she wasn't listening to the broadcaster. She clicked off the TV, grabbed her cell phone, and had half-dialed Grammy Nora before realizing what she was doing.

Oh Grammy. How I miss you. Beverly hadn't even made it for the funeral—probably didn't even know Grammy was gone.

Ember had called all Beverly's friends, but if they knew where to contact her, they weren't telling. Ember had been left to make all the arrangements alone. She stared at her cell, grasping for a name of a friend—anyone—she could call. But Grammy Nora was the only one she'd trusted with her private life.

And Grammy Nora was gone.

* * * *

It wasn't necessary to shower at four a.m. to prepare for an eight o'clock appointment, but since Ember wasn't sleeping anyway, that's what she did. She chose her clothes carefully, dressing in her favorite power suit—a fitted black blazer over an expensive red shell. With her four-inch heels she could look most men in the eye, giving her equal footing, something she desperately needed this morning. She locked her door, took the elevator to the front of the complex, and strolled down the street. The walk would calm her nerves.

Trisha, her favorite barista, greeted her. "The usual?"

"Please."

"Out a little early, aren't you?"

Ember toyed with the idea of telling Trisha the whole, crazy story. But one didn't tell family secrets to the Starbuck's lady. "A little."

Trisha made small talk as she prepared Ember's Americano, and the tension in Ember's stomach eased. Funny how seemingly insignificant relationships were comforting in the face of the unknown. Ember shoved everything out of her mind as she sipped her coffee and soaked in the bustle of the world around her. In the corner a man with salt and pepper hair read the newspaper. Two teenagers giggled as they left with tall white chocolate lattes. Trisha flirted with a young man in khakis and a pressed blue shirt.

As the business at hand pressed upon Ember again, she feigned hunger and bought a vanilla scone, just for an excuse to chat with Trisha and get her mind off her fears.

She chose a round table for two in the corner and had just sat down when an older gentleman with snow-white hair entered the shop. As he surveyed the patrons instead of the menu, she surmised this was the lawyer, James Williams. Evidently his research was thorough, because he came directly to her and extended his hand. After a brief greeting and introduction, he said, "May I?" and indicated the chair.

"Of course." Ember surveyed the man's Armani suit, polished shoes, and crow's feet around his eyes.

"My mission today is quite unusual."

Ember pushed back the sarcastic "Ya think?" that wanted to roll off her tongue. "Mr. Williams, as far as I know, the last anyone in my family heard from Thomas Keaton was before the *Titanic* sailed in 1912."

The older man's eyes twinkled. "I've had a lot of interesting cases over the years, but this one has the most intrigue." He leaned over the small table. "Instructions were given to my grandfather of Williams and Williams—no Smythe in those days—by Olive Stanford in 1925, two days before her death. My grandfather's business journal indicates that he visited her in her home, where she gave him this key." Mr. Williams pulled an envelope out of his breast pocket and laid it on the table. "Then she gave him most unusual instructions, which he wrote up in legal jargon and both of them signed. I have the document for your perusal." From his briefcase came another envelope, legal sized and yellowed. He handed it to her.

Ember shuddered as she reached for the envelope. She pulled out the document and scanned it. Her mouth went dry. "Is this saying what I think it is?"

The lawyer leaned back. "It seems you are in the possession of a hundred-year-old secret to be revealed on the anniversary weekend of the sinking of the *Titanic* to the eldest remaining descendent of Mr. Thomas Keaton. The key is to a safety deposit box located in one of the oldest and most prestigious banks of New York City."

Ember's gaze dropped back to the document. "It says here the box is to be opened Friday, April thirteenth."

"Unfortunately I have left you little time to make travel arrangements. I had thought to contact your mother—and only called you after having exhausted every lead."

"I can't travel then. I could go today—or after the sixteenth."

Mr. Williams's steady gaze never faltered. "I'm afraid that is quite impossible. You did read the entire document."

"Yes, but surely other arrangements can be made."

"I'm afraid not. Mrs. Stanford was quite explicit. The safety deposit box is to be opened, by you and only you, on the thirteenth, before noon. If you are unable to do so, the contents of the safety deposit box are to be retrieved by me at precisely five minutes after twelve, and I am to deliver them to the museum of my choice by five o'clock. If you are unable to participate in this process—or simply not interested—I am most eager to carry out my duties. This particular case has been passed down, father to son, for generations in my family. We've long speculated as to the contents of the safety deposit box. You may say it's been *our* family secret for almost ninety years."

"What did Mrs. Stanford have to do with my great-great-grandfather?" Ember tried to tamp down her exasperation. "Do you have any clues as to what's been hiding in that box?"

"I know nothing more than I have told you."

"But it has something to do with my great-grandmother Elizabeth's father, Thomas Keaton." Ember grimaced.

"So it would seem."

"And the contents will be made public if I don't retrieve them."

Mr. Williams's eyes reflected a glimmer of compassion. "Yes."

"But I can't possibly be in New York on the thirteenth." Ember hated the rising panic in her voice. "I'm closing the biggest deal of my life that day. My future depends on it."

Mr. Williams reached across the table and gave her hand a grandfatherly squeeze. "It would seem that you must choose between your past and your future."

Ember jerked her hand away and stared out the window. "How important do you think this is?" She looked back at the man.

"Important enough to hide for a hundred years. Important enough that Mrs. Stanford couldn't take it to her grave."

"Is there monetary value?"

"Ms. Keaton-Jones, I have told you all I know. The decision is yours now." His voice softened. "Take the key. Should you choose not to use it, I will employ the duplicate just after noon on the thirteenth." He stood and gave a formal little bow. "I wish you the very best." With that Mr. James Williams picked up his briefcase and disappeared out the front door of Starbucks.

Ember stared at the unopened envelope on the table before her. So much for Friday the thirteenth being her lucky day. She grabbed the unwanted intrusion into her life, slid her finger underneath the flap, and let the old-fashioned key fall into her palm. Its cold metal blazed into her skin.

Chapter 2

You know how this works, Ember." Dean's dark eyes never flickered.

She knew. Dean had waited for just such an opportunity to get his claws into her commission. There is no way her greedy boss would let her reschedule such a big deal. If she didn't make it to the closing, the sale would be Dean's, not hers. "You could agree to split the commission. It's done all the time."

Dean leaned back and put his feet on his desk. "But not required."

"You *know* I deserve it."

"Business is business." He gave a dry chuckle. "You don't follow through, I take the sale."

She fought for composure.

"The closing is day after tomorrow. I need a decision."

Ember set her chin and met his gaze. "Give me a few hours. I'll let you know first thing in the morning."

"I have a schedule."

How had she ever thought him attractive? "Don't even go there, Dean. We both know you'd drop everything to be the one to close the Dowling estate."

"Eight o'clock. No later."

Ember flinched at his gruff voice then crossed Dean's plush office in long strides. Why had she given so much of herself to this selfish, driven man? Men were all alike. She wanted to stomp her feet, to slam the door behind her, but she refused to give him the satisfaction.

It was raining again. Figured. She climbed into her Saturn and slammed the door. Cranking the engine and then cramming the gearshift into reverse, Ember peeled out of the parking lot.

The man's greed was out of control. She pointed her car toward US 26. Teary rivulets made their way down her windshield, interrupted by each swish of her wipers. Her boiling emotions gentled to a simmer as the miles splashed beneath her wheels in a wet mess. In less than an hour and a half she turned onto 101 and slowed to watch the ocean. Some people had comfort food; Ember had a comfort drive. It began in Cannon Beach and went south until she calmed. Today's drive could take a while.

The angry waves to the west were in turmoil, tossed about by the whim of an external force.

Like her.

Dean and his ego. He couldn't stand that she had landed the biggest deal the agency had seen.

How easily he took what was rightfully hers.

Drippy, dreary, dreadful day.

Ember released a humorless chuckle. Ember and the terrible, horrible, no good, very bad day. How many times had she read the story as a child? She loved the book, but there was no mother to rescue things at the end of *her* bad day then—or now.

She glanced at the clock on her dashboard and willed herself to think outside of emotion.

The facts: She could close on the biggest sale of her life and make enough to start her own agency, but it meant ignoring a hundred-year-old secret that might expose Grammy's grandfather to censure.

And it meant never knowing what had happened.

No it didn't. She could visit the museum. In dark glasses and a decorative scarf to hide her identity.

Then again the museum might not find anything too interesting in whatever the safety deposit box held, and the secret would be archived away where only a stuffy historian here and there would give it attention. Safe from prying eyes, but also beyond her reach.

Ember slowed the Saturn as it splashed through an especially wide puddle.

Unless, of course, the secret was interesting enough to make the news. And draw traffic to the museum. And cause them to up the price of admission—after a private showing to their biggest donors and the press corp.

So what if they did? Who would ever connect her to the whole sordid mess?

There could be money involved.

But what was the old saying? Something about a bird in hand.

The Dowling Estate. That was her bird, not the dubious contents of a safety deposit box.

The present and future. That's where she belonged, not in the shadows of the past. Ember exited the highway, turned around, and headed home. She'd call Dean at eight o'clock after she'd let him drool overnight.

She wasn't missing this sale.

* * * *

Bleary-eyed, Ember downed another cup of coffee—black—and stared at her monitor. It would take more than a quick makeup application to cover the dark circles this morning. She glanced at her watch. Other than breaking the news to Dean, there was nothing pressing until the closing tomorrow.

She should be relaxing.

Her fingers flew across her laptop, unbidden. She typed *Thomas Keaton* into Google, digging for anything on her great-great-grandfather. Eventually she found a record of his survival of the sunken *Titanic*. From there she followed links to a short blurb following the lives of survivors in the news after the sinking. There was a brief notation that fit the bits of family history she'd heard. Thomas Keaton abandoned his family after making it to safety, was traced to St. Louis then disappeared from all good society.

Lifting the framed picture from her desk, she traced the lines of Grammy's face and wrinkled her nose at her little-girl self, staring wide-eyed back at her. It was her favorite picture, taken on one of their rare trips to the beach. The ocean crashed upon a cliff in the background, its white spray adding energy to the photo.

Grammy had taken her the day after Beverly left for one of her "trips." Ember had cried long into the night, not knowing when her mom would return. The next morning Grammy greeted her with a picnic basket. She'd even taken the day off work.

"How important would this Olive Stanford thing be to you, Grammy?" She talked to the photo. "Surely you'd want me to close the deal, to seal my future."

Then again Grammy might want to know more about the event that had caused her mother, Elizabeth Keaton, so much pain.

"Could it hurt us in any way if this secret became public?" She put the picture on her desk. It had to be quite a story if Olive Stanford hid it for a hundred years. Not that Grammy was here to know or care. And would anyone really connect Ember to the infamous father of Elizabeth Keaton?

Typing Elizabeth Keaton into the search engine, she gasped when the third entry referred to Ember Elizabeth Keaton-Jones. Maybe it was easier than she thought to link her with the past.

When the cell jingled she glanced at the unfamiliar number. "Ember Keaton-Jones here."

At the sound of Beverly's high-pitched voice she sat up straighter. How long had it been—a year? More?

"Mom?" The word slipped out, breathless and irritating.

"Now, babycakes, don't you worry about me. I'm safe and sound."

I'll bet you are. "Really, Beverly, where are you? A cruise in the Pacific? A yacht south of France? I'll bet he has deep pockets."

"Touchy, touchy. Listen, Ember, I have only a moment, not long enough for one of your childish outbreaks. I was thinking about zipping in for a day or two. I could be there Friday. I called Mom, but she didn't answer."

"About Grammy—"

"Yes?"

Ember's stomach clenched at the impatience in Beverly's voice. "Um . . ." How could she tell her mom Grammy had been gone for two months?

"Really, Ember. I thought you had quit stammering."

"I . . . need to—"

"Do you have something to say or don't you?"

Hot tears filled Ember's eyes. "Not a thing, Mom. Not a thing."

"Whatever. I'll be in town Friday morning. Tell Grammy to make up my old bed. I'll be traveling alone."

"But—"

The click was followed by the silence of twenty-nine years. *Thanks, Mom. You always know just what to do when I'm needy. Invade my world and make it worse.*

The clock flashed 7:59. She stared out the window at the gloomy Oregon morning, complete with fog. Then she dialed. "The Dowling Estate is all yours, Dean. I have to take care of that family emergency."

Ember punched the OFF button on her phone before she could hear him gloat. A few clicks of her mouse and she was booked on the next flight out. No way would she let her mom in the middle of all this. If there was money, Beverly would blaze through it. If there was a dark secret, Beverly would exploit it. The whole world would know, and Beverly would bask in the attention without a thought for what Grammy would have wanted.

To leave the secret in the hands of a museum historian was one thing—to take the chance her mother would get her hands on it was quite another.

* * * *

It was the bright yellow daffodils that caught Ember's eye. She grabbed two bunches from the grocery store display and hurried through the checkout and to her car. She had plenty of time before she had to catch her flight. The lump already in her throat swelled to the size of a baseball, or so it felt, when she pulled up to Grammy's white-shuttered home. With a click of her key she was inside, frowning at the closed-up, musty smell.

She'd cleaned it top to bottom after the service, but a closed house was still a closed house.

Her favorite antique vase, the one Grammy promised to her, still sat in its proper place. She loved the cream-colored, hand-painted porcelain with the gold-tipped edges as much today as she had when she was a little girl. The vase stood tall and elegant on its pedestal. She used to pretend it had once graced the throne room of a castle.

Perhaps she should take it to her townhouse, but she'd wait until Beverly decided what to do with Grammy's home. Until then she'd rather have the vase gracing the decorative table by the picture window, fresh flowers in it every week, just like when Grammy was alive. She picked up the vase and glanced at the bottom as she always did, enjoying the distinctive scroll of her grandmother's hand declaring two simple words: For Ember. Carrying the precious vase to the kitchen, she emptied the old water down the sink and took the lavender roses, now tinged with brown, to the outside trash. Once the delicate vase was filled with the cheery yellow flowers it felt as if Grammy were home again.

Almost.

With a ragged sigh she sat at Grammy's desk and pulled a piece of her favorite stationery from the drawer. The pen trembled in her hand, making her penmanship shaky and untrue. *Dear Beverly, I tried to tell you when you called, but couldn't find the words . . .*

By the time she finished telling her mother of Grammy's death, her cheeks were smudged with mascara and her eyes puffy. Knowing the battle against emotion was lost, she climbed onto Grammy's bed and curled up with her pillow for a cleansing cry. Then she marched to the bathroom and splashed several waves of cold water on her face. After reapplying her makeup, Ember made Beverly's bed in the extra bedroom and placed the note on top of the envelope containing the legal papers from Grammy's lawyer. It surprised her when Grammy chose to leave the house to Beverly. She said the gift might finally give her daughter roots.

Fat chance.

Ember sighed and forced her thoughts back to the business at hand. One last detail required attention before she flew to New York. She curled up in the safety of Grammy's recliner, dialed Diana, and explained she could no longer afford the loan on her dream office. When her throat constricted, she feared she couldn't finish the phone call. But with practiced determination Ember controlled her voice as she thanked Diana for her hard work and expressed her regrets. Then she made a cup of chamomile tea and returned to Grammy's chair. Grammy had often made tea for Ember when life hurt.

Ember sipped slowly as she stared out the picture window. It was finished. She'd put a firm hand to the door of the future and shut it. Now to door number two: the past. Ember stood and began the ritual of closing up the house. With a gentle brush of her fingertips across the yellow flowers, she left the haven of Grammy's home, hid the extra key where her mother was sure to find it, and headed to the airport.

Thankfully the line through security wasn't long that afternoon, and she walked briskly to her gate, enjoying the almost woodsy, northwest feel of the decor. Soon Ember stood in the stuffy airliner, waiting for the unending stream of people ahead of her to store their carry-on bags and take their seats. Typically, she loved to fly. She loved the sense of freedom, the way the world as she knew it became more and more distant, looking first like kiddy land and then dollhouse pieces. The car she worked so hard to pay cash for, her townhouse, the realty office—none of them were big enough for her to recognize in the myriad of miniatures.

The separateness of it all usually distanced her from responsibility and stress, if only for an hour or two. But this flight was different. When Portland became a tiny playland, panic reigned instead of freedom. Ember's breathing grew rapid. She'd taken one step too far from reality.

Her seatmate leaned toward her. "Are you afraid to fly?"

Ember shook her head.

"Asthma?" The concerned face peered at her. The woman signaled the flight attendant. "I think she's having trouble breathing."

"Fine." Ember managed to gasp. "I'm fine."

The attendant and the woman stared at her.

"I . . . just need . . . a moment. Really . . . fine." Ember leaned back and closed her eyes. She felt the flight attendant move away but sensed the concerned gaze of the lady next to her. Ember willed herself to breathe naturally. She hadn't had a panic attack in years. She wouldn't succumb now. Maybe if she kept her eyes closed, the woman would quit staring.

Guilt. That was what was eating at her. Leaving her mother to arrive at Grammy's without even telling her. When her breathing slowed, she sat up and pulled out her laptop. Maybe work would get her mind off things. But it only reminded her of all she'd sacrificed in making this decision.

She pulled up a document she'd downloaded from the Internet and scanned the firsthand account of the sinking of the *Titanic*, written almost a hundred years before. What could possibly be in that safety deposit box, and what did it have to do with Thomas Keaton, Grammy, and her?

But no matter how she tried to distract herself, guilty thoughts buzzed around her like gnats on old bananas. The flight had become a grueling exercise in mind games. When the wheels finally touched the runway at JFK, Ember exited the plane and rushed to a private corner, where she tried to call Beverly. Whoever answered said she'd reached a pay phone in Florida. She moaned. Even when Ember tried to do the right thing, Beverly made it impossible.

Dragging her carry-on behind her, she went in search of a taxi. She was more than ready for a hot meal, hot bath, and long sleep. However, once at the hotel, fed, clean, and warm, sleep eluded her. Every direction her mind traveled led to assaulting thoughts of Beverly, Grammy, the lost sale, and the secret of the safety deposit box. She saw one a.m., two, and three. Then she must have dozed off. When she gasped and jerked straight up in bed, afraid of the water filling the little rowboat she was on, it was four. With a moan, she put the pillow over her head and counted sheep.

Chapter 3

Plink. Plink. Plink.

What was that noise? Jeff Dawson lifted one eye to look at his alarm clock and groaned.

6:00 a.m.

Plink. Plink. Plink.

He'd only been in his sister's spare room in the basement for a couple of nights, so he wasn't yet familiar with all the sounds in the spacious two-story Victorian. Had he not turned the faucet off all the way in the bathroom? Or maybe the toilet was leaking.

Plink. Plink. Plink.

He tried to burrow deeper into his nephew's blue and green comforter. He didn't mind the spaceships with humanoids and aliens warring in galactic scale. He loved that movie. Oh, crud. Now he had the theme song in his head.

6:01 a.m.

Plink. Plink. Plink. Plink. Plink.

The leak, or whatever it was, came faster with more insistence. He'd probably have to get up and fix it before leaving for Dad's shop.

Another groan escaped his lips. Last month he was a young upstart in an Internet company dreaming of going global. He shared an apartment with his best bud from college and life was good.

Now, however, he found himself unemployed, one of the first to get cut from the flailing company, his buddy ended up in Vegas honeymooning with the girl of the week, and Jeff was living with his sister, her husband, and their 3.4 children.

Another groan. He hoped to be out of there and on his own before the baby was born. Late night crying. Uncle Jeff babysitting and changing toxic diapers.

Plink. Plink. Plink. Plink. Plink. Plink. Plink. Plink. Plink. Plink.

He threw the comforter off and yelled at the ceiling. "What is that noise?"

Giggles came from the bathroom down the hall, and he saw it. A small tin cup set precariously on the shelf above his bed. A tube ran from his bathroom, thinly disguised in the floral border and anchored with cup hooks to the wall. The tube dripped water into the cup.

"No freakin' way!" He bolted upright, but not in time to avoid the drenching.

Three nephews of various sizes rolled out of the bathroom in spastic fits of laughter.

"Happy Birthday, Uncle Jeff!"

Friday the thirteenth. The traditional day of torture on his birthday. He should have known.

* * * *

It was pitch-black in the cave. Funny how a place with no light could be warm and cozy. Trying to ignore the muffled tune in her head, Ember pushed deeper into the feathers. Who had made such a safe, soft resting place? And why did music play in this remote area? But the sound was insistent, and it brushed away the last tendrils of Ember's sleep.

She stretched. The room was dark. Gotta love hotel curtains. She rolled over and gasped.

10:45!

Oh, no! She'd set the hotel alarm and her cell phone! She pushed the buttons on the alarm clock, moaning. It was set for seven *p.m.* But where was her cell? She followed the muffled music until she found her cell atop a washcloth, behind the closed door of the bathroom.

What had the lawyer said? She had to be to the bank before noon to open the box. According to Google maps the bank was a fifteen-minute walk from the hotel—or she could hope a taxi would be faster.

Flipping on the coffeepot she threw on her clothes and ran a brush through her hair. She skipped half her makeup routine but dressed professionally. Grabbing the complimentary Styrofoam coffee cup provided by the hotel, she rushed from the room. One look at the crawling New York traffic, and she set out on foot, carried by a flow of bustling humanity.

She quickened her pace, weaving through the crowd. Her Google map, printed at home before she left, seemed accurate until the last left turn when the street sign proclaimed Lincoln Avenue instead of Buffalo. Seriously! Google was failing her now?

Ember glanced at her watch and fought the tears pricking her eyes. After everything she'd sacrificed for today's mysterious deadline, there was no way she could be late. She studied the information on her paper and took her best guess.

* * * *

Jeff stood in the heart, no, the corroded artery, of Old Town Portland and hovered at the entrance of the elderly brick building, hating the mustiness of generations. Not only had the architectural ogre been there too long, with its cracked foundation and graffiti, so had the contents of the antique shop his dad ran. He'd inherited it from his father who renamed it *Dawson & Son*, which prompted Dad to ask each male offspring to continue with the family legacy.

Jeff was his last hope, the first three forging their own ways in different directions.

It wasn't supposed to be this way. Jeff swallowed hard as he stepped over the threshold, leaving his future on the sidewalk to be trampled by the smattering of pedestrians.

"Hey! There's my boy!" Dad grinned from under his graying bushy mustache. He stood from the tall stool behind the counter, a glass enclosure that held "valuable" pieces of tarnished jewelry. Rounding the counter, he joined Jeff in the middle of the store and slapped his shoulder. "Glad you're here, son."

Jeff winced, not because of the masculine love tap, but because he knew Dad expected him to make the shop his career, especially in light of his recent failures. He loved the old man, but as soon he developed his own computer company, he was out of there.

"You're just in time. I need to log in last week's acquisitions." He handed him a ledger and a pencil.

Jeff looked at the items in his hand. Why not a stone slate, hammer, and chisel? Following Dad to the backroom, he asked, "Wouldn't it be more efficient to list your stuff onto a computer? I could create a spreadsheet for—"

"I don't have a computer here."

Blood drained to Jeff's toes. "You don't have a computer? How do you conduct business?"

Dad moved to the counter and reached behind it. He pulled out yet another ledger and a receipt book. "I don't trust machines. If anything goes wrong, it will be because of me, not because of system failure." He replaced the items and motioned for Jeff to follow him into the storeroom.

Jeff glanced around the small space, where a high window layered with grime filtered the sun into a dusty ray of amber light. A bare bulb hung from the middle of the ceiling with a chain dangling from it. Dad reached up and flicked it on. It helped, but only minimally.

"Dad." Jeff fanned the ledger in his hand toward the ancient items stacked on shelves and lining the floor. "These were all fancy new inventions at one time, all to help make someone's life easier. Computers are no different. They're just today's convenience that will someday be tomorrow's antiques."

Dad scratched his nose as he seemed to consider this idea. "How many people do you know clamoring to get their hands on a Commodore 64? Or the first cell phone? Now, take this coffee grinder." He picked up a wooden box with a crank on the top and cradled it in his large hands as if it were a living, breathing thing. "Near mint condition. Made by Yorkcraft. See? It still has the label on the bottom." He turned it over. *Sure 'nuf.* "I've had three calls from people looking for this in the last month. I finally found one. Each customer is willing to pay top dollar for it."

"And how much might that be?"

"Bet I can get a good hundred-and-twenty for it."

"Wow, Dad. You and Mom could retire on this sale alone." A hundred twenty dollars? Seriously? Jeff hoped there were more valuable items lurking in the dark corners of the storeroom.

Dad's bushy brows drew together in a frown. "It's not about the money. It's about preserving our history."

"And computers are part of my history."

"Well, right now inventory is your future. It will probably take you all morning to log these in." He pointed to the wall, the entire length supporting five shelves, and each shelf filled with junk. History so thick it would choke a feather duster. "Get crackin', son."

About mid-morning, Jeff heard a familiar feminine voice. "Helloooo!"

"Back here, Mom!" He stood from his cross-legged position in front of the lowest shelf and stretched his stiff back. "I'm in the Wormhole."

Mom appeared in the doorway. "Wormhole?"

"My name for the storage room. I'm convinced it's an anomaly designed to suck me into the past."

She laughed, the sound refreshing. "Where's your father?"

"He left to pick up an old thing for a customer. Don't ask me what."

"I came here to see you, anyway. Happy birthday." She kissed his cheek. "I'm making your favorite dinner for tonight."

"Strawberry stuffed clams on the half shell?"

She frowned, her eyes reflecting confusion. "Your other favorite."

"Octopus tentacles in cranberry sauce?"

Light dawned as she apparently realized he was teasing her. "Lasagna."

"Ooo, with Limburger cheese and a dandelion salad?"

She wandered away from him and pulled out the receipt ledger from under the counter. "I should make those things and force you to eat them. That would teach you."

Jeff leaned on the glass and glared at the ledger as Mom opened it to the current date. "Mom . . ."

"What's wrong, baby?" She continued to glance over the page without looking up.

"How receptive do you think Dad would be if I converted all of his paperwork to a computer? You know. As a surprise."

Mom smiled, still not looking up. "So, you've had that conversation."

"Huh?"

Finally, she met his gaze. "You're not the first. All of your brothers have tried to drag your father into this century. RJ even looked into moving the shop to the Pearl District."

"The Pearl District." Jeff allowed his mind's eye to imagine *Dawson & Son* on the same street as artsy bistros, galleries, specialty shops. "Wasn't The Pearl as run-down as this neighborhood once?"

"Yes, it underwent an urban renewal project a few years ago. Best thing that ever happened to Portland."

"Imagine," Jeff said. "Taking something old and ugly and turning it into something classy."

"Let me show you something." She led him into the office, the only other room off the showroom besides the Wormhole. Three large file cabinets lined one wall. He'd seen them in there before, but never paid much attention to them. She opened the top drawer of the first cabinet. Ledgers were crammed into it, dating back several decades.

Mom tapped the books. "There are more in boxes in our basement."

He pulled one out, opened it, and saw yellowed pages with inky scrawling penmanship. "Why has he kept all of these?"

"Every entry here represents a loving object that he had to let go. You may think your dad is living in the past, but he's only trying to allow the past to live in the future. Does that make sense?"

No.

She went on. "Someday he may bend a little and join the rest of us in this age, but right now, he's happy doing things the way his father did them." She ran her fingers along Jeff's jaw line. "It wouldn't hurt you to take a lesson from that page."

Kicking and screaming, Mom. Kicking and screaming.

Chapter 4

A hushed respect for the past seeped into Ember as she stepped into the bank at 11:35. Its polished and somber atmosphere slowed the pace of her rushing feet, but not the urgency of her heart. She wrinkled her nose. The old building smell wasn't unpleasant, but it was distinct. It reminded her of an old library with dust trapped in books—or mildew in marble. Someone had taken pains to restore, not remodel the elegant structure, and the results were captivating. Only the modern dress of the tellers kept her grounded in the present as she sought her contact. When the woman stepped forward, stunning in a taupe suit with matching pumps, Ember felt her stomach do its little flip-flop thing. She hoped the stress didn't show on her face as she offered her hand and introduced herself.

The woman shook it but gave no further introduction. "This way, please."

A security guard joined them, and Ember suddenly felt like a small-town girl as she followed the woman through the large main lobby, framed with teller booths that looked like something out of *It's a Wonderful Life*, only backed by more money. They traveled down a dim hall, lit by beautiful antique sconces spaced high on the walls.

When they stepped into an elevator and the woman pulled a bronze gateway across the front, Ember caught her breath. Reliving the panicked experience on the airplane, she modulated her breathing.

The woman turned a cool gaze upon her. "Ms. Keaton-Jones?"

She forced a smile. "I'm fine."

Their descent ended with a little bump, and the woman led her through a short entryway then unlocked a copper-colored, accordion-style gate that folded into the wall. Next came a heavy steel door, which she unlocked by pushing numbers on a keypad. Finally, Ember was ushered into a vault lined with bronzed boxes, each guarded by an antique lock. Ember noted the cool, dry temperature and thought fleetingly that it was probably constant year round. The woman stopped in front of a plaque with elegant numerals declaring the box to be number one hundred seven. It looked larger than most of the other boxes, and for a moment Ember was paralyzed.

The woman inclined her head toward the box and then made a show of glancing at her watch. For the briefest moment Ember felt a wild, unjustified hatred for the impatient, cold woman in the taupe suit. The woman stepped back next to the security guard, who waited just outside the vault.

Swallowing hard, Ember willed her hand to rise and insert the key. As she pulled open the door, the first thing that caught her eye was a little polar bear, dressed in a sailor suit. Puzzled, she pulled it out and stared into its black, beady eyes, thinking they held a lonely kind of wisdom. She pushed down the irrational thought and picked up a yellowed envelope. A lump formed in her throat as she read the inscription across the front: *To Mrs. Josephine Keaton and Miss Elizabeth.* The penmanship looked masculine and hurried. She paused to put the letter into her purse, flat against the lining so nothing would wrinkle it.

The last item was quite large. Ember placed her purse and the bear on the table in the center of the room before reaching into the safety deposit box and pulling out a wooden container that looked to be made of polished cherrywood. It was made from two pieces—a larger bottom and a lid—held together by leather straps, metal hinges, and an old-fashioned latch. It took both hands to lift it to the table.

Before her lay treasures of a hundred years before. Olive Stanford, whoever she was, had planned this moment. Should she open the envelope in her purse or the mysterious cherrywood chest? She reached for the copper latch, and her breathing became short. Great. The last thing she needed was another panic attack. She took a slow breath, but still didn't feel like herself. It would be wiser to wait until she reached the hotel room to face the secrets hidden in the envelope and the cherrywood chest.

"Guard!"

"Yes, Miss?" The older man in his security guard uniform stepped forward.

"Is there a way to transport this box more easily?"

He went to the side of the room where a dolly leaned against the wall. "Do you want me to load it?"

"Yes, please." Ember slipped the straps of her purse over her shoulder then pulled the white bear close. The guard loaded the chest onto the dolly and followed Ember out of the vault. Suit Woman locked the doors behind them then led the way once again.

The trip up the elevator and through the long hall lasted forever. Ember imagined the box full of everything from golden coins or carefully stacked one hundred dollar bills to old letters, jewels, or secret documents. As she stepped into the main lobby, a quick glance at her watch told her it was 11:55. Suit Woman directed them to a large desk in the corner where the security guard placed the chest next to Ember, who sat the little bear on top of it. She filled out paperwork declaring she had claimed her property and closed out the safety deposit box.

Just as she contemplated securing a taxi, a deep voice called her name. She turned to discover James Williams, accompanied by a plump, gray-haired woman, dressed in a periwinkle suit and pearls that reminded Ember of Grammy.

"I see you made your decision, Ms. Keaton-Jones. Good for you." His smile was genuine. "Mrs. Williams and I are here on standby, but it looks as if our services aren't needed."

The woman extended her hand, energy emanating from her bright blue eyes. "So you are the famous Ember Keaton-Jones who had to travel across an entire continent to clear up our family secret."

Mr. Williams flushed. "I'm afraid my wife has been intrigued by the Stanford situation, Ms. Keaton-Jones." He shot his wife a pointed glance then looked back at Ember. "And while I did share some of the story with her, I can promise she is the voice of discretion."

Ember held back a smile at the concerned look on Mrs. Williams's face.

"You mustn't think James unprofessional, dear. After forty-eight years of marriage, we share the interesting tidbits of our day, but he would never compromise a client—and I usually know when to hold my tongue." The woman's gaze was clear and trustworthy.

"No worries, Mrs. Williams."

"Call me Cynthia!"

Ember fought back a chuckle as Mr. Williams stiffened. "I'm Ember."

"Well then, Ember, what can we do to help you? We could drive you back to your hotel, couldn't we, James? And we really should have you join us for lunch. It's always nice to have friends in a strange place. Isn't that right, James?"

Mr. Williams shrugged at Ember then grinned at his wife, looking more like a schoolboy than the elegant professional Ember met in Portland. "Cynthia and I would be delighted, of course." He leaned forward. "There's no use arguing with the head of the house, you know," he spoke in a stage whisper.

Cynthia swatted his arm and batted her eyes at him. "Now why would you say such a thing?"

Some of the tension fell away from Ember. "Your help would be appreciated, Mr. Williams. I was just trying to decide the best way to transport these." She gestured toward the bear and cherrywood container.

"My wife has crossed from business associates to friends. You might as well call me James."

Cynthia eyed the stuffed bear.

"Would you do the honors?" Ember handed Cynthia the toy, and Cynthia cooed over the little bear as Ember lifted the chest.

James led the way to the Lincoln Town car. "Would you prefer to keep the box with you or placed in the trunk?

"Do you mind if it sits next me?"

"Of course not."

Once in the car, Ember gave directions to her hotel. Cynthia turned toward the backseat. "What's in the box?"

"Cynthia!" James tone was firm.

"I'm sorry, dear." Cynthia sighed. "James would never ask you, but I know he's as curious as I am."

"Let her have some time with her discoveries, Cynthia. It will likely mean more to her than it would to us." His low tone was kind but definitive.

"I appreciate your concern, Mr. Will—James. And he's right, Cynthia. The truth is I don't know what's inside yet. I felt . . . emotional when I pulled it from the safety deposit box and decided to wait for the privacy of my hotel room to open it. I have no idea how its contents will affect me."

Cynthia's lips formed a little pucker. "Sometimes I get carried away. You'd think I'd have a little more self-control at my age! James is right, of course. I'm sorry I pried."

Ember gave a light squeeze to Cynthia's shoulder. "I'd be curious, too."

"Thank you. Now, how about lunch? James promised me an afternoon on the town—he's semiretired, you know, so he doesn't have to return to the office. He just works a few cases to keep from getting bored. Let us treat you to a good meal and show you around the Big Apple."

"She probably would prefer some time alone, Cynthia—to go through her things."

"But she has to eat, don't you, dear?"

Suddenly Ember did feel hungry—and the thought of company on such a monumental day was soothing. "Could I have an hour?" She'd check out the contents of the box then take a break from this whole surreal world Mrs. Olive Stanford had created and enjoy Cynthia's energy and companionship.

It would be good not to be alone for once.

Chapter 5

She was delaying, of course.

Ember circled the box she'd placed on the hotel room floor. Instead of opening it, she grabbed the little white bear and flopped onto the bed. She lay on her back and held it above her, staring into its beady black eyes. Why would someone pay a hundred years of safety deposit box fees to house a stuffed animal?

"I'm going to call you Bear. Not very original, but until I figure out why you're so important, that's the best I can do."

Ember sat up and tucked Bear into the crook of her arm. With a hard swallow she grabbed her purse, retrieved the aged envelope, and studied the careless scrawl across the front. Flipping it over, she noted the broken seal. Had her great-great grandmother opened it or some other intruder? She started to pull the letter from the envelope but suddenly felt like an interloper herself. "Maybe we should start with the box?"

Bear didn't answer.

Still clutching the toy, Ember walked to the box and flopped, cross-legged, in front of it. Frowning at the slight tremor in her fingers, she reached for the latch and lifted the heavy lid. Once it lay open, she discovered both the lid and the bottom of the box held four cylindrical cardboard containers fitted carefully into pre-shaped holes. Each container had a number on top, beginning with one and continuing to eight. Ember pulled the first from the box, which she now suspected had been built just for these containers, and opened it. She went to the bed and gently urged the contents onto the comforter. A strange wax cylinder emerged.

What the heck?

She grabbed her laptop and typed wax cylinders into Google. A quick search brought new meaning to the eight containers. Wax cylinders were used before World War II by businessmen, who dictated letters and documents into a Dictaphone to be transcribed by their secretaries.

Ember eased the cylinder back into its container and returned it to the cherrywood box. What was on the cylinders, and who had dictated the contents? The historical magnitude settled upon her, and she reached for her cell phone. Something like this—intact wax cylinders from almost a hundred years before—belonged in the hands of a professional, not hers. She Googled local museums, picked up her cell, then faltered.

"Maybe we should read the letter first, Bear."

Bear's knowing gaze was unsettling.

Ember reached for the envelope and using a light touch pulled three brittle pages from it. She quickly looked to the end of the missive for the signature.

Thomas.

Of course.

She began reading from the top.

April 8th, 1912

My Dear Josephine,

As promised, I attempt a faithful narrative of my travels. I know your inquisitive mind and would not deny you the joy of experiencing this journey, though secondhand. One day I will achieve the means to make separation unnecessary, and I will never have to leave you like this. We will pack up little Elizabeth, a nanny, and any other children given us and travel together. Until then I will try to satisfy your curiosity. I must warn you though, my darling, that being of the male persuasion I know I shall fail in the attempt to give you all the little details that cause you such interest.

Perhaps I can assuage some of your disappointment at my poor attempts at narrative by telling you the most important of my thoughts. They are, by far, of you. Yes, I work hard to improve our situation, but, dearest, I do it for your comfort—and that of our sweet Elizabeth. How I love and miss you both! I long to pull the pins from that silly bun of yours (that never really contains your curls) and run my fingers through your

thick, lovely tresses. I'm glad Lizzy got your hair—full of wave with that
delightful tinge of red brightening the brown.

With a little gasp Ember reached for the clip that held her
hair and released it. She stared across the room into the hotel
mirror as curls tumbled onto her shoulders, brown with a tinge
of red, wavy and unruly. Setting the letter aside, she fell upon
her pillow and stared at the ceiling.

* * * *

The aroma of French cuisine and gentle strains of Pachelbel
calmed Ember as James pulled a chair for her at the table
clothed in white. The old-fashioned courtesy warmed her. She
couldn't remember the last time a man had treated her with
such careful attention. Then again except for her short—and
bitter—time with Dean, she hadn't dated much, and nothing
about that experience gave her any hope a man was worth the
effort.

Still, something about the way James immediately turned his
attention to Cynthia and settled her into a chair at the elegant
Café Affaire gave Ember a twinge of longing. "Have you two
really been married for forty-eight years?" She hadn't meant the
question to sound so abrupt.

Cynthia's tinkling laughter put Ember at ease. "And I've
even enjoyed most of them. Do you have a boyfriend, dear?"

"Really, Cynthia—"

"Now James, this is girl-talk. Ember doesn't mind." Cynthia
turned her bright blues eyes on Ember. "Tell me all about
him."

"There isn't anything to tell. I mostly focus on my work."

"I can't imagine life without James. I met him when I was
nineteen—just a baby! You wouldn't have known him back
then—he wore a black leather jacket and slicked down his
hair—just like Fonzie from Happy Days. It aggravated his
father something terrible. In fact—"

"The waiter is coming, sweetheart. Do look at your menu."

Cynthia reached for her menu then peered over the top of it
and winked at Ember. "We'll chat later."

Ember grinned at James, who sat stiffly in front of her, a slight blush across his handsome, genteel face. He caught her gaze and shrugged. "I eventually did settle into the family business and learn to wear the proper attire." He swept his hand down the lapel of his pinstriped navy suit.

"But I still have that leather jacket under plastic in the closet." Cynthia sighed. "He looked so—hot—in it."

James's eyes widened, and the blush became bright red. Ember couldn't help it, her laughter bubbled out and Cynthia's giggles joined in. When the sound of James's low chuckle mingled with their revelry, Ember felt as though she'd come home for the first time since Grammy died. She loved how comfortably the meal progressed. Conversation flowed freely, the wine, handpicked by James, was superb, and their meal mouthwatering.

"Thank you for not asking about the box." Ember looked toward the couple when the conversation lulled.

"I gave James my solemn promise." Cynthia reached for her husband's hand then wriggled her eyebrows. "He said he'd make it worth my while."

Ember grinned. "I'd love to tell you about it."

"We're all ears." Cynthia leaned forward, eyes sparkling.

"The box is full of wax cylinders—the kind used by businessmen in their Dictaphones before World War II. There were eight of them, preserved in cardboard containers. The box was designed for perfect storage and protection."

James gave a low whistle. "Dictaphone cylinders. In all our years of pondering the contents of the safety deposit box, I never once thought of that."

"Who do you think dictated them?" Cynthia leaned back. "It could be anyone."

"More than likely it was someone connected with Olive Stanford—or perhaps the woman herself." James rubbed his chin. "My grandfather told me about the day he met Mrs. Stanford. He said she was quite thin and sickly but sat ramrod straight in her fancy parlor and handed him the key like she was bestowing a great treasure. He would have loved to have known the contents of that safety deposit box."

"Cylinders and a teddy bear. What a strange old woman to keep such things secret for a hundred years." Cynthia took a generous bite of her *mousse au chocolat.*

"There was also a letter."

"From Mrs. Stanford?"

Ember shook her head. "No. Thomas Keaton. It was begun on April 8th, two days before the *Titanic* sailed." She looked away from them. "It's a love letter to his wife." She hated the husky sound that crept into her voice.

Cynthia reached out and squeezed her hand. "Your great-great-grandfather."

Ember nodded. "The family was told he lived through the sinking, but his wife, Josephine, didn't find him among the survivors, and he never came home. I found reference to a newspaper clipping on the Internet that said he was traced to St. Louis. Then he just disappeared."

Cynthia gave a sympathetic *tsk* around another mouth full of mousse.

"When I saw the movie, *Titanic*, I pestered my grandmother until she told me what she knew of our family history." Ember paused and toyed with her dacquoise. The first bite of meringue, lemon filling, and fresh raspberries had awakened her palate, but now it was hard to enjoy.

"Grammy said Josephine was heartbroken when Thomas never came home. She'd given up her life as a socialite to marry a young man with great promise but little money, thinking he was in love with her. She was destroyed when he abandoned her and Elizabeth. She eventually remarried, but he turned out to be a philanderer. Great-grandmother Elizabeth was unhappy in marriage, too. Grammy never told me much about her father, but when she was of age she went to court to take her mother's maiden name, so he must have been a real honey. I guess the Keaton women are destined for heartbreak."

"But why would Thomas write a love letter then disappear?" Cynthia's dessert was gone, but she cut a small piece of James's strawberry savarin as she spoke. He didn't even seem to notice.

"Grammy said Josephine eventually decided the love she thought they had must have been a farce to help an ambitious man climb in society. Josephine's father didn't approve of her marriage, though they hoped he'd come around, especially after Elizabeth was born. Josephine thought Thomas must have decided her father wasn't going to share the wealth. When they struggled financially, he just moved on."

"Is that what you think, now that you've read the letter?"

Ember cleared her throat. "I don't know. . . . I couldn't . . . finish the letter."

"Why ever not?"

"Cynthia!"

"It's okay." Ember smiled at James and shrugged. "I'm not really sure. I just suddenly felt so . . . connected to them, despite the years and generations between us. I just couldn't read on. Maybe I needed to come back to the twenty-first century—to reality—have lunch with two delightful new friends, and let the past be for a few hours."

"James said you gave up a lot to unearth the family secret."

A knot formed in Ember's throat. "My dreams. I was about to close on a deal that would have secured a small-business loan. I wanted to start my own realty."

"I pray your journey will be worth your sacrifice." James's quiet voice caressed Ember.

"And so do I." Cynthia grinned. "As Maria would say, 'When God closes a door, He always opens a window.'"

Ember grinned at Cynthia's perfect imitation of Julie Andrews. "That was Grammy's favorite movie."

"You must have been very close to your grandmother. How long has she been gone?"

"Two months. But it feels like forever." Ember frowned at the crack in her voice. "She was my best friend and more like a mother to me than my own." Her final words were barely a whisper.

"I hope you don't think I'm too intrusive, dear"—Cynthia grabbed Ember's hand again—"but I want to keep in touch. Would you let me be your new friend? I have Facebook."

Ember laughed. "That's one friend request I won't ignore."

"And I have a plan for tomorrow."

"I'll bet you do!"

"The museum is running the *Titanic* display for the hundredth anniversary of the sinking. James and I would like to take you, since you don't fly home until Sunday. We won't take no for an answer."

James cleared his throat. "Unless, of course, no is your answer."

"I'd love it!" Suddenly the dacquoise tempted Ember again. She took several slow bites, allowing the tang to roll on her tongue before swallowing.

After the meal, James treated Ember and Cynthia to a carriage ride around Central Park. The huge Clydesdales tossed their massive heads and snorted as the three climbed aboard. Ember settled in across from the Williamses, who sat close together, holding hands and beaming at her. James pointed out local attractions, and then everyone fell silent.

Ember closed her eyes, breathing in the damp air of spring, feeling the start and stop of the horses, and listening to the *clip-clop* of their huge feet upon the pavement. She imagined what it must have been like one hundred years before, when horseless carriages mingled with those like the one they rode in, socialites married dreamers, and great-grandmother Elizabeth waited for her father to return. "I met her once, you know."

"Who, dear?"

Ember opened her eyes and felt the assault of the New York day. "Great-grandmother Elizabeth. She was glad I had her name."

"Her name?"

"Elizabeth is my middle name—after her. My mother chose Ember, and Grammy talked her into adding the Elizabeth. Grammy adored her mother, despite her disdain for her father. Said Elizabeth was a survivor, and I would be, too."

Cynthia patted her hand again, a gesture Ember was quickly becoming attached to. "I'm sure you are."

By the time James dropped her back at the hotel, Ember felt connected to the old couple in a way she hadn't been connected to anyone except Grammy for many years. The thought of another excursion with them gave her the courage to ride the elevator to her empty hotel room and pick up the letter by Thomas Keaton.

She made herself a cup of tea in the hotel coffeepot, flinching at the coffee taste barely disguised by the chamomile tea bag she'd brought from Grammy's house. She fluffed her pillows and propped them against the wall, climbed under the covers, and leaned back. It took three lingering sips of the tea before she found the courage to read the rest of Thomas Keaton's letter. As she read, her heart pounded in her ears. If the letter before her was true, it changed everything.

Chapter 6

Dawson birthdays were always celebrated in the house where they grew up. Achingly delicious aromas wafted from Mom's kitchen, reminding Jeff of his favorite Italian restaurant. Hints of sauce, cheese, and garlic with a tinge of chocolate cake made his stomach growl.

Jeff sat in the living room awaiting his special dinner while everyone arrived, beginning with the three culprits who had doused him with water that morning.

"That was pretty funny, wasn't it, Uncle Jeff?" Ten-year-old Bobby smiled so big all of his crooked teeth showed.

"Yeah. Hilarious. You better hope my pillow dried out, or I'll have to challenge you to a water-gunfight at high noon." He reached out to tickle the lean ribs, but the preteen was too fast and squirmed away.

"Tickle me, Unca Jeff!" The youngest of the culprits at age four, Marcus, fell into Jeff's lap and erupted into a fit of giggles.

"I'm sorry for this morning, Jeff." His sister Claire entered the room from the kitchen. She said the words, but her expression suggested she was probably in on it. "Anything else happen today?"

"You mean any more Friday the thirteenth shenanigans?"

His oldest brother entered the room. "Shenanigans? How long did you hang with Dad today? You're using antiquated language."

"It's the Wormhole," he murmured, more to himself than in answer to the question. He glanced up at RJ squinting one eye. "Are there anymore birthday surprises I can look forward to?"

RJ chuckled. "It wouldn't be a surprise if I told you, now would it?"

Great.

"Dinner's on the table," Mom called from the dining room.

All five of his siblings—two sisters, three brothers, and their spouses—clamored for their favorite spots while the children were corralled at a separate table. All but a couple of infant nieces who kicked pudgy legs and slapped their highchairs in anticipation of a shared bread stick broken in half.

Jeff sat to Mom's right. Watching the rest of the family, he realized this had been his spot since he was little so that Mom could take care of him. Everyone in the room, with the exception of the children, had a mate, even Lacie who had pushed out of the womb a mere ten months before him. Did that make him the world's oldest rug rat?

During Dad's prayer, Jeff internalized that observation. Today he was turning thirty, and what did he have to show for it? A failed company and all his worldly possessions crammed into his sister's basement. Even though his eye was on technology, he was forced to work around old, dead things at the antique shop. His life sucked.

He missed the "Amen" and sometime during his musing, a plate of lasagna appeared in front him. He plunged a fork into the soft noodle, and it sprang off his plate, cheese, sauce, and meat landing in his lap. Every person at the table laughed except Mom, who stood quickly and issued a reprimand. "Ron Junior, Brett, and Matthew! All of you are grounded!" Before she could correct herself from slipping into the Mom-mode she'd been in for years, the rest of the family roared with laughter.

All but Jeff, who quietly removed the mousetrap from his plate and left the table to clean up.

Hours later, Jeff finally extracted himself from the pole in the basement. Back in the day it only took one roll of duct tape to immobilize him. Good thing RJ found the extra roll in Dad's toolbox. He allowed a mirthless snort at the sarcastic thought. He'd put up a good fight, though. This time his three brothers needed help from the two brothers-in-law.

Claire had brought an extra pair of pants for him, which he changed into before the duct tape incident. She tried to look apologetic, but Jeff was struck again with the thought that she may have been the mastermind. Thankfully, she offered to soak the tomato sauce out of his jeans.

As he entered the kitchen from the basement, he noticed Mom and Dad cleaning the last of the dishes together. Once again, he felt a twinge in his gut reminding him that not all was right with his world. When would he share kitchen duties with the love of his life?

"Did everyone leave?" he asked while poking his head into the dining room and scanning the silent house.

"Yes," Mom answered. "Didn't they say good-bye?"

"Yeah. They all walked past me and wished me a happy birthday while patting my head." He took Dad's dish towel and finished the drying. "Dad, don't they make breakable duct tape? Something with scores maybe?"

Dad chuckled as he grabbed a clean mug and poured freshly brewed coffee. Then he walked out without a word.

"He loves this stuff, doesn't he?" Jeff fisted his hip and regarded his mother.

"Half of what the boys do to you he did first to his little brother. Who do you think started the Friday the Thirteenth birthday tradition?"

That explained so much, mostly about Uncle Mark, who often flinched when he and Dad got a little rowdy.

Would he end up a flincher? He squeezed his eyes shut. Man, he hoped not.

He kissed Mom and thanked her for the meal then trailed Dad into the family room where he sat with his coffee and a newspaper.

"Guess I'll go now. See you tomorrow, Pop."

"Sit down a minute, son."

Crud. He'd hoped to avoid the heart-to-heart talk he knew was forthcoming after his first day working with Dad.

"It was great having you in the shop today."

Here it comes.

"Can you see yourself really learning the business, digging in to take over for the old man?"

"Dad, it was only one day."

"I know, I know." He held up a calloused hand. "But hear me out."

Jeff settled into the cushions of the couch and folded his arms.

"None of your brothers had the patience to run the shop."

"I don't think it was lack of patience, Dad. More a lack of desire."

"But you"—he pointed his finger, deftly avoiding the comment—"you have potential."

Was Dad delusional?

"The only potential I can see is if you let me computerize the shop. You don't even accept credit cards!"

Dad rolled the newspaper section he'd been reading and smacked the arm of his chair, as if he were disciplining the family dog. "No computers. I told you that already. We'll do it the way my dad did it. It worked for him—"

"But that's not the way the world works." Jeff leaned forward and pressed his elbows into his knees. "How profitable is this business, anyway? Are you and Mom doing okay? I noticed more noodle than meat in that lasagna."

Dad stood, and a vein popped from his neck. "We're doing just fine. We raised the six of you on what we made from that shop."

The shop and the home accounting business Mom began when Jeff was ten. How could Dad be so blind?

Jeff now stood to be almost eye-to-eye, wishing he had grown to be as tall as his father. "Let's get this clear. I'm only going to work with you until I can get my own Internet company up and running. Then I'm out of here!"

Dad's face registered pain. Oh, how Jeff wished he had pulled that punch to lessen its blow.

However, Dad countered with a right hook. "And how stable are Internet companies? Isn't that why you're working with me now?" Okay, maybe that was a sucker punch. "What are the statistics of those things going under?"

"Dad—"

"Stick with a stable job. *Dawson & Son* has been on that same corner for two generations. You can't get more stable than that."

Jeff sank back onto the couch and drooped his head to his clasped hands. "I'm sorry. I know what the shop means to you, but why try to push it off on someone who clearly does not love it like you do?"

"Push it off. Is that what you think I'm doing?"

Yes, that's exactly what he felt he was doing. "All I'm saying is let it be what it is. When you retire, sell it. Why does it have to stay in the family?"

Dad now leaned on the mantel over the fireplace, staring at the long dead ashes. "You coming in tomorrow?"

Jeff sighed. "Of course I'm coming in tomorrow. I need the money."

"Fine. I'll see you then." He walked out of the room, leaving Jeff wondering if he'd won that argument.

Chapter 7

If Ember hadn't seen how James and Cynthia's relationship worked, she might have felt sorry for James as Cynthia flitted about the museum, teasing him.

"Look at me, darling." Cynthia held up the boarding pass she'd been given when she entered the *Titanic* exhibit. Each pass had the name of a passenger, the class they traveled in, and a tidbit about their life. "I'm Miss Edith Corse Evans. Socialite, first class. Single and rich, thirty-six years old. And you, poor dear, Charles is it? You're traveling steerage—third class."

James grinned at his wife. "Good solid man, Charles. A forty-five year-old Norwegian carpenter. Salt of the earth."

"Oh my!" Cynthia grabbed James's arm as she read the rest of her card. "A few days before boarding a fortune teller warned me, 'Beware of water!'"

Ember glanced at her own card. For the morning she would be Alma Pålsson. A Swede, third class, traveling with her four children, all under ten. She prepared herself for the worst and went through the exhibit with a pit in her stomach. There was little chance someone in third class would survive—and she didn't even want to think about what happened to the children.

Full of artifacts actually retrieved from the ocean floor, the exhibit took her breath away. Ember grinned at Cynthia's antics as she pranced through the rooms, exclaiming over every beautiful item "she" would have used as a wealthy passenger. Eventually they walked down a replica of a first-class hallway. Gilded doors and fancy sconces on pristine white walls lined either side. A lush carpet softened each step.

Soon they found themselves in a luxuriant dining room. "Oh look, darling!" Cynthia pointed to a glass goblet. "What beautiful crystal. Imagine something so fine touching my lips. Oh, but you wouldn't have drunk from that down in steerage, would you, dear?"

As Ember admired ornate china rimmed with gold and decorated with the White Star insignia, her thoughts flickered to Thomas Keaton. Had he touched the silver fork in the display case or walked a hallway lit by the expensive sconces? An eerie shiver coursed through her.

Each display offered new insight into the wealthy, whose collective assets totaled more than six hundred million dollars, quite a sum for 1912.

"Those, my dear, were my evening jewels—for weekday dining only. I had several sets, of course."

Ember played along with Cynthia as she exclaimed over each new find, but then they turned a corner, and even Cynthia's playful mood sobered as they entered a stark hallway. Lit by service lights, its ceiling was latticed with exposed piping. A sound, almost like that of a steam engine on an old train, filled their ears.

They were entering the heart of the RMS *Titanic*. Tension rose in Ember as the annoying rhythm assaulted her hearing and continued, endless. What would it have been like to cluster in this barren place, listening day after day to the drone of the engine? Her overactive imagination saw poor, hungry people, stomping numb feet and blowing into red hands, cold and weary. The bitter reality of their impending deaths climbed up Ember's spine, creating goose pimples on her arms.

The artifacts in this area were simple—no gold, silver, or ivory here. No nameplate declaring its owner.

"Best food I ever had!" James took Cynthia's hand, and she turned a confused expression his direction.

Ember frowned. "Excuse me?"

"It may seem stark after all we just saw." James squeezed Cynthia's hand and smiled at Ember. "People say the third-class amenities were lacking, but for Charles Dahl the food would have seemed a feast. His cabin would have been warmer than his own home."

Ember tried to process James's comment as she looked to the middle of the room where a lighted silhouette of a lifeboat showed on the floor. No matter how comfortable the third-class passengers were aboard RMS *Titanic,* most of them died in the chilly waters when the great ship went down. Ember shivered as she stepped into the shadowed lines of the lifeboat silhouette, shocked by how small the boat was. It stood in contrast to the enormous propeller hanging on the wall. Ember joined with the others in reaching for it, awed that she touched history, feeling closer to Thomas. The sense grew as she entered the next room, walked to a huge block of ice, and pressed her hand onto it. How had anyone survived such temperatures?

By the time they emerged at the end of the exhibit, heaviness had settled over her. It deepened as she stared at a wall of 2,200 names, divided by class, most followed by a single, gut-wrenching word: deceased.

Ember scanned quickly, looking for Thomas Keaton. She knew he'd survived, of course, but it comforted her to see it in print. As soon as the positive feeling came, it twisted to anger. What a waste—for such a man to beat death only to remain forever separated from his family. For the first time she felt Josephine and Elizabeth's loss as her own. She shoved aside the vulnerable feelings that welled, unbidden, within. It was that stupid letter summoning emotions she'd never felt and contorting her insides.

She pushed aside concerns of grandparents she never knew and turned toward third class. A quick search for Alma confirmed her suspicions. Her malaise was complete when she found four more Pålssons, all marked "deceased."

James glanced up from where he studied the wall. "What do you know? The poor bloke survived." He pointed to the name Charles Edward Dahl, listed underneath the third-class placard.

Cynthia searched the wall then let out a whimper. "I can't believe it." Her eyes glistened as she turned toward them. "Edith didn't survive. I was so sure—a first-class woman, single and in her prime . . ."

James put his arm around his wife. "There are no guarantees."

"No." She sighed. "Not then or now."

"Look." Ember pointed to a name in first class. "Olive Stanford, survivor. And Charles Malcolm Stanford III, deceased. Do you think he was her husband—or son?"

James shrugged. "It would be interesting to know."

Ember found it hard to shake her somber spirit as they left the museum. She thought about all those names with *deceased* next to them. About Alma and her four children. About Thomas Keaton and the letter in Olive Stanford's safety deposit box. For the first time she wondered what Olive Stanford was doing with Thomas's letter. Then she remembered the movie, the water rushing into the ship, the screaming and panic. She envisioned the ship breaking in half and disappearing into the icy waters. What horrors had Thomas Keaton lived through? Did the tragedy change him? Make him desert his family?

When they stepped from the museum into a gray New York, complete with congestion, diesel fumes, and honking horns, Ember sighed. The gloom of the city matched the gloom inside her.

Cynthia grabbed her hand. "There's the most wonderful little bistro, right around the corner!" The next thing Ember knew she was ushered into a corner restaurant, fed the best Italian sub she'd ever tasted, laughing again at Cynthia's pert remarks. One didn't stay somber very long when Cynthia was near.

Soon the conversation turned to the cylinders. James surprised her by offering to help her get them home safely. They spent the afternoon in her hotel room, Cynthia dozing lightly on the queen-sized bed while James and Ember researched safe packaging, temperature control, and transportation of her treasures. James was thorough. By the time the Williamses left, the cherrywood box had been carefully packed in a climate-controlled container, the airport had been notified of the special needs of the box, and safe transportation had been secured.

Ember ordered room service, devoured a bowl of hot tomato and basil soup, and fell, exhausted, into bed. Before she turned off the bedside lamp, she pulled the letter out and read it slowly. Silent tears traced her cheeks. When she turned off the light she hoped she could sleep the morning away until she had to catch her flight. The thought of one more lunch with James and Cynthia touched upon her melancholy, and a measure of peace came as sleep descended.

The next day lunch went too quickly. Soon Ember and her belongings were crammed in James's car, which inched through traffic to JFK. James surprised her again as he guided her through every step of securing the safe transportation of her box, checking her luggage, and navigating the unfamiliar airport. Used to handling things on her own, Ember made a conscious effort to let James take care of her. It wasn't as difficult as she thought it would be. For a moment she fantasized, allowing herself to believe her father, should she have ever known him, would be so attentive.

As James took care of the details, Cynthia looped her arm through Ember's, talking nonstop. Her antics kept Ember from worrying.

And then it was over.

When Cynthia hugged Ember tight, pressing wrinkled cheeks against her own, Ember felt moisture on the older woman's face. She pulled back slightly, noting the sheen of more tears in Cynthia's eyes.

Cynthia lifted her chin as she stepped away. "I can't help it, you know. I've adopted you."

James stepped forward, slipping one arm around his wife's waist and offering the other to Ember, who gave him a sideways hug. "You'll have to keep in touch with her, Ember. Once my wife places someone in her heart, she is there to stay."

Ember looked down, blindsided at her own rush of emotion. She plastered on a smile before meeting their gaze. "I already accepted your friend request, Cynthia—and your phone number is stored right here." She lifted her cell. "I'll be in touch. I hope one day soon I can tell you what's on those cylinders."

"I can't wait!" The sparkle was back in Cynthia's baby blues as Ember stepped into the security line and waved her final good-bye. She noted Cynthia's wavy white hair, powder blue sweater, and signature pearls, then glanced at James's pressed shirt, gray slacks, and kind, proper face. She stored away the picture to pull from the files of her memory the next time she felt desolate.

Here, with these new friends, she'd found the one place in this big old world where she was known.

Chapter 8

Mother-tension assaulted her as the sun crept in Ember's townhouse window on Monday morning. No use delaying. Beverly would surely be at Grammy's. Ember dressed quickly, found she couldn't eat, and headed for her car. The first thing she noticed at Grammy's was the lack of a rental car in the driveway. The curtains were drawn, and there was no sign of movement.

When she stepped from her Saturn her feet felt chained to the cement. Ember straightened, forced steady steps to the front door, and took a deep breath before inserting her key. It wasn't even seven. If her mother was here, she wouldn't be awake.

"Beverly?" Her breathy tone irritated her, and she cleared her throat, then called more loudly, "Beverly?"

No answer. Ember pulled the door closed behind her, vacillating between relief and disappointment.

She flipped on the living room light. Something wasn't right. Suddenly she knew. Gone was Grammy's favorite painting. Gone was the antique chair. Her gaze darted to the picture window.

"Oh, Beverly! Not the vase!"

Ember rushed room to room, digging through cabinets for china and crystal, thrusting open Grammy's jewelry drawer in the bedroom.

Gone. All of it.

Ember punched the bed and flung the pillow across the room, then snatched it from the floor and hugged it. A faint scent of Oil of Olay night cream wafted toward her.

The sound from within started as a growl but morphed into sobs. They came from deep places inside, places she hadn't accessed in many years, way down in her gut. She curled into a ball on Grammy's bed. It was like birthing pain. If only crying would make it all come out.

She wept until the sobs subsided. Then she must have dozed because she started, awake and weary. She climbed off the bed and surveyed the room. Then she opened the closet door, pulled Grammy's fluffy purple robe from its hanger, and draped the robe across her arm. She grabbed the pillow, went to Grammy's desk and took her favorite pen and stationery. Then Ember headed for the car.

As she placed the items on the passenger side, a familiar car parked in front of Grammy's house. The car door opened. She flinched. "What are you doing here?"

Dean shrugged, opened his trunk, and lifted out a Wright Realty sign. "I'm selling the house for your mom. She said to tell you to clean out all the junk."

Ember lifted her chin, walked right in front of him, and stood nose to nose. "Dean, go to—"

"Watch it."

She stood her ground and glared at him. When he broke eye contact and looked down, she turned and stalked to her car. As she pulled away, Ember ignored his threats to fire her. She would save him the trouble. She drove straight to the office, cleared out her desk and files, and cleaned off the hard drive on the office computer. By the time she reached her townhouse, it wasn't even noon.

Not bad for a morning's work.

She trudged inside, put on her pajamas, and bundled up in Grammy's robe. She plopped in front of the TV and scanned Netflix for old movies, choosing *Beaches* and *A Walk to Remember*. Hugging Grammy's pillow, Ember stared at the screen. She would give herself this one day to wallow.

Tomorrow she'd deal with her life—what was left of it.

* * * *

Tuesday began the fourth day of his sentence.

"Morning, Dad."

"Morning, son."

And he knew that those few words and quick instructions would be the most profound things they'd say to each other the whole day.

In between inventory and dusting, Jeff whipped out his smart phone and began researching software development on the Internet. He thought back to the company he'd just left, what worked, what didn't. If he could learn from their mistakes, he could take it to a whole new level.

Mom had sent lunch for both Dad and Jeff, and he was eating his in the office when he heard the bell over the door jangle, another irritant from days gone by. Dad greeted the customer. A female voice drifted to Jeff as he stuffed the last bite of homemade roast beef sandwich into his mouth.

Man. I gotta marry someone who can cook as good as Mom.

The voice in the shop seemed austere, all business, unlike the other friendly customers who frequented *Dawson & Son*. He tried to imagine who was talking. Certainly it must be a middle-aged lady with her hair pulled so tight her eyebrows met her ears. But then the voice took on a desperate tone.

He wiped his mouth, downed the last of his soda, and threw the can into the recycle box. Jeff considered recycling a small victory to drag Dad into the twenty-first century.

He wandered into the showroom with one eye on his phone and the other on the woman—a pretty woman his age, but with the bun he'd imagined—standing at the counter. What was that she just brought in? A pillar candle? Her hands pressed against his gleaming Windexed counter as she explained to Dad what she needed.

"What do you know about these things?" she asked, her large brown eyes pleading.

Dad placed two fingers inside the cylinder and lifted it carefully, his pupils dancing as he took in the entire thing from left to right. If it had been a fine cigar, he would have sniffed it.

"This is a wax cylinder from a Dictaphone. I'd say probably"—he examined it once again—"era early nineteen hundreds."

"A Dictaphone?" Jeff asked. "Like a secretary uses to dictate something her boss has recorded?"

"Yes, however . . ." Dad disappeared behind the counter and pulled up a catalog. He licked his thumb and began flipping through the pages. "It was a much larger device than the modern ones. I have a picture here somewhere." He gave up on that catalog and bent down to retrieve another from under the counter.

Jeff realized it would take forever to find the item the old-fashioned way, so he Googled the word Dictaphone and had it in a matter of seconds.

"Here, Dad. This what you're looking for?"

Dad's balding head slowly came into view, like a fleshy, graying sun attempting to rise on a gloomy day. His eyes registered horror as he locked them onto the phone sitting on the counter. Then, as he rose to his full height, his gaze jerked to Jeff and his eyebrows met each other in a severe frown.

"Yes." Dad's professional expression replaced the we'll-talk-about-this-when-we're-alone face. "Yes, this picture is similar to the Dictaphone that would have recorded this cylinder."

"What do I do with it? I have seven more at home."

"Seven?" Dad reached up to his thinning hair and gripped both sides. "You have eight cylinders in total? And they're all in this excellent condition?" When he lowered his hands he looked liked Doc Brown from the movie, *Back to the Future*, the first one, when Marty ends up in 1955 and Doc is younger but still having a bad hair day.

Jeff asked, "What is a cylinder? What was it used for?"

"A businessman would dictate into the machine, here." He pointed to the offending cell phone and the clear image on the screen. "He would speak into this tube with the small funnel on the end. The voice would travel through the tube to a membrane with a needle attached. The needle would inscribe a record of the vibrations into the wax tube. That's what made these little grooves." He indicated the side of the cylinder without touching it. "To listen to the cylinder, the speaking tube would be replaced with another tube with a stethoscope-type ear piece. The secretary could then listen to the scratched-in voice and type what she heard."

While the woman seemed to be processing the information, Dad continued on, clearly excited to be sharing what he knew. "Dictaphone is an American brand name, but has eventually been generalized to include any kind of machine that records voice to be transcribed later. Music used to be played on the cylinders, but they were replaced with wax discs and played on the gramophone."

The woman and Jeff looked at each other then back to Dad. "Gramophone?" the woman asked, apparently just as clueless as Jeff. Ah, a woman after his own heart.

Dad's animated face fell. "You know. Phonograph. That plays records?" He made a motion with his finger, like he was stirring a large pot.

"You mean, like a turntable?" She quirked her head to the side.

Dad took off his glasses and ran his hand down his face. He motioned to Jeff's phone. "You got anything on there about a Gramophone, era early nineteen hundreds?"

Jeff brushed his finger from bottom to top of the phone and another image came into view.

"That's it! Haven't you two ever seen one of these things before? Even in old movies?"

Again, the two younger people looked at each other and shrugged.

Dad shook his head. "I've failed you in your education, son."

While the woman continued to ask questions, Jeff picked up his phone and continued to surf through the Dictaphone links. Soon, he interrupted them.

"It says here the information on the cylinder could be recorded onto a CD. That would probably be easier for her."

The woman's face clouded over. "Would anyone hear what's on them in the process?"

Jeff looked further at the site. "Yes. It seems so."

She shook her head. "No, I would like to find a machine and listen to it in privacy."

"Let me see that again." Dad reached out and examined the cylinder. "This one plays on a phonograph, I think. That might be easier to find. Let me jot down the information on here and I'll research it more thoroughly. Then I'll get back with you."

The woman replaced the cylinder into the box. "Either way, you don't have a machine here that would play these."

"No, but I can find one for you. Leave your name and number with Jeff here. He'll spend the day on the phone looking for your machine."

The day? On the phone? Kill me now. "Dad, I can probably find it faster—"

Dad put a hand on the cell phone Jeff held in his palm and gently removed it then slipped it into his shirt pocket. "Land line."

Jeff stormed out of the room, into the office. Just before he slammed the door, he noticed the shocked look on the woman's face. Too bad. Maybe she'll take her business elsewhere. A place where technology was appreciated, if such a place existed in the antiques world.

Chapter 9

Ember sat at the kitchen table, sipping coffee, researching antique phonographs and Dictaphones and getting a pit in her stomach. How could she be sure the one she chose was compatible, worked, was a reasonable price? She pulled a piece off her bagel and cream cheese and stared at the screen.

She sighed. Already word had gotten around that Ember was no longer with Wright Realty, and she'd had a few agencies inquire about her availability. But before she got locked in, she needed to deal with the past. And to deal with the past she had to figure this stuff out!

There was still the option of putting the recordings on CDs. But that meant sending them off to a lab and exposing a stranger to the contents. . . .

She was so over her head.

Maybe the man from *Dawson & Son* would follow through on his promise to help her. He seemed nice enough, but his son had an attitude. What kind of a man let his dad boss him around—then slammed doors like a child? He had to be at least her age. She shut her laptop and finished her bagel.

Like a magnet drawn to the object of her speculations, she went to her walk-in closet and pulled cylinder number one from its cherrywood box. She eased it from the container with two fingers as the antique dealer had and turned it over and over in her hands. It was a good thing she had Grammy's robe. She'd turned the air conditioner up to keep her closet at a constant cool temperature.

Ember sighed. Sometimes she felt she needed a top, like they had in the movie, *Inception*, to spin and ground her in truth. This whole thing was surreal. Maybe the cylinders would be the top, explaining Thomas's letter and sorting out her family history.

She stared at the wax grooves, cut by a stylus almost a hundred years before. What secrets did they hold? A chronicling of old business transactions? Something about the *Titanic*? The voice of Thomas Keaton himself? Or Olive Stanford, whoever she was? The only connection Ember could make between Olive and her great-great-grandfather was that they both sailed the *Titanic*—and Olive's strange unveiling on the anniversary of its sinking seemed to point to that connection. Maybe Olive Stanford was Thomas's rich mistress. They'd met on the *Titanic*, both first-class passengers. Had she seduced him with her money? That would explain him never coming home.

But if she died in 1925 an old woman, wouldn't she be too old for Thomas?

Ugh. That was just sick.

Ember sighed and looked at her watch. Too much time on her hands. She might have enough savings to put off taking another job, but could she stand the lack of tasks to keep her busy?

She carefully returned the cylinder to its case and put it away. Then she walked to the kitchen, opened the refrigerator, saw nothing of interest, and closed the door. The ring of her cell phone was a welcome interruption.

"Hello?"

"Mrs. Keaton-Jones, this is Ron from *Dawson & Son*. I think we've found your phonograph."

Ember's pulse quickened.

"My son called shops up and down the coast—spent most of yesterday at it. Max, over at Dewberry Harbor owns a shop called SOMETHING OLD. He has one at a good price. It doesn't work, but he thinks it could with a little tinkering. He's not sure. He doesn't do that sort of thing."

"Do you know anyone who does?" Ember grabbed a pen to write down leads.

"You're talking to him."

"Oh?" She dropped the pen.

"Since you're not a collector, the phonograph won't do you any good if we can't make it work. I'd like to meet you at SOMETHING OLD. I could go on Saturday. It's a bit of a drive, about two hours down Highway One. If I think I can fix the machine, I'll help you negotiate a good price. If I don't, we'll have had the opportunity to investigate a machine almost one hundred years old. Not a bad reward for a few hours' investment of time."

This wild goose chase was going to milk her savings. "How much?"

"Fifteen dollars an hour to fix the machine. Wouldn't charge you for the trip. I'm always up for interacting with new antiques."

"What's the catch, Mr. Dawson?"

"No catch. I just do business the old-fashioned way. Customer service and integrity. And call me Ron."

Uh . . . Okay . . .

"Oh, and I'd like to bring my wife along. She loves Dewberry Harbor, and I thought you might be more comfortable with another woman around."

Was this guy for real? As Ember wrote down the address for SOMETHING OLD she determined to stay in public places. If Ron didn't come with his wife, she'd watch her rearview mirror after their appointment. The man was too good to be true.

* * * *

Jeff hustled to the shop on Thursday morning. He hadn't planned to be late, but one of the nephews had dragged his feet during breakfast and missed his bus. Jeff offered to take him to school and tried to call Dad to let him know he'd be about forty-five minutes late, but no one answered. And since the man didn't own an answering machine, he couldn't leave a message.

So frustrating!

He asked Dad once how he could run a business when people couldn't get hold of him.

"Someone is always here. Never had a complaint."

"But if you're on the phone with someone else, you'll probably lose customers who can't get through."

Dad shrugged and looked at him as if he were missing a wire connection and Dad couldn't figure out how to get him working normal again. "They'll call back."

Feeling rebellious, Jeff had decided to stop for a Starbucks after dropping his nephew off. He opted for the longest name on the menu, hoping it would take them longer to fix it. Pleasantly, the Cinnamon Dolce Crème Frappuccino hit the spot.

Jeff now entered the shop, his nephew excuse ready on his lips, but once the bell above the door ceased its clanging, the quiet struck him. Normally, he could hear Dad rooting around in the storage room or talking on the phone in the office if he wasn't in the showroom. The door had been unlocked and the OPEN sign had been flipped over to the outside, so Dad had to be there. Maybe he just stepped out back to dispose of the trash.

No. Jeff had done that the night before.

"Dad?" A disconcerting silence greeted him.

As he moved to the back of the counter, a shoe came into view.

Oh, God!

Dad lay on the floor. Was it a robbery?

His eyes were open, but glassy, yet he seemed to be breathing. His face looked odd, too. But there was no blood.

Jeff grabbed the phone and dialed 911, and after relating the little he knew, slunk to the floor and cradled Dad's head. He was conscious but not moving.

What was wrong with him?

Jeff tried to grasp reality, but his brain buzzed so loudly, he could only process small bits at a time.

An increasingly blaring siren.

Sudden silence as the room flashed red.

Activity and dozens of questions of which he knew little answers.

Dad on a gurney.

No, he couldn't ride in the ambulance, but he could follow.

A quick phone call to Mom who expressed her surprise in a cry of pain.

Traffic. Stupid traffic.

Skidding tires as he found one of a handful of parking spaces.

A warm ER and a cool administrator telling him to wait here.

Numb silence.

Chapter 10

Ember arrived early at Dewberry Harbor and parked along the street, across from SOMETHING OLD. When Ron showed up she would know what she was getting into. Rolling down her window she let the light breeze waft through her car, inhaling the tang of the sea. She leaned her head against the headrest, letting the strains of Enya's music pull some of her tension out. She should get away more often—walk the beach, seek the healing of the ocean even when she wasn't angry.

If there ever was such a time.

She sat up. Grammy's death. Dean. Beverly. Olive's Stanford's invasion of her life. She had plenty of reason for the rock that seemed to live in her stomach these days.

She punched the search button on her XM, stopping at the sound of African drums, pulled out her cell phone, and started a game of Angry Birds. There was an almost guilty satisfaction as she flung the birds across the screen and watched them smash into wooden boxes and explode.

This couldn't be good.

A movement in front of SOMETHING OLD caught her eye. The man looked familiar, but it wasn't Ron.

She cursed then bit her tongue as she remembered how much Grammy hated it when she used such language.

But really, what was Mr. Childish doing here? She wanted the professional, not the tagalong. With a frown she raised the electric windows, locked the car, and headed for the shop.

"It's Ember, right?"

She grudgingly nodded. "And you're . . ."

"Jeff Dawson. My dad, um . . ."—he looked away for a moment—"asked me to fill in for him. Shall we?" He opened the door for her and flashed a smile that didn't quite reach his eyes but did add to his masculine appeal.

She bristled. No way was she letting him charm her. He obviously didn't want to be here. Might as well get this over with. She marched to the counter. "I'm looking for Max?"

The man held up a finger. "Just a moment."

He came around the counter and grabbed Jeff in a bear hug. "Is that you, Jeffy? Last time you came in with your old man, you were just getting hair on your upper lip."

Oh, brother! What was this, old home week?

Jeff looked over the man's shoulder and winked at Ember before pulling himself from the man's bear hug. "It's been a long time, Max. Still have Tootsie Pops underneath the counter?"

Max laughed. "Only for the kids."

Jeff grinned—a real, full smile this time—and Ember suddenly wished he'd lit up like that when he smiled at her. She felt her cheeks warm as Jeff walked toward her. "This is Ember Keaton-Jones. I think Dad told you about her."

She stuck out her hand, wondering how much her invasion into the good old boy club of antique peddlers was going to cost her. Good thing she'd researched prices. She may not know a good phonograph from a piece of junk, but she did know the median price.

"So you're the one looking for a phonograph that plays the wax cylinders." Max gave her hand a brief shake, then turned and motioned them to follow. "I've got a beauty." He led them to a small room at the back of the shop where a dusty old phonograph sat in the corner of a table full of junk.

She looked at Jeff and raised an eyebrow.

His gaze flickered acknowledgment, but his face didn't change. "Where'd you find it, Max?"

Ember's mind wandered as the old man told his story. She glanced at her watch, wondered how long it would take her to get home then caught a change in the direction of their conversation.

"Now, Max, you know we can't pay that. You didn't even clean it up."

Ember began listening more intently as Max and Jeff haggled over the price. By the time they finished, Jeff had negotiated a very good deal. She paid Max and was contemplating how to transport the phonograph when Jeff again took charge. Before she knew what happened, the machine was boxed according to some pre-thought specifications and loaded into his SUV. He closed the trunk and turned toward her. This time she was the recipient of his full smile. "We'll do our best to have it in working condition early next week."

"I can't thank you enough for your help today. I'd have paid twice as much if I'd come in by myself."

He chuckled. "At least." His face clouded. "I promised Dad I'd take good care of you."

What was it with him and his dad? The self-confident negotiator of today was a far cry from the man she'd met at his father's store. "When your father first offered to me meet here I wondered what his game was. Now I'm reminded there are actually businessmen still around who have customer service as a high priority."

"That's my Pop."

Ember noted a tenderness in Jeff's voice that surprised her. Her heart warmed toward him. "You've saved me a lot of money." She smiled up at him and realized his eyes were a startling blue. She forced a professional tone into her voice. "I'd like to thank you by buying your lunch."

"That's really not necessary." He looked away from her.

Don't act so eager, buddy. She hesitated, tempted to exit quickly to salvage her wounded ego. But, hey . . . it wasn't like she'd asked him out. She was just doing the right thing. "It's lunchtime. Portland is two hours away. It's the least I can do."

* * * *

As they entered the café, Jeff pulled his cell phone from his pants pocket. Mom said she'd let him know how Dad was doing. They had determined the stroke was the result of a blood clot, and was, thankfully, the less fatal of two possible scenarios. However, Dad's speech and mobility had been severely affected. Yesterday was his first full day in the hospital, and he'd been agitated in between short rest periods. The family took turns sitting with him, although Mom refused to leave his side. The doctor said he wanted to prevent another stroke, or, as happened in some cases, a heart attack.

They were all exhausted, but he knew Dad would want him to meet Ember. Good thing, too. Max was a good businessman but a tough negotiator.

He and Ember sat at a table near a window overlooking the ocean. Beautiful, yet powerful. The scene would have calmed him had he not been so distracted. He shouldn't have taken the time to eat. However, his stomach disagreed with a rumble as the savory smell of grilling meat wafted his way.

He set his phone on the table so he would immediately see his messages.

The waitress arrived to take their order after they'd perused their menus in silence. How could he carry on a conversation when he'd rather be someplace else?

When she left, he was forced to look at Ember, who gazed out at the water, a small frown slowly melting away as she watched the crashing waves.

"It's beautiful, isn't it?" He ventured.

"I often take long drives when I need to clear my head. Somehow, I always find my way to the coast." Her cheek was resting in her palm as she leaned on the table. Her hair, unbunned, curled around her right wrist; such a change from the severe woman he'd met a few days ago. He did a quick mental calculation. It felt as though he'd lived a lifetime in the past week.

"I lose myself in the computer when I need to clear my head. But my dad doesn't allow technology in the shop."

She placed her forearms on the table to look him in the eye. "I noticed that. Was it hard to find the phonograph without—"

His phone alerted him with the Star Wars R2D2 warble. *Finally*, a text . . . not from Mom. But it was from his teenaged niece. Maybe she knew something. He tapped the text to open it, but it was Katie simply asking him to help her pick up some items for her science fair on Monday. After he texted her back, inquiring if she'd heard anything about Dad, he looked up into flashing brown eyes and a quirked eyebrow.

"I'm sorry. You were saying?"

"I was just wondering how you could run a business without a compu—"

The display on his phone lit again. Katie answering him back. Crud. She didn't know anything.

A faint tapping drew his attention to the stranger he was supposed to be having lunch with. Her polished nails drummed a dirge on the laminated tabletop.

"I'm sorry." He held up his phone. "Family stuff." He offered a slight shrug and a grin. This seemed enough to stop the tapping.

"What do you do for a living, Ember?" Perhaps if he got her talk about herself, he could let her carry the conversation. Then he could half-listen while keeping an eye on his phone.

"I'm a Realtor."

"Cool. Do you work for a company, or are you independent?"

That was an easy enough question, but she seemed to struggle with it. "I'm on hiatus." She turned her gaze back to the ocean, the frown settling once again upon her brows.

O-*kay.* That subject closed abruptly.

His phone rang with the robust theme song from *Star Wars* and when he saw it was Mom, he excused himself to take it. "How is he?" he asked without preamble. A seagull shrieked overhead as he stepped outside, drowning out his mother's response. "I'm sorry. Can you repeat that?"

"Good. He's good." She enunciated her words, which melted away his anxiety as effectively as her special hot chocolate. "He's in much better spirits today."

Jeff sank to the steps of the wooden porch, his feet on the walkway and his elbows on his knees. He rubbed the back of his neck feeling the tension from the last few days. "Is he out of the woods?"

"The doctor said his tests are looking better. He recommends starting therapy right away. You got him to the emergency room just in time, sweetie. Any later and it could have been much worse."

"I could have helped sooner if I had gotten to work on time."

"Don't even start that." He knew she frowned when she spoke. "You had no control over what happened."

But he did. He'd stopped for coffee after taking his nephew to school. He'd dragged his feet, not wanting to go to the shop, and now his dad lay in a hospital bed. Could his symptoms have been less severe if he'd gotten there sooner?

When the conversation was over, he sat on the porch a moment longer, his wrists pressed into his temples.

"Jeff?"

Ember stood behind him.

He shot up abruptly. "I'm so sorry, Ember. We've had a family emergency."

Concern softened her features, replacing the perturbed frown. It was then he noticed her purse tucked tightly under her arm. He wouldn't have blamed her for ditching him.

"If you want to leave, I understand," he said. "I haven't been the best of company today."

She took a step toward him, her hand lifting almost hesitantly. "Please, come back inside. I won't pry, but our food is ready, and it looks like you may need a moment before attempting to drive home." Her words soothed, and he found himself being led into the café.

A succulent cheeseburger nestled in a basket of French fries awaited him and roused his hunger. He was suddenly grateful for the woman who had started out abrasive but now calmed his turmoil.

After a couple of bites, he broke the silence. "My dad had a stroke day before yesterday."

"Oh, no!" Her fork clattered on the rim of her salad bowl. "Is he okay?"

"Looks like he will be. But his speech is slurred, and he's lost mobility in his right arm and leg."

"Why didn't you tell me?"

He shrugged. "I don't know. I guess I didn't want to make it real."

"I understand. I didn't want to talk about my job situation for the same reason."

Finally, some common ground.

"You feel like talking about it now?"

She shoved a cherry tomato around in the slurry of her dressing. "I lost a huge account because of a small safety deposit key." She went on to tell him about her trip to New York and her decision to solve a family mystery. "On top of all that, my grandmother passed away recently. I have no one to share all of this with."

"No other family?"

She shook her head but didn't elaborate.

He reached across the table and cupped her small hand under his. "I can't replace your grandmother, but since the day you walked into my shop, I've kinda become invested."

She slid her hand out from under his. "Thank you. I'll keep that in mind." Her words sounded all business, but the small grin on her face convinced him that he'd made the right offer.

The waitress refilled their drinks, pausing their conversation.

Ember thanked her and when she left, she glanced back at Jeff. "I'm so sorry about your father. What will you do now?" Ember asked the innocent question, not realizing those very words had pinged in his brain for the last two days.

"I run the shop, I guess. It's been in our family for a couple of generations, so I can't let it slip out of our hands."

After an awkward moment of silence, he looked out the window. A craggy sea stack waited as a sentinel just a few feet from the shore and water swirled around the enormous rock. A wave ebbed and left a starfish clinging to the exposed side. Jeff took that as a sign that everything would be all right. Dad would come back to them, changed for the experience, but alive.

* * * *

"What are you doing?" Ember stiffened. "I invited you, remember?"

Jeff released the bill then put both hands in the air. "It's all yours."

The cocky tilt of Jeff's head caught her off guard. She softened her tone. "It's just that I wanted to thank you."

Those blue eyes twinkled at her as he leaned forward with his boyish grin. "Then I now, officially, consider myself thanked."

She dipped her head and made a show of digging for her wallet and busied herself with paying the bill. When she finally looked his way, he was gazing at the sea. "How 'bout a short walk on the beach?" He stood and offered his hand.

She allowed him to help her to her feet but quickly let go.

Despite the sunshine, the cooler air near the water made Ember pull her jacket tighter. Jeff walked next to her, hands in his pockets, a navy hoodie emphasizing his strong shoulders. The ocean surged toward the shore, a vast expanse blending with sky in the distance, extending beyond vision. Ember began to breathe a little more deeply, a little more slowly.

"Goes way down deep, doesn't it?"

Ember glanced at him, surprised he could put into words the feelings she had not even processed. "The ocean isn't quiet, but there's a quiet it brings."

He nodded. She appreciated that he didn't try to fill the silence.

The calm followed Ember as Jeff walked with her to the Saturn. She punched the button on her automatic lock and turned to say good-bye, but Jeff stepped in front of her and opened the door.

What was it with men trying to take care of her lately?

She forced a smile as she allowed him to help her into the car. He thanked her again for lunch, flashed that grin, and closed her door. Stepping back with a little wave, he gave a brief nod and was gone—and she was left to drive the two hours home, trying to figure out why the quiet was shattered when he did something as simple as open the car door for her.

At home she went immediately to the kitchen and poured some white zin into a pretty wine glass. Then she kicked off her shoes, curled up on the leather sofa, and pulled her laptop to her. While her mail downloaded, she decided to check in on Facebook, a luxury she had once allowed herself only as a connecting tool with clients. Funny how now that she didn't have a job, she turned to it more and more for mindless distraction.

Ember couldn't help but chuckle when she glanced at the right side of her home page to see, "Cynthia poked you. Do you want to poke her back?" She'd never paid any attention to such time wasters before, but as she imagined Cynthia in her powder blue sweater and pearls "poking" her, she had to respond. She spent a few moments figuring out how to poke her back.

Suddenly a little rectangle popped up in the lower right-hand corner. Cynthia's sweet face and halo of white hair smiled at her from the tiny square picture next to Cynthia's name.

Cynthia: Hi there, sweetie! How was your day?

Ember: Wonderful and confusing all at the same time!

Cynthia: I'm all ears!

Ember: I got a phonograph to play the cylinders.

Cynthia: Oh, my! What was on them?

Ember: Don't know yet. Jeff has to repair the phonograph.

Cynthia: Who's Jeff?

An image of Jeff's impish grin and bright blue eyes surrounded by messy brown hair filled Ember's memory.

Ember: His dad owns an antique shop. They're helping me.

Cynthia: Is Jeff handsome? Married? Your age?

Where was James when you needed him?

Ember: He's okay. Not married. And yes. But don't get any ideas.

Cynthia: Oh, dear. I'm doing it again, aren't I? Don't be cross.

Ember chuckled and was startled by the sound of her own laughter in the empty house. How long had it been since she laughed like that?

Ember: How could I be cross with you?

Her fingers clacked a cheery rhythm on the keyboard.

Cynthia: I'll leave you alone about it if you promise to tell me if there are any juicy developments. Old ladies like me look to young romance to keep their own alive!

Ember: You're looking to the wrong gal for that.

Cynthia: You just haven't met the right one yet.

Ember: He pulled out my chair and opened the car door.

Ember: Very upsetting.

Cynthia: It's wonderful! About time you met a young man with some manners. Women your age need to learn how to let a man show them care and respect instead of being so insufferably self-sufficient.

Ember: I'm insufferable?

Cynthia: FOTFRAL. Talking in general. Not specific.

Ember: FOTFRAL?????

Cynthia: You know. Falling on the floor rolling and laughing.

Leave it to Cynthia to jumble the letters all up.

Cynthia: I have to go now, dear. James says I've been on Facebook too long. Men! Lol (lots of love) xoxoxoxo

Should she tell her? Nah.

Ember: Lol to you, too!

Ember closed her laptop, pulled the throw off the sofa, and wrapped up in it. She pushed the remote and a cozy fire sprang up in her gas fireplace. She stared at the flames thinking about independence. Grammy had encouraged it, and it served her well in life—didn't it? She took another sip of her zinfandel and gazed at the flames, drowsiness caressing her shoulders. But she fought the sensation.

Independence was survival.

Chapter 11

Jeff sat in the armchair next to his father's hospital bed. Weird to see him incapacitated that way. His face looked like a half-melted candle, the right side drooping from his eye to his chin.

"I met with Ember today, Dad. It went well. Oh, and Max says 'hi.'"

The left corner of Dad's lips curved upward in a freaky half-smile. Was he remembering the little league baseball tournaments when he and Max coached rival teams? Or maybe their good-natured feud that stemmed from bidding wars on the same estate sales?

"The phonograph isn't operable, so I got her a good deal. Max assured me all it needed was a little cleaning up."

"Address book . . . Rick . . . Reynolds . . ." His *r*'s came out sounding like Barbara Walters', reminding Jeff of a comedy skit on You Tube he'd seen parodying her. *Wepohting to you, this is Bahbwa Wawa, wive fwom the pwesidential debate in Wode Island.*

"Who is Rick Reynolds, Dad?"

"Can help . . ."

"He fixes antiques?"

Dad nodded.

"I got this, Pop. You just get better, okay?" He couldn't let the old man down.

For the rest of the evening, family came and went. They all visited and even got Dad to chuckle a little. Jeff and his mother were the only ones left when the nurse reminded them that visiting hours were over. Mom refused to leave, and the night nurse—the one from Georgia with the large doe eyes and a smile that lit up the room, not the sour-faced alien who looked ready to pull out her light saber at any moment—brought in a recliner with a pillow and a blanket.

"I understand your need to stay, sugar," the kind nurse said, "but I suggest tomorrow night you go home and sleep good in your own bed."

Mom thanked her and walked out with Jeff after he placed a kiss on his sleeping father's forehead.

"I want to stretch my legs a little before I settle in for the night," she told him as they wandered through the waiting room, her hand tucked into his elbow.

"He's going to be okay, right, Mom?"

She shot him a concerned look that was more to protect him than to express her own fears. "Of course, darling. He's a strong man, and the doctor has already seen some improvement. This was a warning for him to start eating right."

Jeff moved away from her loving grasp and shoved his hands into his pockets.

"What?" She followed him. "What have you been trying to not tell me?"

Oh, she was good.

"Is it his diet, or is it the last few days of fighting with me over every little thing? I know I'm a disappointment right now." If he had caused this, and then exacerbated it by not getting to him in time—

She grabbed both of his forearms and swung him around to look her in the eye. "You stop that right now. Your father is very proud of you. You don't think he's ever had battles with your brothers and sisters? Have you met Lacie? Remember what we went through when she was dating that . . ."—her voice dropped into a whisper—"musician."

Jeff chuckled. "Oh yeah, the guy in the rock band with all those piercings. Nearly got her busted for carrying his drugs in her purse."

"Shhh! We don't need the whole hospital knowing about that." She started giggling and before long both were engulfed in healing laughter. "Kept me on my knees for a year."

"Well"—Jeff wiped his eyes—"she married a good guy. At least, we've never found cocaine in the house. They do have a suspicious looking bush in the backyard, though."

"I love you, you nut." Mom slapped his shoulder. "Don't worry about Dad. He'll get through this, and the two of you can continue your little spat."

Jeff smiled. "I hope so. I'd rather have him mad at me all the time than like this."

The two hugged, and Jeff left her pondering what soda she wanted from the vending machine.

* * * *

On the way to his car, Jeff looked at his watch. It was too late to call that Rick guy. The next day was Sunday, so he doubted he'd be available then. He ran by the shop and unloaded the machine so he wouldn't have to carry it around in his car until he opened on Monday. He'd call Rick then.

In the darkness, the Wormhole seemed even more depressing. He flipped on the fluorescent shop light over the workbench and while it sputtered to life, he retrieved the phonograph from his car.

"How hard could this be?" he voiced aloud as he inspected the machine. "It's not like it has a million working parts or memory chips." He decided to work on it the next day after a good night's sleep. Thankfully, he wouldn't be interrupted on Sunday.

The next afternoon, he arrived at the shop ready to dig in to the phonograph.

The outside looked good. No dings or scratches. Jeff found a screwdriver and proceeded to take the casing off. Inside was a different story. Dust had made a comfortable home there, but with a little vacuuming and oiling, he'd have this bad boy submissive in no time.

Around two o'clock in the morning, Jeff glared blurry-eyed at the monster eating up his beauty sleep. "What's wrong with you?"

He wound the crank on the side and still nothing.

The address book called to him from Dad's office. Rick Reynolds could probably fix it in a flash.

"I accept that challenge." Jeff set his jaw and continued to work until time to unlock the door and flip the OPEN sign. He had taken the machine apart and put it back together again, oiled and cleaned, checked out all the parts to be sure it was all there, but still no go.

As he stood in the Wormhole contemplating his next move, the bell over the door jangled. He looked at his watch. Who shopped for antiques so early in the morning?

A quick peek into the showroom revealed Ember striding in. "Hi, Jeff. Have you had a chance to look at—" She stopped short. "Are you okay?"

Jeff glanced toward the old mirror with the gold ornate frame. A haggard man with two-day-old stubble glared back at him. He quickly smoothed the tufts of hair on his head with splayed fingers. "I'm fine. Why do you ask?"

He couldn't admit he'd worked nonstop eighteen hours trying to get her phonograph to work.

"You look a little . . . tired. Is it your dad? Were you at the hospital with him?"

He thought about using Dad as an excuse, but knowing her concern for him, he didn't want to mislead her. "Nah. Dad is doing great."

"Oh, that's good to hear." Thankfully, Ember moved off the subject but kept a wary eye on him. Judging by the man in the mirror, she probably feared she'd have to call 911. "I know it's early, but I was in the area and couldn't resist checking in." She placed the same box she had carried in that first day onto the counter. Really? Did she expect it to be done so she could listen to the cylinders? Well, after eighteen hours, it should have been done, but she didn't know he had worked on it over the weekend.

"Uh . . . Yeah. My dad gave me a guy's name. I was about to call him, actually."

"May I see the phonograph while you do that?"

"Sure, it's in the back there." He thumbed toward the Wormhole but then followed her. "I cleaned it up. Oiled and inspected it. You know . . ." He sniffed and hitched up his pants. "Prepped it for the fix-it guy."

She ran her fingers along the top, as if she were caressing a cherry T-bird. "It really is beautiful, isn't it?"

Beautiful? That old thing? The bane of his last eighteen hours? She had no clue that her machine nearly became wall art. "Yes, I suppose it is."

"What does this do?" She flipped a small metal part to the left and it purred to life.

Jeff cuffed the back of his neck. "Really?"

She glanced at him in surprise. Apparently too much venom in his sarcastic comment.

"Really, really good job there," he backpedaled. "I think you solved the problem."

"Oh! That's wonderful. Now we don't have to call anyone and wait for it to be fixed." Her face lit up the gloomy Wormhole, and Jeff wanted to bottle the beams of happiness radiating from her. He knew he'd need it later when he did inventory.

"I'll get your cylinders."

When he returned, they found the first one and together figured out how to place it in the machine.

"Would you like some privacy?" Jeff remembered Ember's reaction when he suggested putting the cylinder recording on a CD. She didn't want anyone else to hear.

"Actually . . ." She grinned. "Since you're already invested, as you mentioned the other day, I'm fine with you staying. And frankly, I don't think I want to listen alone now."

This pleased Jeff to a depth that surprised him. "Okay then. Let's unlock this mystery together."

He pushed the same lever Ember had. As the cylinder groaned to life, the voice of an older woman filled the air. Distant, like the ancient recordings of Roosevelt's fireside chats that Old Miss Hatcher made him listen to in history class. He still felt the sting of her knobby fingers thumping his head when he fell asleep. Thankfully, the words coming from the cylinder were intelligible. With a glance at Ember's wide eyes, he leaned forward as the story unfolded.

* * * *

Cylinder One
Olive

Some stories are meant to be told; others go to the grave with the one who keeps them. I, Olive Stanford, long assumed the latter. As sole possessor of the knowledge buried deep within the Atlantic with the final cries of the unfortunate, it is within my power to encapsulate the tale, push it down within my bowels and silence it, until I cross to the other side.

Ah, but therein lies the issue. What awaits one who passes on? Are secrets afforded there as they are here, or must all be laid bare?

As my eyes dim and time slows to a crawl, I find the story clawing, climbing, demanding a way out, convincing me that now is the opportune time to unload the secret clutched to my breast. I can no longer deny the forces which compel me to tell it.

I first thought to pen the tale and keep it in some secret place to be discovered after my death, but these contrary arthritic fingers sketched their chicken scratch for less than a page before I knew such recourse to be futile. Still, I have never been one to be denied once I set upon a plan. This crafty old mind, coupled with the indulgence always given to those who have the means with which to obtain it, devised another route to the same end.

They think my requests the eccentricities of an aged woman, but they afford me my way, as they always have. And so, under the ruse of dictating memoirs, I steal away to solitude and unburden my soul—memoirs the likes of which the vultures of my day will never hear. These words, over which I have long ruminated, are for the ears of a future age. I know not who you are, son or daughter of the future, but your listening person shall forever silence the compulsion I have to speak. This story will perchance be of particular import to you, if all goes as planned. Through this story the truth of Thomas Keaton will finally be known.

* * * *

"You're stopping now?" Jeff glanced at Ember who appeared physically shaken. She had flipped the lever and without speaking lifted the needle and took the cylinder from the phonograph and placed it in its cardboard box with the others. For a moment, she simply stared at the larger box and its contents. Then she closed it up.

"Thank you for your help, Jeff."

He followed her out the door and to her car parked on the street. "Wait! Don't you want to hear any more?"

She turned to him, her expression unreadable. "Actually, I want to process what I've learned so far. Besides, I don't want to take too much of your time."

He reached out and gently grabbed her arm. This was not the woman who walked with him on the beach. "I'm very interested, Ember. I can see something has upset you, and I want to help."

She shook her head and wriggled from his grasp. "No, really. I have some things to do today. I'll leave the phonograph here and let you know when I'm ready to listen again."

She slid into her car, but before she drove away, she rolled down her window. "Thank you, again. And thank your father for me. You both have been very helpful."

As she drove off, Jeff wondered if he'd ever see her again. He now felt more determined than ever to help the beautiful woman with her mystery.

Chapter 12

Ember's hands trembled on the steering wheel. Where did this violent reaction come from? She drove mindlessly, taking one turn after another, not truly conscious of where she was going until she pulled in front of Grammy's house. Evidently she was like an old dog finding its way home. She grimaced at the SOLD banner across the Wright Realty sign and briefly contemplated how much Dean had made on the commission. Her stomach lurched, and she fought the urge to throw up.

Oh, Grammy.

She'd thought she wanted the truth about her family heritage, but this whole Thomas Keaton thing was messing with her. Was she strong enough to know his dark secrets? Time crawled, mocking her weakness, as she stared at the house, wishing the curtains were open in the picture window. She found herself dialing Cynthia. "Please answer." She swallowed hard at the pathetic whine in her voice.

"Hello, dear Ember!" The voice, though aged, was full of life. "Don't you love these cell phones? Know who's calling you before you ever pick up. 'Course it does take some of the mystery from life. I can't imagine you're Robert Redford calling, now can I? Not that he's ever called."

It was like finding a grassy spot underneath a shade tree and listening to a gurgling stream. "You amaze me, Cynthia."

"Whatever for?"

"Your zest for life."

"Gotta have a lot of zest at my age to keep at it. Now tell me all about it."

"About what?"

"The cylinders of course—or that handsome Jeff who's helping you. Figure it's gotta be one of those subjects to warrant a phone call."

"You're too good."

"I have a little experience. Did you know I not only raised five daughters, but counseled nine granddaughters through boyfriend troubles?"

"You think you're tricky, don't you?" Ember leaned her head against the back of the car seat, surprised by the hint of a smile reflected in the rearview mirror. "This isn't about the man."

"Oh, poo."

"But you're right. It's the cylinders." Darn her voice. Did it have to crack on that last word?

"That bad?"

"I don't even know. Couldn't make it through the first one."

"Is the cylinder damaged?"

"No. Clear as a bell. But she started talking about my grammy's grandfather, about this deep dark secret, and I shut it off and practically ran from the shop. Jeff must think I'm an idiot."

"Who was talking, dear? And why was Jeff there?"

With a deep breath, Ember started at the beginning.

When she finished, Cynthia said, "So you stopped the phonograph because . . ."

"I don't know!" She was wailing now. Disgusting. Ember clicked the ignition and started driving, fast.

"You there, dear?"

"Why am I so upset?"

"Maybe if you knew why you turned off the phonograph, you'd understand your emotions."

"What if he's the world's greatest jerk? After he wrote that letter to his wife. After he talked like that to his little girl. What if . . . I'm going to hate him still?" She headed west on the highway. How far away was the ocean?

"Ember, he won't even know."

"That's not the point."

"So what exactly is the point?"

Before she could stop it, another wailing "I don't know!" escaped her lips.

"Sweetie, are you driving?"

"Ummm . . ."

"Why don't you go home, dear? Have a nice cup of tea. Think this through logically. Chamomile is a good choice. Always calms the nerves."

Chamomile tea. Grammy's answer to everything. The tears started then. Silent and wet.

"Ember?"

"I'll call you when I get back home." She managed to get the words out without sounding like she was crying. No reason to worry Cynthia further.

She sped along the highway until the tears stopped their silent streaming, then took the next exit and headed back east. She wouldn't go all the way to the ocean. Cynthia didn't need to wonder where she was. After she'd parked in the covered garage and begun her ascent in the elevator, she was thankful Cynthia urged her home. She unlocked her door and headed straight to the teakettle. It took a full cup before she was ready to call Cynthia back.

"Better, dear?"

"Yes."

"Chamomile works every time. Did you figure out why you're so upset?"

Ember swallowed hard. "I want Thomas Keaton to be good."

"I'm not sure I understand."

"My grandfather was an idiot. I guess I loved him in my own way, but he was just . . . not really there. Detached." Ember cleared her throat. "I don't know who my father is. Grammy's father was a . . ." Ember stopped to find a more acceptable word. "A jerk who broke Grammy's heart. When I read that letter from Thomas to his wife, I wanted to believe in it. That there might be men out there who actually care about their families." It all sounded so irrational, pouring out like that.

"There are good men, Ember."

"Not in my world." She hadn't meant the words to come out so snippy.

"So you stopped the cylinder because you couldn't bear for your great-great-grandfather to let you down."

"I know I've never met him, but what if . . . What if there was a man in my family who was actually good?"

"You're sure he's going to turn out bad?"

"I . . . guess not."

"There's only one way to find out."

Ember took another sip of her second cup of tea. "I know," she whispered.

* * * *

"Yes, Dad, I'm being good." Jeff spoke into the shop phone. "Not an electronic device on the premises."

Jeff hated lying to his dad like that. Seriously. How could Dad expect him to function in these extraordinary circumstances? He'd been allowed his cell phone, but that didn't keep him from feeling like a fish out of water. His laptop provided life and breath.

It pleased him, though, that Dad was feeling well enough to challenge him. This day could have been so different.

"Hey," Jeff said before Dad became too tired to talk. The sun already cast long shadows through the windows as another day drew to a close. "Remember I told you about Ember and the phonograph?"

"Yes." Dad still slurred his words and spoke haltingly. But he didn't seem as confused.

"About how she came in a couple of days ago and only listened to part of the first cylinder?"

"You . . . said she seemed . . ."

Jeff had gotten used to waiting for Dad to come up with the right word. He'd heard the phrase "new normal" before but never considered it would ever apply to them.

". . . troubled."

"Yeah. She went through all of this effort but then dropped the whole thing."

"You . . . haven't . . . heard from . . . her?"

"No. It's been two days. Should I call her? See if she's all right? Maybe I should offer to take the phonograph to her so she can listen to it in private."

"Good . . . idea."

Just then a familiar car pulled up and parked in front of the shop. "You'll never believe this, Dad. She's here."

"Atta girl." It was a weak cheer but told Jeff he was on the right track to be sure she followed through.

Before hanging up, he got in an admonishment of his own. "Don't give the nurses a hard time, you hear?"

Dad chuckled. What a beautiful sound.

Ember entered, a little sheepish as she tried to avoid looking him in the eye. "I know it's late, and if you have other plans, I totally understand. I mean, if you need to go, I'll come back tomorrow."

Jeff clasped his hands behind his back and circled her, pretending to be a jackal stalking his prey. "Ember. What are you trying to say?" Would she admit to wanting to listen to some more from the phonograph?

She pulled one cylinder from the large canvas tote bag slung over her shoulder. Apparently she didn't feel she could listen to all of them in one shot. "Please?"

Well, that was close to an admission.

"Let me lock up."

They were soon sitting in the Wormhole—that always seemed brighter when she was there—and started up the cylinder. Not knowing how to start where they left off, they listened to the first part again. Jeff watched Ember for signs of agitation, but all she did was take a deep breath when the new part started, as if she were about to dive into the icy waters from the *Titanic* itself.

Chapter 13

Cylinder One Continues
Olive

When I met Thomas early in the voyage, I thought little of the exchange. Like many others, he seemed an upstart seeking his fortune in the world—of little consequence to me. I couldn't have been more mistaken. The lives of Thomas Keaton and Olive Stanford intertwined, changing me forever. Ours was not a premeditated union, but one circumstance thrust upon us. Opportunity appeared, and I took advantage of its offering.

But I get ahead of myself. The story must unfold for you as it did for me.

It started that fated Wednesday, April tenth, 1912, in London. If only I'd understood the gravity of all that was to transpire, perhaps I could have stayed it. But I had not the benefit of foreknowledge, and that Wednesday seemed as any other.

I arose early, eager for our departure on the first-class boat train. London's Waterloo Station was an easy distance from our hotel, and the boat train would deliver us within a few steps of the famed *Titanic.* The sooner we made our departure, the better.

It was my habit to awaken with the sun. Louise heard me stir and came to my aid, opening the curtains to welcome the light as she does each morning.

I stepped into the peignoir she held for me. "Please see that Calvert has awakened Mr. Charles."

"Yes, Madame."

As I watched Louise bustle from the room, I had second thoughts about lingering there myself. Leaning on my favorite cane, I walked to the doorway to watch the proceedings. Calvert seemed none-too-eager to enter my grandson's room.

And no wonder. Charles Malcolm Stanford III wouldn't be in the mood for civility. Calvert slipped in quietly, pulling the door behind him, and Louise glanced my way. Perhaps they thought I didn't hear Charles Malcolm's drunken entrance in the wee hours of the morning.

"I'll take tea and toast here." I arranged myself on a parlor chair near my grandson's chambers and listened for the tongue-lashing Calvert was sure to receive. When it came, I made my way to the door and rapped upon it with the silver end of my cane. "Charles Malcolm, you will join me for tea and toast immediately."

He cursed under his breath before answering. "Yes, Grandmother."

Though some may dispute the idea, I am not without heart. When Charles stumbled from his chambers with red, bleary eyes and complained of a pounding headache, my anger was tempered by sympathy for his condition. "For God's sake, Calvert, get him something for the pain."

Calvert rushed to do my bidding as Charles leaned in and planted a kiss upon my cheek. "My apologies for my appearance." He slid into the chair across from me.

"The shenanigans of your night will haunt you this day."

He offered a wry smile.

"We haven't much time before we board the train. You will pull yourself together."

He sat straighter. "I thought to stay in London."

"I see."

He held my cool gaze only briefly before breaking eye contact.

"You have the means to finance this delay, I presume." We both knew he did not, but I would play his bluff. I reached for my tea and pretended a delicate sip.

"I thought perhaps you might offer an advance in my allowance." Charles fidgeted, toying with the seam on his jacket, as he spoke. "There is much to learn in London. We could employ a tutor to accompany me to all the sights. And perhaps I could tour Cambridge and Oxford."

"I assume there are card players at Cambridge and Oxford same as where you go now. Don't toy with me, Charles." The rap of my cane upon the floor caused him to grab his head. I suppressed momentary amusement at his discomfort then steadied my voice. "You will accompany me to the station, the *Titanic*, and New York, where you will find a way to curb your appetite."

He hung his head, and I stood. "Louise!"

She came scurrying at the sound of my call, but before we left the parlor there was a terrible clamoring at the door of our suite. Calvert argued with someone, a distraught female by voice. Charles stood, panic in his eyes, as a teary young woman pushed her way into the room. Her too flashy dress and jewels spoke of poor breeding, as did the way she grabbed at my grandson. "Charles!" Her wail filled the shocked silence.

I was sure to be sick to my stomach.

The woman clung to his arm. His eyes darted from her to me.

"Do you intend to introduce the intruder?" I dared him to humiliate me.

"I think not." He turned to the young woman. "I will walk you home."

"The train, Charles."

"You promised to stay with me!" The woman began her wailing again.

Calvert stepped forward, coat and hat in hand. Charles shrugged into them then led the woman toward the door. "I will not be late, Grandmother."

I nodded toward my maid. "Let us prepare for departure. Calvert, see that Charles's belongings are loaded into the car." Louise followed me into my chambers where I fought to control the trembling of my hands. Whatever trouble Charles had gotten himself into this time would be left behind in London. Or so I believed.

At the station I held my head high. I am a Stanford as Charles Malcolm is after me. Pretending confidence I didn't feel, I greeted Mr. Astor and settled myself to wait. I hoped my demeanor was casual, but my breathing quickened as the train whistle blew a warning without Charles Malcolm's appearance. As I stood to make my way to the railroad car, suddenly there he was, placing a trembling hand at my elbow. He looked worse than he had when he arose a few hours before. I raised an eyebrow. "I assume all is under control?"

A stricken look filled his eyes. "There will be no further encumbrance."

Determined to act like a Stanford I eased into a padded chair, covered in a beautiful navy and gold fabric. A full breakfast would be served on the table before me, covered in a thick white cloth that matched the pallor of my grandson's face. I flicked the gold napkin open and watched it billow to cover my lap. If only life's mistakes were covered so easily.

We pretended to enjoy our meal as I remarked on the highly polished and comfortable arrangements, but in truth we ate very little as the train clacked upon her tracks carrying us to the *RMS Titanic*.

When we arrived at the great ship, I was in no such mood to celebrate her grandeur. It wasn't far to the gangplank which boasted "White Star Line" painted in tall, pristine letters. Once aboard, I watched the rather ordinary departure with little interest due to the sickening that had taken residence in my stomach. Charles stood next to me, posture erect, but when he offered his arm, I sensed a tremor. A horrible premonition filled me, and I stiffened my back. I had to keep up appearances.

To an outside viewer, I'm sure, we were two socialites taking our proper place in history, boarding the most famous ship ever built. It was the very behavior expected of those of our station—to enjoy the luxury designed for us to partake. We had, of course, no conception of what we would experience when we set foot on the "safest ship ever built"—the ship "designed to be unsinkable."

We joined the others at the port side rails, my grandson waving to no one in particular while I observed. There were three blasts from the *Titanic*'s throaty whistle, and then five tugboats began their work, pushing and pulling at our massive hull like hardworking little ants, dragging weight many times their own. Soon we were in the River Test, where Southampton is built, and we felt the rumble of our engines beneath.

As we came upon the steamer, the *New York*, there was a bit of excitement that distracted me from musing upon the horrible scene in the parlor that morning. Reports, like those of a revolver, rang out. I whipped toward the sound to discover that the coils of thick rope, which had held the *New York* to the dock, snapped. They flung through the air and fell upon the crowd at the shore. Evidently our great ship had displaced a huge volume of water causing the *New York* to rise on the swell. When she dropped back down with the water, her lines had broken as though they were sewing thread.

The *New York*'s stern swung out into the river toward us. Anxiety mounted as it drew nearer, steadily, as if drawn by some unseen magnet to our massive ship. A tug came around our stern, passed to the quayside of the steamer, and made fast to her. How strange to watch the tiny tug strain against the weight of the *New York*, like a toddler trying to pull a loaded wagon.

Outside I believe I was the picture of composure. But the incident, on top of what I'd experienced before sailing, pushed my fortitude to the limit. I insisted Charles Malcolm take me to our suite for a nap. I heard later the two ships avoided collision by a mere four feet. While I am unconvinced of the accuracy of such a small number, my nerves would easily believe the estimate.

Even with the emotion that simmered beneath my reserve, I couldn't help but note the beauty of our ship as Charles guided me from the deck. We entered the *Titanic* by the Grand Staircase. The large glass domes built over it allowed a bath of natural light. The glow of sunshine danced upon the gilt bronze garlands and illuminated the intricate carvings in the polished oak. I brushed a hand across the leg of a cherub on the middle railing. The stairs were aptly named. Grand indeed.

My cane made no sound on the plush carpet that lined the alleyway that led to our parlor suite. Once there, I was not disappointed—an unusual experience, I assure you. Nothing was spared that would mark my comfort, the RMS *Titanic* replete with every modern amenity the age afforded. While only twenty percent of London had electricity, the *Titanic* was electric from bow to stern. Our suite boasted electric lamps and an electric fireplace, as well as rich furnishing. I felt completely at home.

"What do you say, Charles?" I turned toward my grandson, smiling, but he didn't return my gaze. Instead he dashed away to our private lavatory. He didn't close the door, and I heard him retching. Calvert and Louise were finishing the last of the unpacking, and I suggested they finish their tasks later and take some time to explore the ship. As soon as they left, I went to Charles and held a damp, cool cloth to his face. He allowed himself to be led to a settee, where I perched beside him.

Charles fell against me, and I brushed his rich brown hair from his forehead. "What is it, Charlie?" I whispered the intimate name of his childhood. In that moment many of his twenty-one years faded, and he looked like a boy again, vulnerable and heartbroken. He began to sob, and I held him until he quieted enough to tell his story.

Would that I'd never known the truth of that ugly business in London!

As his words tumbled forth, heart palpitations overtook me. I grabbed the back of the settee, fighting for control. Another sob escaped Charles, and fierce emotion tore through me— repulsion, then grief. I stood and paced about the suite, wanting to retch as he had done.

Finally his tale was finished. For an awkward moment we stared at each other. The pain in his eyes begged me to understand. When he excused himself and disappeared into his quarters, I wished for a cup of tea to calm myself, but could do nothing but gasp for breath and stare at the walls of my cabin.

After a time Charles reappeared and informed me he was off to the gymnasium. I don't know how my grandson had the nerve to go about at that moment, after the situation in London, but the Stanfords are taught from a young age to hide any hint of inner turmoil. Charles Malcolm Stanford III did just that. He disappeared out the cabin door, leaving me to what was now a raging headache and full-fledged stomach malady.

I didn't come out at Cherbourg, but chose instead to spend the rest of that day and night in solitude. Charles did burst upon my berth in a rare moment of consideration to suggest I partake of the excellent cuisine of the evening meal. The thought of ingesting made my stomach roil further.

When I refused to dress for dinner, Charles tarried and regaled me with stories of the instructor in the gymnasium, with whom he was obviously enamored. The mustached Mr. McCawley, dressed in white flannels with matching plimsolls upon his feet, had taught Charles to conquer the rowing machine, the riding of an electric camel, and heaven knows what else. His stories of the man made me wish for such a figure as a constant in my grandson's world. Perhaps if Charles had the modeling of a man of character he could overcome his vices.

For a moment I was carried away by the shine which replaced the deadness in my Charles's bloodshot eyes, but when he paused between tales, I saw the shadow sweep across his expression once again, and my stomach lurched. Maybe Charles could work off the emotion by physical exertion, but I was not yet ready for the public. He excused himself to change for dinner, then returned, strutting like a peacock, and made for the dining room. To this day I'm astounded he could behave as he did.

I passed a sleepless night but made it to breakfast the next morning, Thursday, April eleventh, as we approached Queenstown Harbor. There was no use reliving the distasteful business in London every moment, dreaming or awake. We were Stanfords. Between money and ingenuity there was always a way to manage things. I would get Charles Malcolm out of this mess, just as I had lesser situations before.

After breakfast, I took to the deck, hoping fresh air would calm my nerves. In truth, I could no longer abide waiting in my room, ears straining for the footsteps that would bring the news I most feared to my door. With a determined gait I stepped into the chill of morning to witness the final passing of the Channel and the coast of Ireland. The bitter cold bit through my coat, but I was resolute. I'd often longed to see the Irish coast, a craving begun in childhood when my mother whispered of her secret descent. It did not disappoint.

Rugged gray cliffs fringed the shoreline, and the morning sun sparkled upon them and the deep green hillsides above, sprinkled with a smattering of dwellings. For a moment my spirits lifted, but they soon plummeted at the thought of who might board at Queenstown, looking for Charles. I could only hope he would not be discovered until we were upon the open sea with only the telegraph to connect us to those who would surely seek him.

When the ship stopped still rather far out to sea, I caught my breath. I suppose we were too large to come closer to dock. Soon little tenders, small boats used to ferry people from the dock to the ship, worked their way toward us. Watching them gave me a greater sense of the magnificence of the vessel I was upon.

The *Titanic* rose, deck after deck, above the bobbing tenders, who looked like mere toy boats in comparison. The bouncing crafts below emphasized the grace and strength of *Titanic*. It seemed she didn't even ride the swell, so stately and solid was she. Still, when I compared her bow to the little white house to the left of Queenstown, I realized we indeed rose and fell with the slight swell of the ocean in the harbor. But so gentle was the dip, so regal her recovery, it was hard to perceive any movement unless I fixed my gaze upon this landmark positioned on solid earth. This experience filled me with a security which, knowing all I do now, was of course preposterous. But premonitions of danger that day all centered on Charles.

As the tenders unloaded its cargo onto *Titanic* I felt momentary panic, strained to recognize a badge, a uniform, anything which might mean harm to my grandson. I soon realized the futility of such concentration. When the bugler signaled lunch with the traditional "Roast Beef of Old England," I forced the morbid thoughts away and turned toward the first-class dining room. I had to keep my strength up. I needed all my faculties about me to design an escape for Charles Malcolm.

Chapter 14

Jeff watched Ember closely, even while caught up in Olive's voice and its implications. "You okay?"

Ember seemed confused, her brow furrowed as she stared at the cylinder still in the machine.

"Ember?"

"Oh! Uh . . . yes, I'm fine. There's no more mention of Thomas." She turned her large, brown eyes toward him.

A guy could slip and fall into their chocolate depths if he weren't careful.

"Thomas?" he asked. "Why are you interested in him?"

"Just curious." She stood abruptly, nearly knocking over the chair. As she removed the cylinder from the machine, she asked, "Are you hungry?"

Jeff stood and reached for his jacket slung over the Venetian chair Dad had acquired before his stroke. With its squat legs and scrolled carved back, he imagined it looked like a plump woman settling in for tea.

"I'm a guy. I'm always hungry." He held out his hand. "Come on, let's get out of here."

She put the cylinder back in its cardboard box and carefully slid it into her tote. After depositing it into the trunk of her car, she offered to drive them both to a nearby pizza parlor.

She wound her way slowly through the downtown traffic where surrounding them were tall office buildings with street level shops and eateries. Finally, the green awning of the restaurant came into view. Finding a place to park proved a challenge, but Jeff was impressed how deftly she negotiated the streets.

Once inside, they perused the blackboard where the menu was scrawled in colorful chalk. They agreed on sharing a Pepperoni Supreme pizza and then found a table toward the back where a candle glowed in a red globe on a checkered tablecloth.

Ember shed her jacket. "Not the fanciest place, but they have great pizzas."

As curious as Jeff was about Thomas Keaton and his effect on Ember, he decided not to push the issue. He liked this Ember—relaxed, and she laughed easily.

"So tell me," she spoke over her white wine, clasping the glass in both of her hands. "What's a young techie like you doing working in an antique shop?"

Wow. Hadn't she gotten the message that this was a sore subject with him?

"I was working as a graphic designer for an upstart Internet firm. We all thought it was going to go somewhere. Stock options, the whole nine yards. But the economy turned, and I suddenly found myself living in my sister's basement, working the family business. I was just about ready to shop my résumé around when Dad got sick." He took a swig from his microbrew beer. "Now, I'm stuck working with old, dusty merchandise in an old, dusty building." He almost added his old, dusty father, but given the circumstances thought that might be tacky.

"Can you do both? How busy are you at the shop?" She clamped her lips shut for a moment. "Oh, your dad won't let you have your laptop, will he?"

"I love my father, and I will do anything for him. But since he's been gone, I've moved in my laptop. And you've given me a good idea. The job I had would have included an office and a hefty five figures with the potential for six. However, in the interim, perhaps I could go into a side business. I love web design, no matter what the level. Maybe I can find a few clients that would at least help get me out of my sister's house." His hopeful heart dropped again as he thought of his situation there. "But then, there's the baby."

Ember's face went pale in the flickering candlelight. "Baby?"

"Not mine!"

"Oh!" She fanned herself with her napkin. "I was worried there for a minute."

He laughed with her but then thought about it. Why would she care if he had a child?

"My sister is pregnant, and she already has a houseful of boys. I had offered to help out."

A look passed over her face. "You would do that? Stick with your family despite your own discomfort?"

"Of course, that's what families do."

The shadow he had become familiar with returned, and he thought he'd heard her mumble into her wine glass, "Mine doesn't."

* * * *

What was it with him and family? Did he really stick by people as he claimed? She couldn't help comparing him to that scumbag Dean. Not that there was any love lost there, but since Dean was the only guy she'd dated since college, he provided the only contrast. Wait a minute. This wasn't a date, was it? She stared at the mound of ingredients on her slice of pepperoni supreme. Had she asked him out?

Of course not. They were working and hungry. She'd simply done the polite thing. Not any different than when she'd asked him to lunch by the ocean. The picture of him sauntering along the beach in that navy blue hoodie filled her mind. Dean may have had all the fancy, name-brand clothes, but there was something genuine in Jeff's casual look and attitude.

"I wouldn't dare offer you a penny."

"Huh?" She glanced up to find his gaze trained on her.

That boyish grin filled his handsome face. "I'm sure your thoughts are more valuable than that—especially with inflation and all."

She could feel the blood rushing in. Drat her face. "I doubt they were worth even a penny—just nonsense."

He didn't look convinced.

"So, what's your impression of Olive?"

"Rich. Spoiled." He shrugged. "Hiding a secret. Cares about her grandson."

"Sure. State the obvious. But who is she? You know, is she good or bad?"

"Villain or heroine?" He took another swig of his beer. "I suppose most everyone is a bit of both."

"I always supposed people were one or the other."

"That's pretty black and white."

She didn't like the way he pinned her with a direct look.

He leaned forward. "Have you ever met anyone perfectly, completely good?"

Ember snorted. "I know some who are rotten all the way through."

"Not a redeeming quality to be found?" The typical tease was gone from his face, and the studied gaze of those blue eyes was too intense for comfort.

It unnerved her to realize how quickly a list of offenders and a litany of offenses filled her mind.

His cell phone went off while she thought about the top two in her inventory.

Beverly and Dean.

He glanced at his caller ID. "I'm sorry. It's my mom. She may have news about Dad."

Ember nodded, and he swiveled away from the table. Ember noted how his reaction to the disruption contrasted sharply with how she would react if Beverly called.

His eyes had lit up upon seeing his mother's name. Ember would have glared at the phone and let it go to voicemail. He sat casually, one arm draped over the back of the chair. She would have tensed up. He laughed easily. When was the last time she laughed with Beverly?

"Thanks for letting me know." Jeff said as he pivoted back toward the table. "No problem. I was just having dinner with Ember." He made sudden eye contact with her then his cheeks flushed. He darted his gaze away. "Mom! We were just taking a break."

Ember chuckled. Apparently Mom was teasing him about having a meal with a girl. He quickly said good-bye and stuffed his phone into his shirt pocket.

Ember waited for him to take a long draw from his drink. "Is everything okay?"

He cleared his throat. "Uh, yeah. She was just letting me know that my dad should be coming home by the end of the week."

"Oh, that's wonderful."

"Therapy is going well, and they think he's ready for a home nurse."

"Will he be back to work soon?"

Jeff frowned. "I don't know. I can't imagine he'd be in full commission too quickly." He sighed. "I'll probably have to continue to fill in for a few more months."

Ember reached out and laid her palm over the back of his hand. "I know this wasn't your dream. But I'm glad you were there to help me." She almost continued with *help me . . . through the mess that was dumped in my lap.* She tried to shield her angst over learning anything about Thomas Keaton. But should she? Could she trust Jeff not to make a mockery of her feelings?

Jeff wasn't Dean.

And if anyone understood family, it would be Jeff.

Before they parted ways that evening, Ember stopped Jeff as he was about to get out of her car. She had driven them both back to the shop. "So, should we listen to the next cylinder tomorrow?"

"Absolutely. You know, you can bring all of them over so we can finish them."

Ember almost agreed. But if she did, she'd have no more excuse to see Jeff every day. Of course, that wasn't the only reason to drag her feet. The truth? She was not ready to learn about what happened on the *Titanic*. Or hear any excuses about why her great-great-grandfather abandoned his family.

No, one cylinder at a time, thank you very much.

Chapter 15

Ember wrapped herself in Grammy's robe after her shower and rubbed the soft chenille across her cheek. She imagined the wrinkled fingers drawing lazy circles on her face, an action that never failed to calm Ember when she was a child.

She'd been clearing out Grammy's house for the past week, moving the things her mother hadn't taken to a storage shed. Some things she simply couldn't relegate to a dark, concrete room. Her house now had pieces of memories decorating the walls and shelves of her apartment. Grammy's miniature teacup collection, the lace doilies she had tatted herself, the creaky wooden rocker she claimed had belonged to her grandmother. All of these treasures brought Grammy into Ember's home.

With a plethora of pillows against her headboard, she settled in with her laptop to see what the rest of world was up to. She logged into her Facebook account and perused her newsfeed. She didn't know many of her *friends* as she used the social network more for networking purposes than social. However, she found herself mildly amused as she read nonsensical updates and watched You Tube videos. She particularly liked the one of foxes jumping on a trampoline.

She noticed she had one friend request. When she was working, these came in with a regular rhythm, but lately she wondered if she fell off the face of the earth if anyone in cyberspace would notice.

A click on the dropdown list revealed it was Dean who was trying to "friend" her.

Dean?

The nerve! She had already *unfriended* him months ago . . . when he broke her heart with his two-timing and lies. Stealing the deal of a lifetime out from under her nose did not bode well for a rekindled relationship, either, or the fact he'd sold

Grammy's home. And yet, she found herself hovering the pointer of her mouse over the accept button.

There had been good times. But good times never last.

She pounced on the ignore button. Why couldn't real life be that easy? Just click away those problems with a flick of the pointer finger.

A box popped up in the lower right-hand corner. Cynthia?

Cynthia: Hello, Ember dear. I see u r online right now.

Ember: What are you doing up? It's 1:30 in NY, isn't it?

Cynthia: I had to go potty.

Okay . . . Ember shook her head and smiled.

Ember: Must I be stern with you and tell you to march yourself back to bed?

Cynthia: LROTFIFOL!

Ember: ?

Cynthia: That means Literally Rolling On The Floor In Fits Of Laughter, silly. Don't you young people have this all down by now?

Ember: We'll learn eventually.

Cynthia: I decided I wasn't sleepy anymore, so I made myself some chamomile and logged on. Oh! James downloaded something called Skip on my computer. Do you have Skip?

Ember: I'm not sure what that is.

Cynthia: It's where we can see each other while we're talking.

Ember: Do you mean, Skype?

Cynthia: Oh! That's what it's called! Do you have it?

Ember: Yes, I do.

Ember got Cynthia's calling information, and soon was face-to-face with her friend via computer monitor.

"Why, Ember, you look lovely."

"You do too, Cynthia." Both women wore no makeup, Ember's hair was damp and Cynthia's was in spongy curlers.

"I think we're ready for a night on the town. What do you say?" Cynthia laughed.

Ember thought it the most beautiful sound in the world.

"So," Cynthia said, "what did you do today?" She spoke in hushed tones, probably to keep from waking James somewhere in the house, but that made her no less effervescent.

"I listened to the rest of the first cylinder."

"Wonderful! Can you share?"

She told Cynthia about Olive Stanford and her account of boarding the *Titanic*. "It was odd. Here is the most impressive ship ever built, and Olive acts as if it serves for no other reason than to get her from London to New York."

"Well, that's the way many of the wealthy viewed it. How awful to be in a prison of society's making and miss the truly beautiful things of this world."

Ember could identify. Now that her career was on hold, she had no one to enjoy cozy business luncheons with. Her dating life was a bust, so no more intimate evenings over wine. And with Grammy's passing, she now had no one to share her deepest fears.

Ember slipped her hand under the built-in camera's range and reached out to draw lazy circles on Cynthia's cheek. The older woman sipped her tea, oblivious to Ember's sentimentality.

"Anyway," Ember continued. "Olive didn't mention Thomas Keaton after that first time. It seems she wants to recount her experiences from the beginning of her voyage."

Cynthia's face brightened. "What a magnificent opportunity, Ember. A firsthand account that I would guess no one has heard for a hundred years."

Ember went on to tell about the grandson, Charles. "He was a rogue, apparently. Kept his grandmother on her toes."

Cynthia giggled. "There must be one in every family. James was quite a rebel."

"Really?" Ember remembered the image of the staid lawyer as a teen with his leather jacket.

"Oh my, yes. My parents worried when we started dating."

"Cynthia. Did you own a poodle skirt and wear your hair in a ponytail?"

Cynthia's cheeks flushed pink, and Ember was grateful for technology that gave her the ability to see her elderly friend turn into a teenybopper even though she was thousands of miles away.

"I loved that skirt."

After a moment more of small talk, Cynthia yawned.

"You'd better go to bed, young lady," Ember said, feeling the sandman dusting her, as well.

"Guess the chamomile worked. I'm so glad we connected tonight, though. Happy dreams, sweetie."

"You, too."

The connection ended, and Ember smiled at the tiny, static picture of Cynthia, still animated even in a still pose.

Ember laid the laptop aside and snuggled into her comforter where she drifted easily into sleep.

* * * *

"Are you kidding me?"

Jeff had just entered his sister's chaotic kitchen and took in the scene before him. Food lay everywhere, and the racket sounded like Saturday night at Chalmun's Cantina in *Star Wars Episode IV*.

He filled his lungs. "QUI-ET!"

Three boys turned surprised faces toward the sound, one they had never heard coming from Uncle Jeff. Surrounding them were the ravages of a food fight involving bacon, English muffins, and Marcus's sock that was now soaking in honey on Tyler's plate.

"Good morning, Uncle Jeff." Bobby, the ten-year-old, the oldest of the ruffians, the one who knew better, grinned at him as if he were enjoying breakfast on the veranda.

"How long has your mother been gone?" Jeff tiptoed through crumbs of food, some unidentifiable, to reach the broom.

"Just a few minutes. She fixed us breakfast, then told us to be good for Daddy."

"And this is good?" His foot crunched on something that now looked like a flattened Froot Loop. "Where is your father?"

They all shrugged.

Great. Jeff needed to leave for the shop, but how could he trust that Muffin War III wouldn't break out again? He handed the broom to Bobby.

"Aww . . . do I hafta?

"No. You don't *hafta*. But if your dad comes in and sees this mess, you're going to wish you had." He glared at the other two. "Tyler, get a rag and wipe the table. Be sure to use the trash can. Don't wipe it onto the floor. Marcus, what are you doing?"

"Licking my sock. It tastes like honey."

At least the child was still. "Good man. Keep it up."

He found his brother-in-law in the garage bent over his old '83 Ford Mustang. Sweet little car but way past its prime. "Hey, man. I gotta leave. You might want to keep an eye on those aliens you call sons in there." He thumbed toward the door leading into the house. "Food fight doesn't even begin to describe what I just saw."

Cameron stood and wiped his greasy hands on an orange shop rag. "They're fine. I remember getting dirty with my brother. I'll check them in a few minutes."

"Okay, suit yourself." Jeff hoped there would still be a kitchen in a few minutes. Didn't matter to him. He was leaving.

"You got plans?" He hoped Cameron would take the boys somewhere and get them real tired so they wouldn't use him as a trampoline that evening.

"We're going to take advantage of their teacher workday and go the Children's Museum. They love the Dig Pit. Lots of dirt to play in."

"Where did Claire go again?"

"A scrapbooking seminar. Said she wanted to be sure to chronicle each child's pictures so no one feels left out."

"Yeah, coming from a big family and being the youngest, I can understand that. I don't think there are even a dozen pictures of me by myself."

"She especially wants Baby Girl to feel special."

Jeff chuckled. He loved his sister for already including her unborn child.

A war whoop rent the air and a shirtless Tyler ran into the garage with older brother in hot pursuit and baby brother trailing. Marcus now wore both socks but had to go slow because the left one kept sticking to the floor.

"Have a great day off." He waved to his brother-in-law as he walked out of the garage. Before sliding into his car, he pretended to shoot each of the nephews, effectively stopping them in their tracks as they fell *dead*, helping him to make a clean getaway.

Once at the shop, the day dragged in an agonizing time warp that caused the minute hand on the antique clock to only go half as fast. He'd learned that afternoon that Dad was coming home on Friday, and he knew that meant he'd probably try to come in to work on Saturday. But Mom would stop him. The question was, for how long?

The only bright spot in his day was anticipating Ember's return with another cylinder. To his delight, she came in early and hung out for an hour until closing.

"Do you mind if I grab a dust rag while I'm waiting?" she asked.

He glanced around and only then noticed the place was grimier than usual. "Knock yourself out." He probably should have refused to let her clean, but when Dad decided to come back to work, it would be nice for him to see the place spiffed up.

The bell over the door jingled and a customer walked in. Jeff assured Ember he would help as soon as he was free, but he never had the chance. If there wasn't a customer in the store, there was one on the phone. The last call was from someone searching for a 1920s metal telephone cabinet. Apparently, they had lost one to someone else at an estate auction and decided nothing else would do in a particular corner of their living room. He had no idea what this item was until he Googled it online. It looked like a square birdcage on legs. Thank goodness for his laptop! He promised to search for one and get back to them.

When Jeff hung up, he glanced around the room. "Wow. The place looks better already."

"Thank you." Ember twirled her rag.

Jeff glanced around the area. "You moved some things." He noted that she had created areas that seemed to tell stories. Some kitchen items were pulled together in a living snapshot of what they would look like in a home. A sideboard now housed a hand-cranked meat grinder, a ceramic set of canisters with roosters painted on them, and a set of two cast iron skillets.

She did the same for a parlor area where a Victorian floor lamp with a marble base was paired together with a Queen Ann chair. A side table had a set of original Zane Grey novels pushed together with a pair of bronze bookends depicting children reading. She had even placed an ivory pipe in a carnival glass ashtray.

"I hope that's okay." She twisted the dust rag. "It might help people find things if they can go to groupings. In the real estate world, this is called staging. Making a place look lived in."

"I think it's more than okay. This looks great." He looked around the shop. "I can see where we can do more of that, too. This whole place could look like someone's house."

"Do you think your dad would mind?"

Mom walked in at that moment. "Mind what?" She stopped short as she noted the change. "Wow! If he does, I'll change his mind for him. This looks beautiful."

"Ember did it." Jeff puffed his chest, feeling pride for his new friend.

Ember thrust out her hand. "Hi, I'm Ember. You must be Mrs. Dawson."

Mom reached out with both of her hands. "Please, call me Frannie. I'm happy to meet you."

Jeff watched this exchange. *No, not the look. Do not give me the look.* But Mom peeked over Ember's shoulder and gave him the look, the one that said, *She's cute, you should date her, get married, give me grandchildren.* As if she didn't have enough already.

"Did you need something, Mom?" Jeff raised an eyebrow. He knew what she needed. To meet Ember.

"I just came down to see if you needed any help with the . . . um . . . ledgers."

"Done."

"Phone calling for order pickup?"

"Done."

"Got any—?"

"Done."

"Good. You have everything under control then."

"Yep."

They stood there, rocking back and forth on their arches.

"Then I should go." Mom thumbed toward the door.

"If you must."

Ember broke the standoff. "I hear Mr. Dawson is coming home tomorrow."

"Yes. He's asked for his kids to be there, so I thought I'd send the boys outside to barbeque. It's supposed to be nice. Why don't you join us?"

Jeff wanted her to say yes.

"No, thank you."

Crud.

"That's a time for family," Ember said. "I don't want to intrude."

"Nonsense." Mom, the sheepherder. It didn't matter if someone wanted to go one way, she was determined to get them through that gate. "Ron probably won't even know you're there. We have a large family." She waited for a response. When none came, she threw in the clincher. "I'm sure Jeff would love to have you there. He's usually relegated to keeping the young ones entertained but having you along would probably be a nice change for him."

111

Gee. Thanks, Mom. Why not tell her he was just a step up from the grandkids and a step down from the adults?

"Well . . ."

Could Ember really be considering this?

"Sure, why not? Do you want me to bring anything?"

Ember and Mom disappeared into the office where he could hear them discussing dinner, the Realtor business, and girly stuff.

Jeff bided his time by playing Alien Blastem on his phone.

It wasn't until a half hour after closing that they emerged, linked arm in arm, and looking like old pals. He wasn't sure if he should be worried or happy they'd hit it off.

"I'll let Jeff tell you how to get there." Mom's face beamed.

After she left he shrugged. "Sorry about that. If you felt railroaded into—"

"Oh, not at all. Your mother is charming."

"Yeah." He grinned. "And she just charmed you into accepting a dinner invite."

Ember leaned against the counter and studied her hands folded before her. "The fact is, since my grandmother died, I've been craving family." She took in a sharp breath as if that was hard for her to admit.

"Well, you might as well jump in with both feet. I have plenty of family to share." After an awkward pause, he said, "So, you ready to listen to a cylinder?"

She moved slowly to the backside of the counter where she had stashed her bag. With a sigh, she bent to retrieve it. He couldn't figure her out. If it were him, he would be all over these cylinders. Even though he wasn't into antiques, he recognized that this opportunity—this gift—didn't just happen to anybody.

They settled into two folding chairs he had set up near the phonograph. With a crank and a flip of the tab, they were once again thrust into the past.

Chapter 16

Cylinder Two
Olive

Friday, April twelfth, offered us calm seas, and *Titanic* plowed through the waters with nary a care. Her passengers paraded about in fine clothes and partook of the ship's many delights. I did my best to join the gaiety despite the heaviness in the pit of my stomach.

Charles Malcolm was frenzied in his enjoyment, and may the gods forgive me, I indulged him, padding his pocketbook so he had free reign of *Titanic*'s entertainment. He cleansed his pores in the Turkish bath, played a few rounds on the squash court, and even donned one of those ridiculous swimsuits to take advantage of the heated, saltwater pool. I might have argued with him about these things, but most consisted of active engagement and kept him away from the women. It's no small thing to keep Charles Malcolm away from the ladies—or the ladies from him.

And I too wanted to forget the nasty business in London.

On this particular Friday, I first met Thomas Keaton. I'd passed an hour in the reading and writing room, settled comfortably next to the crackling fire. The warmth, combined with the elegant situation of the room, replete with soft white paneling and a beautiful bow window overlooking the Promenade deck, calmed me. Doing my best to avoid conversation by looking very busy, I took care of some pressing correspondence. It undoubtedly lies on the floor of the Atlantic now. But even as I worked, I knew the women wouldn't leave me to my solitude for long. Idle female chatter is more wearing than that of mixed company, so offering polite nods and very little comment, I made toward the door.

I did pause to speak to Miss Edith Corse Evans. More than once over the years I'd spent a tedious few hours at one of her mother's teas in their New York mansion. Inevitably the woman turned the conversation to the latest undertakings of the Colonial Dames of America. Edith and her mother were proud to belong to this patriotic organization, and I suppose I resented being outside of this bit of society. With a membership restricted to women directly descended from residents in the American Colonies, neither my name nor my bank account could grant me access.

"Good afternoon, Mrs. Stanford."

Edith's smile was genuine, and I reminded myself her impeccable pedigree didn't have to preclude my friendship. Despite my envy, I admired Edith's poise and pluck. Though she was thirty-six and had never married, Edith had the respect of our circle.

"Do you know my aunt, Mrs. Robert Clifford Cornell?" Edith nodded toward the woman next to her. "I'm traveling with her and her sisters."

A fiftyish woman smiled at me. "It is good to meet you, Mrs. Stanford, but please, call me Malvina."

I accepted her salutation with a nod of my head and made my excuses to move on. As I walked away, two more women joined Edith and Malvina, a flutter of conversation and smiles. They so obviously enjoyed each other's company I felt a momentary envy. An only child born to an only child, I never enjoyed extended family.

Needing to keep up appearances, I prepared myself for the meaningless conversation expected of me as I entered the lounge. The elaborate room, with its elegant carvings and oak paneling, had a French Louis XV feel, and the stripes and laces of the women's dresses as they moved about acted as breathing decoration. It was a fine scene but rather too full of people.

I stepped toward one of the large, bay windows to survey the sea. Endless blue-gray met my gaze, filling me with a surreal sense of safety. We were far from London, separated from all but the society of those within *Titanic*'s decks. If it weren't for the blasted Marconi wireless, I could rest, at least for a few days. But the advances of the age had its downside too, and my nerves were constantly on end, afraid a telegraph would interrupt Charles and my game of well-being.

It's rarely necessary for me to seek out conversation, as the Stanford name draws people around it, and such musings were soon interrupted. An acquaintance of many years, Samuel Jacobs, greeted me then referred to the young man with him. "I'm pleased to introduce my friend, Mr. Thomas Keaton. He married the lovely Josephine Lester."

Everyone knew the Lester name, and I'd heard rumors the daughter had married a nobody. I nodded at the young man, taking in his impeccable grooming. He was not a big man, his stature similar to Charles's. But where Charles's hair was a deep, rich brown, almost black, Mr. Keaton's was lighter, like creamed coffee. His eyes were blue to Charles's brown.

"I'm pleased to make your acquaintance, Mrs. Stanford."

Those blue eyes were intelligent, but too eager.

Samuel slapped Mr. Keaton on the back. "Has quite a head for business, this Thomas Keaton. I've invested in his prospects."

Ah yes, another entrepreneur who needed only my money to make him wildly successful.

"There you are, Grandmother." Charles appeared to my right. No wonder the women were drawn to him like a bee to nectar. Though slight of build, Charles's handsome features carried a masculine magnetism—and he was rich. I didn't try to stay the pride swelling within as my gaze swept over Charles's expensive, dark suit; stiff, white collar; and silk cravat. A flash upon his pinky finger captured my attention. It was a gold and garnet snake ring—the symbol of eternal love. Where had he procured such a thing?

Charles slipped his hand in his pocket, and when I met his gaze, it held a rare determination. But this was no time for questions.

I turned to the men. "Samuel, you know my grandson, Charles. And Mr. Thomas Keaton, this is Charles Malcolm Stanford III."

Charles gave the polite half bow in acknowledgement.

"He's the image of his father, God rest his soul." Samuel's whispered words caught in his throat.

I remembered then that Samuel once was quite a favorite with my son, and a twinge of pain surprised me as remembrances of things long buried rose to the surface. A forgotten memory assaulted me—two little boys sneaking treats from ornate platters as their mothers gathered for those infernal women's teas. They thought we didn't notice, but how I enjoyed my son's boyish ventures. Yes, Samuel was a good friend before Charles II grew into an immature manhood, gave into his wild nature, and left good society behind.

With a swallow, I raised my gaze toward the grown-up man, the man my son should have become. Pain flickered through Samuel's eyes, and this act of genuine care for one most of the world had forgotten made me determined to pay closer attention to him and to his protégé.

"You knew my father, then?" Charles spoke casually, but I didn't miss the almost breathy tone. He was hungry—no ravenous—for morsels about his father. My husband never allowed us to talk of him, and after he was gone I found myself living in the same rut, the hurt of losing my son buried too deeply for safe reflection. I suppose I was never allowed to truly grieve him.

"We were good friends, once." Samuel's gaze softened even further.

"Might you . . . " Charles faltered, fussing with the hem of his sleeve, losing his polished image. "Perhaps I could buy you some refreshment, and you could share some stories of the old days. I . . . never knew him, you know."

Samuel clamped him on the shoulder. "With Mrs. Stanford and Mr. Keaton's permission?"

We nodded, and the other two moved away, leaving Thomas Keaton and me to the awkward conversation of people only recently introduced. It was a chore to focus on Mr. Keaton. I too longed to hear the good stories of when my son was alive and happy.

". . . and little Elizabeth, of course." Thomas grinned at me.

I forced my attention back to Thomas, aware that I'd not followed a word of his conversation. "And Elizabeth is?"

"Our sweet daughter. I couldn't be more pleased with her, Mrs. Stanford. She has all her mother's good traits, with her thick, auburn waves and extra helping of spunk, and none of my bad quirks."

I chuckled politely.

"I had no idea one could miss a child so much." Mr. Keaton's voice softened. "I count the hours until I can be in my family's company, with little Elizabeth snuggled into my arms, and my wife's good conversation ringing in my ears."

Unused to such wholesome discussion from men, I peered more closely at this Thomas Keaton. I'd tuned him out, expecting grandiose description of his prospects. Instead, he talked of his wife and child.

"Have you been separated long, Mr. Keaton?"

"Not even a month!" He laughed. "But it seems an eternity."

"Why didn't they travel with you?"

"Next time I hope they will." He stared at me for a moment. "Do you and your grandson travel alone?"

"Yes. With our maid and valet, of course. As you probably know, Charles Malcolm's parents have been long gone, and my own husband passed five years ago."

The honest sympathy that warmed his eyes unnerved me.

"Grieving must be a long and difficult occupation. I hope you have found as much healing as possible in this life."

"You believe in another?"

"Of course." He placed a gentle hand on my arm. "It brings me great comfort to think of my deceased loved ones in a better place, and gives me something good to aim my life toward."

His touch wrought emotion within me that jarred me out of my collected reserve. I took a step back. To believe in heaven, in God, was a frightening prospect.

"I'm sorry, madam. I didn't mean to pry."

I lifted my chin. "You caused me no discomfort, Mr. Keaton." I lied as I gave what I hoped looked like an unconcerned smile. "Each of us has a right to our own perspective on such things. Now, tell me more about your wife. She sounds like an admirable woman."

Concern flicked through his expression, but he smiled. "The very best. I met Josephine while employed by her father. I never thought one so beautiful and intelligent would notice me, but she did. I am a very lucky man."

Especially if Josephine's wealth accompanied her hand in marriage. Surely, Johnson Lester provided well for his daughter, even in marriage to a lowly employee.

"Are you still employed by Mr. Lester?"

A cloud passed over his features that belied the confident smile on his face. "As Samuel alluded, I have my own aspirations."

Here it came, then. The conversation I'd first expected. I settled into it. It was much safer than the more intimate subjects we'd danced around. "Please, Mr. Keaton, tell me all about your endeavors."

Looking back today, many years after, I believe Thomas Keaton could have been quite a success if not for the events that unfolded on *Titanic*. Samuel was right. He had a brilliant business mind, one the world never fully discovered. But again I rush ahead of the story.

My conversation with Mr. Keaton unnerved me, so I signaled Louise, who always waited just beyond sight, and excused myself. "I'm in need of a cup of tea. I'll take it in Palm Court." She nodded, and I made my way to the back of the Promenade deck, to the portside of the men's smoking room.

Bright sunlight streamed through the large, arched window of the Palm Court room. They stretched ceiling to floor, and I paused a moment on the checkered tiles, just to let the sunshine bathe my head and seep into my mind and soul. I imagined it burning away the discomfort of Thomas Keaton's conversation. I chose a white wicker chair in front of one of the false arched windows that held a mirror reflecting back the sunshine that streamed through the real windows on the other side. Walled trellises with climbing plants made me feel as if I sat in a conservatory, and all that fresh, dark green soothed me as only nature can. Soon Louise appeared with my tea.

In our suite that night, I dismissed the servants after they attended to our grooming. When they left, I beamed at Charles. Dashing in his top hat and tails, his collar pushed down into wings, he stood erect before me.

"Did you enjoy your conversation with Mr. Jacobs?" I adjusted his white bow tie.

"He had wonderful stories of my father as a boy." Charles took my hand and led me to the settee. "Why did you never share them, Grandmother?"

"What's the good of such things?" Turning my head so Charles Malcolm couldn't see the mist in my eyes, I fought for control. "He's gone."

"Yes, but surely you can understand why I'd want to know of him."

I nodded.

"Mr. Jacobs made him sound wonderful." Charles sighed. "An adventurous young man full of potential. Someone I should be proud to know." He hesitated. "You and Grandfather never seemed to hold him in the same regard."

"The past is over and done." I stood. "It's better to focus on the demands of the present." I pointed to his left hand. "Where did you get the ring, Charles?"

He jumped to his feet. "Why do you do that?" Charles's face flushed and the pitch of his voice rose. "You ignore my honest question and begin an interrogation."

"You dare question me after what happened in London?"

His prideful stance melted away. He fell back upon the chair, mumbling.

"Speak so I can hear you!"

"I love her still!" he shouted.

"The ring, Charles. Was it from her?"

"It is a promise of her love," he whispered, a tear trailing his red checks.

"It's an indictment! Don't you see? It ties you to her. How many people have seen you wearing this ring? One hundred? Two?" I grabbed his hand. "Give it to me."

"I will not."

"Think about it, Charles." I would reason with him, lead him like the child he was. "There must be nothing about you that ties you to her. No one must know about your . . . your . . . indiscretions. Surely you can understand this."

He stepped back, frowning, twisting the ring about his finger. "It would dishonor her to take off the ring."

"It will mean your demise if you don't!"

He faltered.

"Come, Charlie. Let me have it."

"I will not." His voice held unusual determination. "But I will hide it." He went to his quarters and returned with a chain. "I will wear it underneath my collar."

My fingers itched to jerk the blasted chain from his neck. How easily I could make this evidence disappear. But I would bide my time to ensure success. Charles was much too emotional at present.

"Wash your face, Charles."

He did so and returned, the picture of polish and ease.

Yes, we are Stanfords.

I smoothed the golden folds of my evening dress. The elaborate lace and beaded accents bespoke elegance. I fingered my jewels. The ensemble gave proper regard to the Stanford name. I would make a striking picture, even at my age.

Charles checked himself once again in the mirror. "Do you suppose we'll see Mr. Jacobs and Mr. Keaton this evening?"

"There will be ample time for mingling as the orchestra plays before the meal."

"Did you know Thomas Keaton was a mere employee of Mr. Lester?"

I nodded.

"Mr. Lester fired him when he discovered his daughter's regard."

Ah, here was the information Mr. Keaton did not share with me.

"Josephine married Thomas Keaton against her father's wishes. Thomas told her they should wait for her father's approval, but Josephine insisted it would not be forthcoming, and that they should marry anyway. Her mother insisted on a society wedding, but her father disinherited her."

"That must have disappointed Mr. Keaton." Charles had no idea how the story he told made emotion bubble within me. I steadied my voice. "He was surely after her money and position."

Even as I spoke, the words rang untrue, and I stepped to the mirror and adjusted my necklace to break his gaze. He came behind me, towering over my head.

"Samuel says Thomas wouldn't have taken his father-in-law's money anyway." Charles watched my reflection in the mirror. "He married for love and is determined to make his own way in life."

I turned toward him. "People with wealth do not marry for love, Charles."

He looked away but otherwise ignored my comment. "Samuel says Mr. Lester is a fool—that there's no better person or smarter businessman than Thomas Keaton."

"The fact remains that Mr. Lester is left with a daughter who married beneath her." I grabbed his chin and made him look at me. "Which is an embarrassment and a waste of family resources."

"Samuel also says that Josephine is a dear, sweet girl and deserves a chance at life." His gaze held steady. "That's why he's promoting Thomas Keaton."

"Samuel Jacobs fills your head with silly notions about love." I'd had enough of the nonsense. "Love is childish fancy. Position. Money. Protecting our assets. That is what is real.

Emotions like love come and go, but a strong income and a strong name withstands the test of time."

"Is that why you never talk about my mother? Did you disapprove my father's choice?"

"What all did Samuel Jacobs tell you?" My pulse raced.

"Just answer me." Charles's voice was husky. "Am I of low birth, grandmother? Is that why grandfather hated me?"

"You're talking nonsense." The lies came easy this day. "What a notion! That your own grandfather would hate you!"

"I want the truth." He grabbed me by both arms. "Who is my mother? How did she and father die?"

"You need to calm, Charles. You've read the newspaper accounts yourself." I fought to keep from trembling. "Let go of all this foolish speculation."

"All my life you tell me tidbits of nothing. Can't you understand that it is hard to forge my future when my past is kept wrapped in secrets?" He stepped away. "I no longer trust you, Grandmother."

Opening the door, Charles strode into the alleyway.

Stunned, I rushed after him, "Charles!" My call disappeared into the long hall, and soon his youthful strides carried him beyond the reach of polite voice. I stepped back inside, leaning my head against the papered wall. Silent tears filled my eyes, and I dabbed at them with my lace handkerchief.

For the briefest of moments, I'd had my Charlie back. His questions were vulnerable and sincere, not the distant politeness we'd lived under for the last many years as he reached a tenuous manhood. But I'd pushed him away with my silence and half-truths. Once again, the sweet boy was lost to this angry and confused young man.

I'm not sure how long I stood there, twisting my handkerchief, but I know it was a long time. Not only did I need to find a way to rescue Charles from the nasty happenings in London, but now I also would have to fight to regain control over my grandson before he did himself more harm. As I yanked the lace this way and that, I wrestled with the many secrets and half-truths I held within. How much would Charles have to know for me to regain his good favor? How much could I admit to myself and still survive?

Chapter 17

The cylinder ceased spinning. The motor stilled. Ember sat in the shadowed storeroom struck by the silence.

Without a word, Jeff stood and removed the cylinder from the phonograph. He replaced it into its box and slid it into her bag. A light glowed from the other room, and Ember realized only then that he had slipped out and was now in the office.

A part of her was intrigued to hear about Olive and her relationship with Charles. If that had been the only thing the old woman talked about, that would have been fine with her. But there was more mention of Thomas Keaton. And it was not what she expected to hear.

Olive had said he could have been a success if not for "the messy business" on the *Titanic*. What did he do to screw things up? Apparently, he loved his family. At least that's what Ember came away with. Samuel Jacobs told Charles that Thomas had married for love.

How then could he have walked away? It didn't make sense.

Knowing that Jeff couldn't leave without her, she gathered her bag and turned off the storeroom light. She found him in the office with his laptop, frowning at the screen.

"Penny?" she asked.

He glanced up and smiled at her, chasing the Thomas gloomies from her thoughts. Or, at least made them scramble to a corner where she could deal with them later.

"Excuse me?"

"Or is it more with inflation now?"

Understanding dawned. "Oh, my thoughts. Nah, a penny will do. I'm just researching possible career leads."

"So you're not going to become the 'Son' part of Dawson & Son?" She pulled up a folding chair and sat hugging her bag on her lap.

He sighed and closed his computer. "I'll admit, there are parts to this job I like. Finding stuff for customers, seeing the look on their faces when they get excited about an item. But, no, I can't see myself here at Dad's age, hocking antique iPhones."

"What are you going to tell him?"

Pain entered his face.

"I'm sorry." She realized she was prying. "This isn't any of my business." She fumbled in her bag for her keys. "I need to be getting ho—"

"No, it's not you. Actually, it's kind of nice to talk about this with someone outside the family. My brothers are all pushing me to convince Dad to sell. None of them wanted to be the 'Son' either. My sisters are a little more sentimental, but neither of them expect to take over. Mom just wants me to be happy, but deep down I know she fears for the day when Dad will close these doors forever."

"It must be nice to have family, even if you can't get the answers you want from them."

Jeff rubbed his face. "It's not all it's cracked up to be. I'd love one moment of silence when I get home. Just one."

Ember studied the strap on her bag. Silence was all she had. "I'm looking forward to meeting your family. I'll need an address."

Jeff pulled a piece of scrap paper off a small tablet on the desk. "My mother could have given you the address, but she was hoping I would pick you up."

"Playing matchmaker, huh?"

"I guess that's what moms do."

Ember steeled herself not to react to that. He didn't need to know about her crazy mom.

"I can do that, you know. Pick you up. Unless you want the freedom to leave when things get overwhelming."

"I take that as a challenge." She accepted the paper and looked at the address. "I live between here and your house." She wrote her address down for him. "If you wouldn't mind, I'd love a ride."

"Great! I'll be by right after work." Jeff stood and put away his laptop into a black leather case with a shoulder strap. "Oh! But what about the next cylinder? Would you rather do that and then leave from here?"

"May I be honest?" She'd already confided in Cynthia, why not include Jeff?

He glanced at her and tilted his head. "Sure."

"There's a lot I'm processing right now."

"Care to discuss it over a burger?"

"No. I'd rather not have others around."

"Okay." He lowered himself back into the chair and offered her an encouraging, if not curious, smile.

"I'm dealing with a heavy issue right now regarding this voice from the past." She told him how her great-great-grandfather, Thomas Keaton, had abandoned the family.

"Wait. You're related to him?"

She nodded.

His eyes rounded, and he ran both hands through his hair. "That's why you ended up with these cylinders."

"Yes. They were bequeathed to the family of Thomas Keaton. Ever since Thomas disappeared, not one man in my family has stood the test of love, marriage, or fidelity in five generations. So you can see that I blame him. I find him no different than my great-grandfather who hurt my great-grandmother Elizabeth, or my grandfather who abandoned my Grammy Nora, or . . ." She stopped herself before she admitted she didn't even know who her father was. She might shock him knowing he came from a strong, moral family. "The point is, I'm afraid to find out this man did something truly evil."

Jeff tented his fingers against his lips and appeared to ponder her words. "So you're telling me that you're letting a ghost control you."

Ember bristled. "That's not what I'm saying at all."

"Think about it. He's dead. He can't hurt you or your family. It's like you've chosen to live under this curse. Curses are meant to be broken."

"Very pragmatic of you. But your family isn't the one with a horrible past."

"And what do you know about my family?"

That stopped her short. She didn't know a thing about his family, other than it was large and boisterous. "I'm sorry. That was unfair of me."

He scratched his neck. "No, I'm sorry. I can see you're in pain, and I want to help. Can you trust me to do that?"

Okay. That was pretty much what this whole thing boiled down to. Trust. Should she trust a man? Any man? Should she trust Jeff?

"I can try." She knew her words came out small and thin. But it was the best she could do. "Since you have your father's homecoming to deal with tomorrow, we can skip a day of listening."

"All right, but let's get back to it on Saturday. I'm really getting into this Olive and Charles thing."

"Agreed."

They parted ways from the shop. This last conversation exhausted her, and she didn't have any small talk left in her.

* * * *

Ember awoke that morning to rays of sunshine playing through her lace curtains. She looked at the clock. When she was working, she would be up by six thirty and out the door by eight. Now, she forced herself to sleep as long as she could, unless she had somewhere to be.

Most days, she spent her unplanned vacation sprucing up her apartment. Somehow, covering walls with fresh color boosted her mood, if only temporary.

But today, a trip to Dewberry Harbor for some shell collecting appealed to her. That was one thing about Oregon. You had to take advantage of the sunshine, no matter what time of year. If she left soon, she could be back in time for the Dawson dinner that evening. She threw off the covers and dressed quickly. The breeze would be chilly, so she opted for her white Abercrombie & Fitch sweatshirt and khaki capris.

After slipping into her beachcomber shoes and lined, hooded windbreaker, she hustled out the door.

She left without breakfast, deciding to stop at her coffee shop for an Americano and blueberry scone. Not bothering to go inside, she pulled up to the window. It had been just over two weeks since she'd been there, and that was when she met James had who issued the ultimatum—go to New York to open the mysterious safety deposit box, or stay and fulfill her dream.

Not surprisingly, her little car took her by way of the Dowling estate. She parked near the gated drive and looked toward the house. With it set back from the road, she could barely make out the red tiled roof through the evergreens.

Two weeks.

How had her life taken this odd turn in two short weeks? She looked down at what she was wearing then glanced up to see herself in the rearview mirror. No makeup and her hair pulled up into a loose bun, she was a far cry from the high-powered Realtor she'd imagined herself to be.

When she decided to protect Grammy's past from Beverly's exploitation, she had no idea the crap it would stir up within her. She groused for several more miles about the men the Keaton women had chosen, and even threw Dean in there since it was his fault she wasn't setting up her own office in that cute little cottage with the striped awning.

By the time the ocean came into view an hour and a half later, she'd played the "Men Are Scum" recording in her head so many times, she was ready to get out and run on the beach to get away from the awful tune.

It wasn't long, however, while she tried to catch her breath from her short sprint in the sand, before other memories began to push her problems aside. Walking this same beach with Jeff, their gentle conversation, the ease she felt by his side.

A sand dollar caught her attention, and she bent down to retrieve it. It wasn't perfect with its chips where it had bumped against who knows what, but it was whole. She couldn't remember the last time she'd seen a perfectly round sand dollar.

Beyond the beach, waves rolled, their violent beauty striking her as a metaphor. It had begun in an ocean where the Keaton lineage had first chipped. Generation after generation, it took more hits. And yet here she stood. Maybe not perfect but somehow whole.

She raised her hand, rearing back to throw the shell into the waves thinking, "Take that, Thomas Keaton!" But she stopped, hand in midair, and slowly slipped the sand dollar into her pocket. She may be battered, but she was whole. Through whatever she was about to face, she would hold onto that truth.

Chapter 18

When Ember arrived home from the beach, she figured she'd have an hour before Jeff came by to pick her up. She'd stayed too long in Dewberry Harbor, but thought it too therapeutic to cut short. She felt eighty percent better.

As she was laying her clothes out before her shower, the doorbell sounded. Annoyed at the interruption, she looked through the peephole.

Jeff!

She performed a quick check. Her hair had become a loon's nest after a day in the wind, her legs were encrusted with sand dust, and she desperately needed a shower.

But she couldn't keep him standing in the hallway.

With a deep breath, she patted her shirt unsuccessfully removing the wrinkles, put a hand on her hip and a smile on her face, then opened the door, trying to look as normal as possible.

He took one look at her, then checked his watch.

"You're early."

"I'm sorry. Didn't my mom tell you I'd be closing the shop at five today? She wanted to have dinner before it got too dark outside to cook."

"No. I've been at the beach all day." She fussed with the rubber band tangled in her hair, hoping to tuck the wayward strands back in.

"That explains it."

"What?"

"I thought you were wearing perfume." His eyes twinkled. "Eau de Mackerel."

She quickly dropped her arms, torn on whether she should fix her hair or keep her armpits covered.

"I'm kidding." Jeff chuckled. "You look great for a day on the coast."

"Since I'll assume that was a compliment, you may come in." She stepped aside.

He strode into her home, glanced around, and whistled. "Nice place."

"Thanks. Please forgive the paint smell. I'm finished in the living room, and I've moved to the bedrooms. I've done my best to make this little space comfortable." She was grateful she'd never been a drop-it-and-leave-it type of person.

When she was selling houses, she was rarely home. Her apartment looked like one of her staged houses. But in the last two weeks, besides painting, she'd added little touches here and there. A colorful afghan draped lazily over her plum sofa. Pretty candle sconces on the wall. New frames for the photos of Grammy Nora, both with Ember and without, displayed on the marble mantel of her gas fireplace.

"This is the newest member of my family." She pointed toward her little white polar bear, all twelve inches of him in his place of honor on a child's rocker she had found at an antique mall. "You'll be interested to know that he has a connection to the cylinders."

She walked over and picked up the bear, straightened his crisp white and blue sailor uniform, and held him facing outward as if she were introducing a child. "This is Bear."

Jeff tilted his head. "Bear? Did you name him?"

"Let's just say, when I acquired him, I was too tired to be creative."

"Rick. That's a good name for a bear."

"Rick?"

"I had a dog named Rick. Got his name because he had rickets when we found him."

What an unusual man. "I'll stick with Bear."

"Suit yourself." He shrugged.

"Are you interested in hearing more about him?"

Jeff pinched his lips shut, a silent promise, Ember assumed, not to interrupt anymore.

"*Bear* was made in England by the Steiff Company, as you can see by the button tag." She wiggled his ear. "He's very well made." She twisted his arms and legs to demonstrate that they were jointed.

"He looks ready for inspection. The admiral must be coming aboard."

"I know, it's amazing how well preserved he is. He was in the safety deposit box with the cylinders."

"Really. This toy is one hundred years old?"

She nodded.

He reached out, and she handed it to him. "Hello, old chap."

Her heart melted as this grown man looked deep into the black glass eyes.

"I'll bet you have some stories of your own to tell, don't you?" Jeff asked.

"According to the letter Thomas Keaton wrote, Bear was a gift to his daughter. Since that was my great-grandmother Elizabeth, I felt entitled to keep him for myself."

"What a shame she never got to meet Bear."

"What a greater shame her father never took it to her in person." Ember felt the familiar anger rise from the pit of her stomach. "How did Olive Stanford end up with it? And why didn't she make sure Elizabeth got it?"

He seemed to be contemplating her questions when she glanced at the clock. "Goodness! We're going to be late! You're welcome to go on ahead. I'm sure I can find the place. I have a GPS."

"I'd like to wait if you don't mind. I'm sorry for the confusion, but please, take your time. It's just family, and besides, it will make for a more dramatic entrance."

Ember had a hard time tearing herself away from those gorgeous eyes, almost as vibrant a blue as Bear's uniform. But she directed his attention to the television remote, the iPod dock, and reading material on a bookshelf.

"Go, I'll be fine." He shooed her out of the room.

After the world's shortest shower, Ember blow-dried her hair and twisted it back up into a neater bun than when she'd left the house that morning. She dressed quickly then applied minimal makeup. Nothing worse than floating foundation on a moist face. When she emerged, Jeff was sitting on the sofa with Bear still by his side and listening to Vivaldi's La Stravaganza. The violins greeted her in a cheery romp, and she now felt ninety-five percent better. Up fifteen from her outing at the beach.

"Do you like classical music?" she asked as she struggled to put on a bracelet.

"I think I do now. This is beautiful." As the melodious strains danced around them, he stood and approached her. "Here, let me help you with that."

His fingers warmed her wrist as he deftly slipped the clasp together on the tennis bracelet.

Wow, she could get used to this. But should she? Sweat broke out on her upper lip.

"Um . . . Thank you." She backed away, disappeared into the kitchen, and hollered out to him. "I know your mother said not to bring anything, but I made a fruit salad."

"You didn't have to do that. There will be plenty to—" He stopped short as she entered the living room with her bowl.

"What?" Why was he staring at her bowl?

A tiny grin tugged at the right corner of his mouth. "Nothing. Whatever you contribute will be appreciated."

When they arrived at his parents' house, Jeff ushered her in. She could see now why he thought her bowl of fruit salad so amusing. What seemed like a big bowl to her wouldn't serve a tenth of the people gathered. The women, his sisters and sisters-in-law she presumed, sat in the living room with several children from toddler on down. She could see older children playing in the backyard. The men must have all decided to congregate under the patio.

Frannie Dawson approached, removed the bowl from her hands, and thanked her as if she'd just brought ambrosia direct from the Greek gods.

"Everyone!" Frannie called attention to her brood. "This is Ember, Jeff's *friend*." Why the emphasis on the last word? Did

Jeff have so many friends that when one entered she was tagged and categorized immediately?

Jeff whispered, "Brace yourself."

A rush of women, two who looked vaguely like Jeff, enveloped her.

"Pleased to meet you, Ember."

"So happy you could join us."

"Whatever do you see in my brother?"

"Lacie!" This came from the other four women.

"What?" Lacie asked. "It's a valid question."

After much chattering and introductions, a hand reached into the flock and pulled her out.

"Dad is waiting to see you."

Jeff. Her hero.

He led her out the back door onto a lovely deck surrounded by plenty of lawn for the innumerable children who were tumbling upon it. Three men stood around a commercial-sized smoking grill. One of them held long tongs and wore an apron that said, "Real men don't cook indoors." Two others sat in lawn chairs near Ron Dawson but stood to shake hands with her.

"Em . . . mer."

Her heart broke as Ron attempted to say her name. This was a mere shell of the man she had met two weeks ago, thinner, older. He sat in a wheelchair, but held out his left hand to beckon her. She felt drawn as a hummingbird to nectar.

"Than . . . you for com . . . ing." She felt his frailty even in the firm squeeze of his fingers over her own.

She kneeled in front of him and stroked his lifeless right arm. "I'm so sorry this has happened to you." Tears sprang to her eyes. How surreal. She had only met this man once, yet she felt connected to him in a way she had never felt before. Not even with her own grandfather.

"Aw." He frowned and waved his hand. "This is a time for . . . cel . . . e . . . bration." He raised his arm toward the heavens. "I'm . . . alive. I'm . . . home."

Frannie appeared at Ember's side. "That's right. And supper is getting cold." A look of pure love passed between Frannie and the husband she'd almost lost. Ember turned, wiping her wet cheeks, feeling like an intruder.

She found herself face-to-face with Jeff, looking into his tender moist eyes. She reached out for his arm, feeling the need to steady herself but was suddenly pulled to his chest. It seemed he needed her at that moment, as well.

* * * *

Jeff and Ember followed the crowd inside to the dinner table. With the sun hanging low in the west, the near seventy degree spring day dipped into a chill.

He still felt wobbly after witnessing Dad's declaration. Why didn't he shake his fist and get angry at his affliction? How could Mom take it all in stride? This was the strength they had always taught their children. To see it in action shook him to the core.

Ember seemed moved, as well. That wasn't the way he had planned on hugging her the first time. But, despite the circumstances, he had to say he enjoyed it. Up until his brothers noticed and started whistling.

In the dining room, platters of grilled hamburgers and Polish sausage sent forth savory curls of steam. Ember's fruit salad sat on the table, dwarfed by large bowls of potato salad, baked beans, and coleslaw. While everyone was preoccupied with helping the children, Jeff pulled Ember's chair out for her . . . to the right of his mother. His chair. He had brought women to family gatherings before, but something seemed different with Ember. He knew he was getting way ahead of himself, but she belonged in that chair.

Talk throughout dinner focused on the cylinders. Jeff noticed Ember made no mention of Thomas Keaton but filled everyone in on Olive Stanford's dilemma with her grandson, Charles Malcolm.

Every adult in the room leaned forward as Ember spoke.

"I just want to scream at her," Ember said. "She thinks her money gives her privileges that the common man has no right to. Yet, she loves Charles and dotes on him, giving him money he doesn't deserve and spoiling him."

"And get this," Jeff interjected. "Something happened to him in England involving a woman just before they boarded the ship. She hasn't been specific. It's almost as if she's not willing to say it out loud yet."

"What do you think happened?" Claire placed her elbow on the table and palmed her chin.

Never before had Jeff commanded this room. He was always the squeaky mouse in the corner that everyone tolerated. But now, every eye was on him, hanging on his every word. He kinda liked it.

Marcus spilled his water all over the kiddie table, and chaos broke out in that side of the room. Claire frowned in his direction but turned back to Jeff, riveted in her chair. "Well?"

He leaned forward, as did everyone at the table. "I have my theories, but I don't want to spoil it for you."

Groans broke out and Claire stood, slapping her napkin to the table. "Marcus, go get a towel and dry yourself off."

Ember tilted her head toward him. "You had them in the palm of your hand."

He chuckled. "Right where I wanted them."

After dinner and a rousing game of Pictionary, Jeff took Ember home. "Thank you for going tonight. It meant so much to my dad."

"Thank you for including me. I'm so sorry he got tired and had to leave his own party." Her eyes darkened with a hint of the pain he'd seen earlier.

"Don't fool yourself. He may have been resting in his bedroom, but he was enjoying the laughter in the house."

She sighed as she unlocked her door.

"What is it, Ember? Even while laughing and having a great time with my family this evening, you still seemed . . . I don't know . . . melancholy." He reached out and stroked her arm.

She turned toward him, so he pressed his luck and with his other hand, held her at arm's length for several seconds, probing the depths of her eyes, trying to find answers.

"I'm fine."

Was she trying to convince him or herself?

She paused, as if she were about to say something more. But she kissed his cheek and in one disappointing move, pulled from his grasp. "I'll see you tomorrow." Then she disappeared into her apartment and closed the door.

Chapter 19

Cylinder Three
Olive

Charles Malcolm avoided me for the rest of Friday night and through Saturday, April thirteenth. I allowed it. I say that as if I had a choice. He came in late at night and slept through breakfast. When I returned from breakfast each morning, he was gone. I knew not where. When we did happen to pass outside our quarters, I kept the Stanford airs. I wouldn't push him in public. He wasn't above making a scene, and I hated scenes.

But he'd return once the money I'd given him played out, tail between his legs, simpering and acting as if he cared. As much time as he spent at the card tables, whiskey within easy reach, it wouldn't be long. I made sure Calvert stayed close to him. As long as his reliable servant was close by, nothing too much could go astray, or at least that's what I told myself.

I retired both nights at a reasonable time, sleeping fitfully until I'd hear Charles Malcolm stumble into the suite, swear at the servants, and finally quiet in his bed. It was grievous, this grasping for distraction in my grandson, this aching distance between us. Oh, it was nothing new for Charles to drink, gamble, and flirt—even to be angry with me, but this time the playboy was carried further, the anger more furious.

My boy was aching in the deepest places, and I had nothing to soothe his pain. I'd tried to feed his ravenous need with greenbacks, pouring money into the gaping, gasping mouth of his agony. It did little but spoil him and offer momentary distraction. I know that now. But at the time the money was the only way I could keep him close, and the only answer I knew to the haunting questions of his existence.

As the hours wore on, that ring taunted me. I feared its connection to the girl in London. I feared the discovery of it around his neck if he swam again in the saltwater pool, or—heaven forbid—found his way into another woman's room in stages of undress. Saturday night when he bumbled into the suite, more drunk than ever, I formed a plan. I lay in my bed, straining to hear. Eventually all was quiet. Calvert retired, but I sat up in bed, listening to the gentle hum of the engines of the *Titanic*, waiting to insure Charles's deep sleep. Then I tiptoed to his room, using my cane to help me feel my way through the darkness. Once there, I slipped as close as I dared, then stood until my eyes adjusted. A slight light came through the window, thanks to the stars, and I edged closer. Charles snored, in the dead sleep of the drunken.

I scanned his neck. Luck was with me. The clasp to the chain that bore the ring was in front, not underneath him. My old fingers were no longer nimble, but they fumbled with the lock until it fell open. I inched the chain off my grandson, holding tight to the ring so it wouldn't fall to the floor and startle him awake.

I wrapped the ring in my fist, then crept from his room and shut his door. I leaned heavily against the wall, thanking my lucky stars for success. My legs trembled beneath me, and I sat for a moment upon one of the parlor chairs. My age, and the fact I was used to being waited upon, slowed my progress, but I was determined. I found my fur coat and pulled it about me, placing the ring deep into a pocket. Careful to not allow my cane to tap upon the floor, I made my way out of the suite and into the alleyway. When I reached the deck, I felt I'd run a marathon. Exultant at my success, I allowed myself a momentary celebration before reaching into the coat pocket. I wrapped a gnarled fist about the hated ring and raised my hand to the railing. I grabbed the rail with my other hand to steady myself. If I held my arm as far out as possible before opening my fist, surely the ring would fall beyond the *Titanic* and into fathomless depths never to be seen again.

I stretched my arm and was about to let go of the hated remembrance of the floozy when a strong hand grasped mine and held my fist closed. I jerked around. Charles glared at me through bloodshot eyes. He squeezed my hand so tightly I couldn't help but yelp in pain.

"Hush!" His whispered threat seared my ears. "We wouldn't want anyone to hear, would we, Grandmother?"

For the first time, I feared my grandson. The alcohol had not completely worn off, and his eyes were dark with rage. He twisted my arm, and I cried out again.

"It's a beautiful, starry night, isn't it?" Calvert's familiar voice caused us to whip around. "I'm sorry I didn't hear you moving about sooner. Were you in need of anything?"

I played his bluff. "Of course not. Charles and I simply had to stargaze this night. We didn't mean to disturb you."

Charles held tight to my fist but held it down low, between us. "Have you ever seen so many stars, Calvert, like a darn canopy of diamonds." He continued to work my fingers, pulled them even as he talked.

I gasped as the ring fell away. There was a slight clatter as it fell to the ground. Calvert reached it first.

Charles was immediately in front of him. "Thank you, Calvert. Your service is rendered impeccably, as always." He turned toward me and offered his arm. "Come, Grandmother. The air is too cold for prolonged enjoyment of the night."

I offered no resistance. What else could I do? Whatever Calvert had seen or suspected was more than enough intrigue. He need not be privy to further indelicacy.

Once back in our suite, Calvert hovered. I suggested he wait in Charles's room until his help was required. As soon as the door closed, I turned toward my grandson. "It was for your good. For your safety." My words were a hiss.

"It was blatant disregard for my desires."

"Come, Charlie, let's reason this out. I only want the best for you. You're all I have." I sat on the settee and patted a spot next to me.

He warred with himself, his emotion more readable when under the influence of the spirits he'd ingested earlier that evening. Finally, he sank into the cushion.

"Who was that woman in London, Charles?"

"Harriet Snow." He hiccupped, his head in his hands. "She loved me, and I loved her."

I bit back the lecture on the folly of believing in love. "How could she afford such a ring?"

Charles hesitated. "He . . . he gave it to her."

"Who, Charlie?"

"The man who . . . who paid for her things."

"Oh, Charles. She was a kept woman?" It was worse than I feared. "Another man's mistress."

"He didn't love her. He . . . hurt her. I promised. I told her I'd help her—that we'd live as man and wife in New York. I would have."

I couldn't control the moan.

"It's your fault." His words were hard. "If you would have just listened to me, I'd be in London now, with her. We'd be married and booking passage to New York."

"Surely you're not so naive as to think that could work—a woman like that married to Charles Malcolm Stanford III? You'd never have been accepted in polite society. Our name. Our fortune would be squandered, all for puppy love." My eyes narrowed as bile formed in my throat. "How could you?"

"It will never happen now, will it, Grandmother?" His tone began cold, but agony warmed it at the end, and Charles began to weep. He fell into my shoulder as he'd done that first night on the *Titanic,* and I dared to pull him into my arms. The talk with Samuel Jacobs had stirred memories I'd long suppressed. Charles's questions about his family—even Thomas Keaton's claims of joy in forbidden love—all pressed upon me as my grandson wept. And after all those twenty-one years of deceit and holding back grief, the truth of it all swept over me. At first I felt disconnected from the wet tracing lines down my face, but once I allowed tears to fall, I couldn't stop them.

I don't know how long we stayed that way, but after a time, I heard Louise's quiet footsteps, felt Calvert lift Charles Malcolm to his feet. They walked, shuffling together, to his room.

Never had Louise's touch been so gentle as that night. She encouraged me to my feet, pulled off the coat still wrapped about me, and eased me beneath the covers of my bed.

Charles and I both slept through breakfast Sunday morning, but Louise brought tea and toast to me and helped me dress for Sunday service, which was to be held at 10:30 in the first-class dining room. I'm not a churchgoing woman, but for appearances' sake I thought it best I attend, even though I knew Charles would not.

Samuel Jacobs found me as I sought a place to sit for the service. As usual, Thomas Keaton was at his side, smiling and conversing easily with all around him. We were seated and, as is tradition, the captain resided over our service. He made quite a fine figure in his crisp white uniform and snow-white beard. His solid build and barrel chest belied sixty-two years, but that beard made it believable. At first glance, I'd thought Captain Edward John Smith quite stern, but the gentle, refined pattern of speech I heard now helped me understand how passengers and crew alike could refer affectionately to him as E.J.

I bored of studying the beloved captain and turned my attention to those around me. It was a good occupation. After the emotion of the night before, I had no wish to listen to religious drivel. The infamous Margaret Brown sat a few rows to my right, Edith Evans and her aunts in front of me and to my left, and Mr. and Mrs. Straus not too far behind them. I recognized many other faces, but an accidental glance toward Mr. Keaton, left me speculating about what sort of man he was. Fascinated by his rapt attention to the speaker, I wondered at his ability to care for religious thought. With such musings I was able to get through the service without giving into personal reflection. It was more difficult to ignore the words of the hymn that sprang from the throats of all around me.

O God our help in ages past,
Our hope for years to come,
Our shelter from the stormy blast
And our eternal home.

Eternity is something I prefer not to speculate upon. I know not if there is a God or an afterlife. Perhaps it is best I never know such things until the other side of the grave.

But I digress.

After surviving the service, I returned to my suite to check on Charles before lunch. He was up and dressed but sat staring aimlessly at the walls. I approached tentatively. Would I be the grandmother who tried to destroy his most treasured possession or the grandmother who held him in his sobs?

"Are you rested?"

He glanced my direction, his eyes guarded. "Well enough."

I left space in the conversation for him to continue, but he did not. He excused himself, and I didn't see him again until he returned to dress for dinner.

I'd saved my favorite gown for this evening. I loved the luster of the beautiful crepe de chine silk, and the steel blue suited my age. I stood and turned before the mirror. The tiny beads on the lace bodice caught the light, casting little twinkles into the mirror. Louise had done well with my hair this night, and as she helped me into the matching lace jacket, I felt only a portion of my sixty-seven years.

When I left my room, I discovered Charles awaited my appearance. He rose slowly and presented his arm.

Grateful for this peace offering, I wrapped my fingers around his coat sleeve and squeezed. He slowed his pace to match mine as we made our way through the great ship. Whenever we entered the reception area, with its dark, rusty carpet and bright white ceilings, gazes often turned toward us, the Stanfords. The old pride rose within me as young ladies fluttered their eyelashes toward my handsome grandson, resplendent in his new swallow-tailed coat, white gloves, and white bow tie.

This latest fashion, with the silhouette cut that focused on his svelte athleticism, suited Charles better than the old barrel-chested look. He looked fine standing beside me. John Jacob Astor himself could expect no better reception than Charles Malcolm and I received that night. And indeed, when he and his young wife passed by, they too offered a respectful nod, as did we.

I had disapproved his divorce a few years before. His marriage to one barely older than his son had the tongues of good society wagging. The newspapers had declared theirs to be a great love, but surely she wanted his money and he her youth.

The Astors didn't follow the crowd to the first-class dining room. I imagine they had decided to enjoy the evening meal in the beautiful A La Carte Restaurant. I'd considered it myself, but after the vulnerability I felt in the church service, I preferred the crowds over the greater hush and intimacy of the restaurant.

The dining room, with its vaulted ceiling, stretched before us. I was told it was the largest ever seen aboard ship, and I would easily believe it as I gazed upon table after table, beautifully appointed with white linen cloths. As the women paraded into the room, in their fine silks and laces, I couldn't help but compare their soft pink, yellows, and creams to the elegant spring flowers in the table centerpieces. All was splendid in that room from people to walls to furnishing. The Jacobean style was said to mirror some very fine houses in Hatfield, England.

People made way for us, and as Charles pulled out an oak chair at a nearby table, the fragrance of roses wafted toward me. Charles seemed pleased when Samuel Jacobs and Thomas Keaton joined us. I was not. Of course I didn't show it. What I'd wanted more than anything upon entering the dining room was to be one of the elite, receiving polite nods, but no real conversation. I had hoped no one of close acquaintance would make their way to our table, but that's not the way the cards fell.

Charles became the charming conversationalist as the first course of oysters was served. I watched in awe as he navigated the social graces with a prowess I could only admire. He had everyone within hearing riveted upon him as he told stories, procured laughter, and asked the perfect questions of those surrounding us. With Charles at his witty best, I was able to let down my guard. Savoring the aroma of my Consommé Olga, I used the soupspoon to take delicate bites. It humored me that Charles had preferred the Cream of Barley. He was never one for the more savory recipes.

Charles's happy chatter soothed my frayed nerves, and I found myself enjoying the meal immensely. By the time they brought the third course, salmon with a creamy Mousseline sauce and cucumbers, I was at my ease.

Charles turned to Mr. Keaton. "I hear yours is a great love, sir. Tell us what to look for in marriage."

My back stiffened involuntarily.

Thomas Keaton raised an eyebrow. "Ah, the young man wants to hear the story of love!"

Charles lifted his glass. "I am no simpering female, but I toast a man bold enough to boast of marital bliss."

I wrenched the cloth napkin lying on my lap but was careful to keep the Stanford composure. How dare my grandson rub his desire for Harriet in my face?

Mr. Keaton winked at Charles. "Then I will regale you with such stories as to make you wild with longing for a wife of your own." He got a faraway look in his eye, and even though I disapproved his marriage into the Lester family, I couldn't help but be drawn into the tale.

He leaned toward Charles. "Josephine is all a man could ask for." His voice lowered, not applied to the masses but spoken in quiet tones to my grandson. "As I'm sure you've heard, she's a great beauty, with her wavy, auburn hair, but while her appearance is pleasing, it is her heart I treasure."

Others around us first sat quiet, straining to hear I suppose, but when they realized the words were indiscernible, the chatter about us resumed. I was close enough to listen, as was Samuel, and we focused on the earnest conversation happening between Charles and Thomas.

"Her love for you?" Charles's eyes never left Thomas's face.

"Of course."

The conversation stalled as our server in his crisp *Titanic* uniform offered the next course. The rich aroma of beef and garlic was a welcome distraction after such conversation. "Isn't it lovely?" I gestured toward my Filet Mignons Lili perched atop crisp potatoes, foie gras medallions, and artichokes. Sliced truffles floated in a rich sauce of Cognac, Madeira, and red wine. "I must have the recipe for cook."

The men ignored me, as well as the china plated delicacies being placed before them. Mr. Keaton leaned forward. "But it's more than emotional love, Charles. Josephine is intensely loyal. As you've undoubtedly heard through the very active rumor mill of our society, she chose me despite disappointment and complication. But it isn't only her loyalty. Or how she believes in my ideas even before they bear fruit. It's her kindness in word and deed. The way she adores our daughter and encourages little Elizabeth to love me. It's the fervency of the prayers she sends on behalf of my safety, my dreams, my daily endeavors."

He paused to draw a breath. I clasped my hands together, hoping to still a sudden tremor. I'd never before believed in love, but the shine in Thomas Keaton's eyes made me almost think it possible.

"Is it true her family disinherited her?" Charles's voice was a whisper.

"It is."

"Don't you care?"

A sad smile filled Thomas's face. "I care for her sake. She is used to more luxury than I can provide, but she bears her reduced circumstances well. The most painful part is the rejection of her father. She loves him still."

An incredulous look filled Charles's eyes. "How do you provide for her . . . and for yourself?"

Compassion softened Thomas's face. "I have always been a working man, Charles. I've never had the opportunity to be idle."

Charles colored and sat quiet. Awed that Thomas Keaton had shared so intimate a discourse with my grandson, I looked to Samuel, a question upon my face. He squeezed my hand. "The three of us have had several conversations." His voice was a discreet whisper. "Your grandson is hungry for such clarity of thought, for lack of pretense."

I looked back toward Charles. Agony was upon his face, and I fought not to give into the tears of the night before.

"And the child?" Charles stumbled over the words. "What's it like . . . to be a father?"

Thomas grinned. "Think of the very best of life. Then double it." He sipped his wine, then grabbed Charles's arm. "To have a child of your own who wraps her little arms about your neck and looks at you as if you've hung the moon and stars . . . well now . . ."

Thomas released his hold, staring into the distance, then refocused on my grandson's face. He leaned forward. "I'm not saying fatherhood is without its challenges, but with a little one like Elizabeth a father does anything to illicit a giggle—crawl upon the floor, growl like a bear, make ridiculous faces. You'd buy her the world if you could. And each night you pray to God to do nothing that would take that respect from her wide, innocent eyes." His voice cracked. "You pray to God to be worthy."

I'd never heard a man speak in such a way. I wanted to scoff, to confront such audacious claims, but the sincerity in Thomas's eyes silenced me. I stood abruptly, right there in the middle of the fourth course of ten. "Please excuse me, gentlemen. I'm feeling a little faint."

Charles looked toward me, and the grief in his eyes ravaged me. "Should I accompany you?"

"Oh, no. Enjoy your friends. I just need a bit of fresh air or to lie down maybe. Perhaps the wine affected me." I tapped my cane upon the floor, walking away as quickly as I dared. How I wished I were far from the staring faces. I cared not I was the great Olive Stanford, woman of wealth and respect, known in all the right circles. Unbidden, the old longing had crept over me—the craving for love, the hunger for a man who saw beneath station and fine clothes and respected pedigree to discover the person beneath all the trappings.

Realization hit hard, like a sudden blow to the stomach. I was sixty-seven years old, and I'd never known true love. I'd glimpsed it on occasion from my mother, but even her attentions were tempered by society and the appearance of my father, who would hand me off to the nanny.

I stepped outside into the cold air, but the bitter temperature stole my breath, driving me back indoors. I made my way to my suite, but once there its opulence mocked me. What good was all that if I was never to be loved? I paced its length, turned, and walked back again. A novel rested on the table, but I couldn't even bring myself to pick it up and pretend to read. Finally, I fell exhausted into the parlor chair.

After a time the door opened, and I looked into the accusing eyes of my grandson. "You said it wasn't possible."

"Whatever are you talking about?" I pretended I didn't understand him.

"Thomas Keaton is an example of true love."

I shrugged. "I've never known such things as he talked about. But I have known love as I have loved you."

"But would you love me if I dishonored you as Josephine Lester dishonored her father? Would you disinherit me as he did?" He turned a sharp gaze upon me. "What if I married Harriet, raised our child?"

"You know that is impossible."

Charles glared then pivoted away from me, slamming the door behind him.

Just as dark had claimed the frigid night beyond the electric lights of our ship that fated night of April 14, 1912, darkness claimed my soul. Like the ship, I was lit with gaiety to all who looked upon me, but inside I was hopeless. I feared I'd lost the only person I truly loved. And I feared for his life if he pushed me away, refused my help at managing it. If Charles Malcolm refused my interference, how would I protect my grandson from the calamity sure to come from the cries of London?

Chapter 20

When the cylinder whirred to a stop, Ember wished her imagination would do the same. She could clearly see Thomas in that dining room, his eyes brimming with love for his Josephine. She could hear the longing in his voice for his family, for his sweet daughter.

Jeff placed the cylinder back in its box, slipped it into Ember's bag, and started to leave as he had a couple of evenings ago.

"Jeff, wait." Ember caught his sleeve as he passed by. "I don't want to be alone with my thoughts right now."

He sat back down on the folding chair and leaned his arms on his knees. His concerned gaze touched her.

"It doesn't make sense," she said. "Thomas is a bad guy."

"Says who?"

She had already filled him in on that part of her family. If he was going to challenge her, maybe she didn't want to talk to him about this.

"Every woman in my family. The men don't care. They're as bad as he was."

"What I just heard didn't sound like a villain. Is it possible something else happened?"

"Like what?" She folded her arms and leaned back into her chair.

"What if he had amnesia? Just wandered off. What if he never recovered, just died a lonely beggar on the streets of New York?"

"He had to know his name in order to get onto the survivor's list."

"True." He tapped his lip as he thought. "What if . . . his injury was so great he was ashamed to go back home? It happens in war movies all the time."

"And usually in those movies, the soldier gets a conscience and comes back eventually. I suppose something like that could have happened, but I find it unlikely. Especially the way he spoke about his. . .affection for his family." He couldn't have felt love of any kind. She squeezed her eyes shut.

"Ember."

She felt his hands gently unfolding her arms. When she opened her eyes, he was holding both of her hands in his.

"Why is this so important to you? Help me understand."

Since when had a man ever had her best interests at heart? Dare she trust him with further information of her messed-up life?

His eyes implored her.

She took in a shaky breath. "It wasn't only the women in past generations who were affected by this curse. My love life has been really crappy." Tears sprang to her eyes.

He stood, dragging her with him, and enveloped her in his arms. This hug was not one of support as it had been on his parents' patio. His arms now offered protection, safety, and—dare she say it?—love.

"It all stops now." His words, spoken softly in her hair, caught her off guard.

"What?" She pulled away, only far enough to see his face.

"Generational curses can be broken. I told you that before." He looked deeper into her eyes. "It stops now." His lips touched hers. Soft, seeking permission. When she leaned in, the kiss deepened, as if the very act itself could sever the curse.

But then again, Dean had kissed her like that.

She broke away, angry with herself—with Dean, with all of stupid men in her family—for ruining this beautiful moment. Why bother giving her heart to Jeff, when destiny would only intervene?

"I'm a good guy, Ember," Jeff whispered. "I can break this curse."

She pushed at his chest to back away. With words on her tongue that would surely end this kind of thought, she found she couldn't refuse the sincerity in his face. "Let's just go slow. Okay?" She grabbed her bag and headed out of the storeroom.

"I'm fine with that. Just don't shut me out."

Her hand was on the doorknob when she turned back to look at him. He'd jammed his fingers into his pockets, and he looked like a puppy that had just been swatted with a newspaper.

"I won't. You're a good friend, Jeff, and that's just what I need right now."

* * * *

The kiss, like cinnamon, tingled on her lips, causing her to toss and turn all night. Could he break the curse? What would happen to him if he tried? What if the Keaton women brought the curse upon the men they loved?

Just after nine o'clock the next morning, her cell phone rang. She'd been lingering over the Sunday paper and a second cup of coffee, and even though she'd eaten breakfast, she wasn't dressed.

"Hey, it's Jeff."

Why was he calling so soon after they'd agreed to go slow? And why was she so glad to hear his voice?

She fought to be nonchalant. "What's up?"

"I forgot to tell you yesterday that I won't be able to meet today to listen to another cylinder. I have to drive to Everett," he said.

"Everett? In Washington? That's what . . . four hours from here?"

"Three and a half. I figure if I leave by eleven, I'd get there before the antique shop closes at four. Dinner there, and then home by nine. You busy?"

"You're asking me to go with you?"

"Yeah." He sounded so eager. "I don't want to make that long trip alone. Can you be ready in two hours?"

If it was just to keep him company and wasn't a date, what would it hurt? "Well, I guess you just solved my dilemma. Other than meeting with you later, I had no plans."

"Then I'll be there. Thanks."

She hung up after saying good-bye and thought about that. It would be good to help him. He'd done so much for her.

* * * *

Jeff couldn't have been happier that Ember agreed to go with him. He filled her in on their trip as he negotiated onto north Interstate 5. "One of our regular customers called yesterday, saying he had found the perfect rolltop desk advertised at an antique shop in Everett. He can't travel anymore due to an auto accident, so he occasionally sends Dad to check out things for him. He pays well." Jeff recalled the phone conversation. Henry Powell hadn't heard about Dad's stroke. He empathized with a couple of swear words, then assured Jeff he'd be there if he needed him. For what, Jeff didn't know, but that seemed a common sentiment as friends heard about Dad.

"So, what if it's just what he wants? How do you get it to him?"

Jeff glanced at Ember then kept his gaze on the road. She looked so pretty sitting next to him. He recalled the first few times he'd seen her, all austere and wearing that ridiculous bun that pulled her face back by at least two inches. But this softer Ember seemed more approachable. Her makeup, if she wore any at all, made her look younger. She actually had a splay of freckles across her nose. The bun was still there, but she allowed small slips of hair to frame her face. The downturn of her mouth wasn't pinched as it had been when she first entered the shop. But there was still a sadness in her eyes that never went away even when she smiled.

"Jeff?"

"Hmm? I'm sorry, you were saying?" He flipped his turn signal and passed an old lady barely peeking over the steering wheel of an eighteenth-century Oldsmobile.

"What if he wants the desk?"

"I call him, tell him if I think it would be worth it. Then he talks with the seller and they ship it to him. Or, if the item is small, I'll take it with me. Like your phonograph. But my job is to be eyes and lend my professional opinion about the piece."

A small grin played on her lips.

"What?"

"You're beginning to sound like an antique dealer."

"Bite your tongue, woman!"

"I think you like this business way more than you let on."

"Okay, get out of my car."

She giggled. "But you're going seventy-five miles per hour."

"Well, don't be surprised if I leave you in Everett."

The first leg of the trip went way too fast for Jeff. If Ember hadn't been along, he would have been bored before reaching the state line. But with her there, he could have driven another two hundred miles.

There wasn't much distinction between Seattle and Everett. The two cities simply melded into one large metropolis. The antique shop didn't take them too far off the highway, and he found it easily.

Buy Gones Antique Shoppe was located in an artsy district, nestled between Misty, Moisty Morning, a shower and bath essential oils store, and Both Ends, a candle shop where apparently one could "Make your own and burn at Both Ends" as the sign said. Once again, Jeff contrasted the difference between a good location and the run-down part of town.

Inside the shop, Jeff began to make mental notes. This place wasn't a hole in the wall, dusty, attic-at-street level place like Dad's. He felt like he was in someone's house. The groupings were what Ember had attempted when she "staged" the showroom. She seemed to be taking mental notes, as well. Her eyes grazed over everything, almost as if she were scanning to make prints later.

"Mmm . . . smell that?" Ember's perky nose thrust upward.

He breathed in deeply. "I do. It's nice."

"Sandalwood. Perfect for a woman but made for a man."

"Isn't that deodorant?"

She giggled. "Not quite. I use sandalwood in houses I'm selling. Usually in the bedrooms, and something more edible in the kitchen, like vanilla or spice."

"Do you miss it?"

"What? Staging?"

"No, selling. I know you said you were on hiatus, but aren't you getting itchy to get back to it?"

"I am, but I want to do it right. I'm thinking of hanging my own shingle, not work for anybody. Of course, it would have happened much earlier if the Dowling estate sale had gone through."

She filled him in on the sale that wasn't, and how one of her coworkers had stolen it out from under her. By the way her cheeks reddened and her nostrils flared, he guessed there was much more to the story.

They moseyed throughout the store as they were talking, picking up little chotchkies, admiring old portraits, laughing at toys from days gone by.

"Ah, here it is." They stopped by the rich walnut rolltop desk in pristine condition. He opened the top, pleased with its ease. The writing part of the desk slid out without a hitch and the moss-green leather writing blotter had no marks. Normal wear spots could be seen in the cubbyholes and tiny drawer inside, but they were devoid of nicks or scratches. The rest of the piece also impressed him, from the burled splashboard and its finials on each corner to the hardware. Jeff felt in good conscience to recommend it to his customer.

They found the owner, a tall, stately woman in her fifties who had been helping someone else. After she told him the desk had just come in that week and had already received some attention, Jeff negotiated a good price then called Mr. Powell.

"I think we have a winner. Would you like to talk to Mrs. Callahan to finalize?"

"I trust you, Jeffy, I really do, but can you send me some pictures?" Jeff was afraid this would happen. Henry Powell had known him since he was a kid, so probably didn't trust him as much he did Dad.

"Hey, Mr. Powell. You got a cell phone that receives picture texts?"

"Sure do. You just called me on it. Kids taught me how to use the text part. Great way to see the grands."

"Okay then. I'm going to take some pictures and shoot them off to you."

He did that and within ten minutes had convinced Mr. Powell to jump on this find before anyone else had a chance. The desk would be shipped since it was too large for Jeff's vehicle, but even so, he thought it was a great deal.

Ember had disappeared somewhere in the store. When he finally found her, she was hugging a porcelain vase.

"It couldn't be, could it?" Her hands trembled as she turned it over. She put it down and began to weep.

"Ember, what's wrong?" He pulled her into an embrace and felt her shoulders shaking.

"Grammy's vase—Beverly." She sobbed into his shoulder, not able to finish her sentences. She glanced back at the vase. "I thought it was hers."

"Whose?"

"Grammy's." Ember hiccupped. "She had a vase like it."

Tucking a strand of stray hair behind her ear, he whispered. "Hey, it's okay." He put a protective arm around her shoulder. Holding her close as he ushered her out, he pointed his cell phone at the vase. He just might need a picture.

Chapter 21

Ember huddled in the passenger seat of Jeff's car as they made their way home. She'd made a fool of herself and now, on top of her grief, she felt humiliated.

Miles went by before she could talk. "I'm sorry you had to witness that back there." She wiped the tears from her face and felt her puffy eyes under her fingers. "Or this mess here."

He cocked his head toward her. "I have sisters."

"I wish it were as simple as hormones."

"We have a hundred seventy miles to go, and I'm a captive listener."

"Oh, I don't want to burden you with my problems."

"Suit yourself. But I'm already burdened. I hate seeing you like this, and if it would help to talk about it, I'm safe."

She eyed him for a moment. Was he?

Another mile went by, and they were coming into Seattle where the traffic flowed easily. Good thing Jeff chose to do this on a Sunday.

"It's the vase," she said.

"I gathered that."

"No, it's not just the vase."

"I gathered that, too."

She looked at his profile as he concentrated on traffic. Strong jaw. Stubborn chin. Laughing eyes.

"I thought it was my grandmother's vase. When she was alive she kept fresh flowers in a vase just like that. Sometimes we would go to her garden and pick them together. In the winter we would buy them. It became our vase."

She didn't mention that she thought her mother was jealous of the time she'd spent with Grammy. Or that the vase had become the solid proof of that. Ironic, since Beverly was never around Ember to seem to care. All she did was criticize in her backhanded way. *Ember, I can see you love spending time with*

Grammy, but if you're not careful you're going be old before your time. Or, *Grammy bought you a new dress! I'm sure we can fix that hemline.* Or, the time Ember made some tissue flowers for Grammy's empty vase because she was too ill that summer to pick them. Beverly ruined it when she said, *Ember, these are really lovely. I hope Grammy won't think them too tacky for her beautiful vase.*

Ember appreciated Jeff's silence.

"When Grammy's health began to deteriorate," she continued, "I entered her house and the vase was empty on her dining room table. She beckoned me over, grasped my hand in hers, and told me she was giving it to me. I knew then that she was going through all of her things, deciding who got what when she died. I didn't even want to think about that. By then, my mother had disappeared into parts of the world I couldn't even pronounce." Ember swallowed. Beverly gold-dug her way to a fortune, always blowing it before the next guy came along. Then repeated the process.

"I assured her I would take it when the time came, but until then, it was to sit in its spot, on the little table in the picture window, welcoming visitors with the fresh aroma of flowers peeking over the gold rim." She blew her nose. "It stayed there until after Grammy's death. But then . . ." Fresh tears began to wet her cheeks. "When I came back from New York, my mother had been to Grammy's house. She'd been gone so long and become so unreachable, she didn't even know her own mother had died. In one fell swoop, she emptied the house and put it on the market. I'm sure that anything she couldn't sell immediately went to the dump."

"And your vase?"

"I don't know. I'm hoping she sold it. I can't bear to think of it smashed under garbage."

Jeff reached over and squeezed her hand. As the miles ticked by, they sat quietly.

Jeff's growling stomach interrupted the silence, loud enough to be heard over the car engine. He rubbed it and glanced at her sheepishly.

"I'm sorry." Ember sat up straight. "We were going to eat in Everett before we left."

"You feel like something now?"

She pulled the vanity mirror down. What an emotional disaster!

"We don't have to go to a restaurant where we'll be waited on." He must have sensed her trepidation.

Thank you, sisters, who had taught him well.

"Would you rather just go to a drive-through and eat in the car on the way home?" Jeff asked.

"Oh, yes. That would be great."

He left the interstate and found a hamburger drive-through. They ordered and were back on the road in a matter of minutes.

Her strawberry shake never tasted so good. The sweet creaminess soothed her aching throat, still raw from emotion.

The conversation for the rest of the drive centered on surface things. Favorite colors. Summers on the coast. Jeff shared that he enjoyed deep-sea fishing. Ember talked about college. All safe topics.

Other than the grueling first few miles of the trip home, Ember thought the rest flew by too fast. He pulled into the visitor's space at her condo and released his seat belt. She put her hand on his arm to get his attention.

"You don't have to go up with me."

"You sure? I was raised a gentleman. Sometimes I actually manage to be one."

"No." She chuckled. "You've endured enough for one day."

He turned in his seat to look at her full in the face. "I had a great time with you today."

She rolled her eyes.

"Well, other than that one hour, but the rest were really fun. Let's hang out again sometime, okay? In this century, not 1912."

"I had fun too . . . other than that hour. Call me whenever you want to 'hang out.'"

She hopped out of the car.

He rolled down his window. "Tomorrow?"

"We're listening to another cylinder, silly."

"Oh, yeah."

The weight on Ember's shoulders lifted with the elevator ride to her apartment. She wasn't sure why. The men in her lineage were still scum. Her mother was still a flake. Dean . . . Dean, who? And her vase was still missing. The only factor that had changed was Jeff's deepened friendship.

She received a text message as she unlocked her door. Setting down her keys, she looked at her phone and smiled at Cynthia's sweet face. The message read: *Do you want to skip?*

Shaking her head, Ember typed: *Do you mean Skype?*

* * * *

Jeff arrived at work the next day thinking about Mr. Powell and his desk. Would he really like it? Was the price okay? Had Jeff proven himself as good as Dad?

The door was unlocked, and he opened it gingerly, wondering if the place had been vandalized. But what he saw alarmed him more.

"There's . . . my . . . boy."

Dad.

He wheeled up to him, more full of life than Jeff had seen in a long time.

"I love the . . . showroom! Mom said Em . . . mer did it."

Jeff glanced around at the cozy spots Ember had created. The shop looked almost as good as the one they visited yesterday.

He moved to the office to set down his laptop on the desk. "Dad, what are you doing here? Isn't it too soon?"

"Nope. Doc said it would be the best . . . thing for me."

Swell.

"Now . . . get in the storeroom . . . take inventory."

What? No *attaboy*? No *you done good, son*? What about saying thanks for learning something that he had no desire to learn? Just sent to the storeroom as if it were his first day?

Uh-uh. It was time to stand up to the old man.

"Dad, if you'll look over the ledgers, you'll see that everything has been logged and categorized."

Dad looked up at him. "Categorized?"

"Yeah." Jeff sprinted to the back of the counter and brought out a ledger. "Ember's rearranging of the store gave me this idea. What if we had a separate sheet for different areas? Kitchen stuff, bedroom stuff, outdoor stuff? When someone calls looking for something, we can go to the appropriate ledger and not have to look through everything in our inventory to find it. Of course, if we had a computerized database system, all we would have to do is a simple search for item, color, era, you name it."

He knew he was stretching his luck with the last suggestion.

Dad pointed at the book still in Jeff's his hand. "I like . . . what you did . . . with this." He wheeled his chair into the office.

Well, he didn't say thank you, but he didn't shoot him down either. That would go into the Victories column in the ledger Jeff was keeping in his head.

The rest of the day exhausted Jeff. Dad thought he could do the work of a healthy sixty-year-old man, but when he couldn't, Jeff had to help him. It took twice as long to hand change back to customers. Twice as long to fill out credit card slips by hand. And even though Dad's speech was improving, it took them twice as long to have a normal conversation.

By the end of the day, Jeff felt as if he'd been playing tug-of-war for nine hours.

Just before closing, Jeff noticed he was alone in the showroom. He glanced into the office, expecting Dad to be pouring over past ledgers, or on the phone with a customer, or anything but what he was doing. He was just sitting at the desk. Staring.

Jeff rushed to his side. "What is it, Dad? You have another stroke?"

Dad turned clear but troubled eyes to him. "I can't do . . . this."

The lost look on his father's face frightened Jeff. "Sure you can, Pop. It's just the first day. You probably should have taken it slow. Maybe only come in a half day or something."

"No." He grabbed his own right wrist with his left and flopped it. "I'm no good with this . . . dead arm. I'm no good for the . . . shop. I'm no good for you."

"Stop talking like that, Pop. You just need to regain your strength." Jeff hated to make the suggestion on his lips, but it really was for the best. "What if we computerized? It's much easier to hit keys than it is to write."

He heard a crack in the limb he'd just climbed onto. Worst case scenario, Dad would fire him. And frankly, that wouldn't be such a bad thing right now.

"Okay."

"Say what?" Jeff leaned his ear in, not sure he had heard correctly.

Dad looked at him, defeat warring with hope. "Okay. If it will help . . . me keep the shop."

Energy burst through Jeff. "Oh, you won't be sorry, Pop. I have so many ideas. We can set up a database for your ledgers. Automate the credit card system. Oh, and a website! I can design a website that will knock your socks off."

When he finally floated back to earth, Dad was studying him as if he were a new species of animal found in the Congo.

But Dad didn't argue.

The door jingled. Jeff wondered if he could replace that stupid bell but thought that might be going too far. Female voices chattered, and he recognized both of them.

"We'd love to have you join us," Mom was saying.

"I'd like that. Thanks for thinking of me." Ember's eyes were still a little red, understandable after yesterday, but she seemed happier. Then again, it would take a clinically depressed woman on serious meds not to match Mom's enthusiasm. Didn't matter what she was doing or how she was feeling, Mom always remained upbeat and encouraging.

"So," Jeff said, "what are you two planning?"

Mom took Ember's hand and stroked it as she did the baby bunnies in their backyard. "We're going shopping tomorrow."

"Well, no wonder you both look so happy."

"And not just any shopping," Ember said with a gleam in her eye. "Baby shopping."

"The girls and I are going to look for some pink things for the nursery." Mom slipped her arm through Ember's. "We don't think Baby Girl would enjoy airplanes and motorcycles on her wall."

"They were good enough for the boys," he teased.

"I happen to know you've already done your own pink shopping for the baby, so you can drop that act, buddy boy."

Jeff shrugged and looked at Ember, who smiled, apparently enjoying the exchange.

"Where's your father?" Mom let go of Ember and brushed past him.

"Um . . . he's in the office. I think he tired himself out today."

"That stubborn man wouldn't listen to me." Mom frowned. "I told him he should just come in for an hour or two at first." She disappeared into the office, leaving Jeff and Ember alone in the showroom.

"Recovered from yesterday?" Jeff locked the door and flipped the SORRY, WE'RE CLOSED sign.

She waved him off. "What you saw is something I deal with on a daily basis. Some days are just worse than others."

"I mean, have you recovered from spending an entire day with me?"

She laughed. "You're not so bad once a person gets to know you."

"Thanks." He grinned, realizing the whole day with Dad was worth it if Ember could show up at the end of it.

She sobered. "No. I want to thank you. It helped to talk things through. I don't usually wear my grief on my sleeve like that."

He glanced toward the office where his parent's voices cooed together like two mourning doves. Waving Ember toward the Wormhole, he led the way in and turned on the light. "I never understood grief until Pop got sick. If I had lost him . . ."

"But you didn't." She placed a soothing hand on his arm. "If that day should ever happen, I hope I can be there for you."

With her face upturned to his, he thought he might kiss her. But he thought too long, and she broke the connection by reaching into her bag and retrieving the next cylinder. She placed it on the machine and cranked it.

"Ready?"

He nodded as he heard Mom's voice calling out a farewell. The bell jangled, the lock clicked, and he was alone once again with Ember, Olive Stanford, and the past.

* * * *

Cylinder Four
Olive

Sleep did not come Sunday night, April fourteenth. Tossing about in my gown, I strained for sounds of my grandson's return to the suite but heard none. Then there was a strange sensation, and my mattress shook a bit. For a moment my heart fluttered, but nothing unusual followed, and I turned my attention again to the task of repose. I couldn't stand guard over my grandson, and rest at my age is of great import. I think perhaps I nodded off for a short time, but soon I was wide-awake. Something was different, though I couldn't discern what.

I sat up, pushing pillows behind my back for support. It came to me. There was an absence of motion, no movement, no hum. After the vibrations of the engines hard at work for the last four days, it was a strange quiet. Suddenly, I had to know where Charles was. I awakened Louise who helped me dress properly. As she buttoned my shirtwaist I turned to her. "Does anything seem different to you?"

Her eyes widened. "The engines have stopped."

I nodded. "My thought as well."

"What could it mean?"

"I am not sure. The alleyways are quiet. I've heard no sound of distress or alarm. Still, I would be more at ease if Mr. Charles were with me." I rapped on Calvert's quarters. "I'm in need of your assistance."

"Yes, ma'am."

Charles could only be one of two places at this time of night—at cards or with a woman. I never thought the day would come when I hoped to find my grandson losing more of my money at the gaming table, but this night I wished for it. The premonitions of tragedy that had nipped at my heels the whole trip now clutched at my throat. Something was wrong, and if Charles was gambling he would be easy to find.

I waited in the parlor chair, my back stiff and straight, as Calvert dressed. I'm sure I drove Louise to distraction, but I couldn't stop tapping my fingers upon the table next to me. Finally Calvert emerged.

"I need you to accompany me to the smoking room."

"Shall I attend you as well?" Louise stood quietly by.

"There is no reason for you to go traipsing about at this hour. We'll return shortly."

Calvert opened the door, and we walked though. A steward passed, and I signaled his attention. "Why have we stopped?"

He inclined his head. "I don't know, madam. But I doubt it to be much of anything." He resumed his brisk gait and left us to our task.

Once we were alone I fought my pride. It was always delicate to discuss personal issues with the servants. "I think perhaps Charles is at cards. The smoking room is no place for a woman."

"I'll inquire after him."

"While you're there, see if you can find anything about the lack of movement of the ship."

My feet ached. I'd heard a gentleman comment that if he stood at Thirty-Fourth Street in New York City, the *Titanic* would stretch all the way to a little north of Thirty-Seventh. It is no wonder I was weary, pacing that distance in the middle of the night. I was too old to parent such a senseless young man, and the opportunities for his escapades were endless on this monster of a ship.

Calvert found a bench not too far from the smoking room where I could rest, and I sat there alone, with nothing to interrupt my musing.

Poor Charles had nobody but me. Even when his grandfather was alive, he'd given Charles Malcolm only the least bit of attention. No wonder the poor boy thought the man had hated him. His suspicion wasn't far from the truth, despite my efforts to contradict such a notion. It had mattered not to my husband that the baby was of his own flesh and blood. He saw only the mother's genes polluting the Stanford name. Charles Malcolm was nothing but a reminder of our son's defiance. If my husband had had his way, we'd have never known our grandson. He'd been left to starve with his widowed mother.

Charles the first would have never married me if my own lineage had been discovered. But I never told him. Ours was not that sort of marriage—to be sharing secrets. By the time my husband-to-be became acquainted with our family, the truth of my heritage was buried to all but myself, and my pedigree seemed impeccable. My English born father also had no knowledge that my mother's linage included poor Irish immigrants. He knew only of the value of her parents' estate.

In the world where I was brought up, marriage was managed for the sake of protecting all that is important—one's standing, one's income, one's name. Class married class. My mother's mother had married well, establishing our station in life, and I had done all within my power to continue the legacy.

But my son, Charles II, had given no mind to our family name and squandered his good fortune upon a poor woman. I've often wondered if blood from my Irish grandmother of long ago had coursed through his veins, taking him to mean places, drawing him to the hidden past.

It mattered not now.

I sighed and shifted upon the hard bench, wishing Calvert would return and rescue me from the direction of my thoughts.

But the area was quiet and my musings, having slipped free from the rigid grasp I usually kept on them, would not be reined in.

It was a bad business, my son's death on the streets of New York—a gambling debt I suspect, though inquiries were never made. It was better to pretend all of it had never happened, so we allowed the killer to run free, and with a slip of money to the right people, the incident was never known.

The society papers reported that Charles Malcolm II and the young wife he'd married abroad had perished in a fire, and that I would travel to England to bring the baby home. That's what I told the reporters, who had been eager to hear personally from the great Olive Stanford. It was this public announcement that forced my husband to allow me to retrieve little Charles Malcolm and raise him as my own.

I've always known how to get my way.

The suffering expression of Charles Malcolm's mother still haunts my dreams on occasion. But what of it? She stole my son away with her bedroom eyes and curvaceous figure.

A life for a life.

The sensation of Calvert's quiet presence next to me pulled me out of such morbid remembrances. I forced my attention to the situation at hand. "Well?" All that mattered now was my grandson, the only family I had left, the only person other than his father I'd truly loved.

"Charles wasn't there."

I sucked in a strangled breath. "Did you learn anything about the engines being cut off?"

"The gentlemen there seem quite at ease. They think perhaps we've grazed an iceberg. They saw a tall one, eighty to ninety feet, one of them estimated. It passed right by the smoking room window. They joke that it scraped off a bit of paint and the good captain doesn't like to go on 'til she's painted up again."

"There's no concern, then?" My cane offered support as I arose from the bench.

"Not to hear them say it." Calvert offered me a reassuring smile. "One of the gentlemen pointed to the glass of whiskey at his elbow then turned to me and said, 'Just run along the deck and see if any ice has come aboard. I'd like some for this.' That brought a round of laughter."

"Very well." I stood at a crossroad, finding myself unable to return to my suite without my grandson but at a loss as to where to look. I swallowed hard. "Did you happen to notice anyone in particular that Charles might be with this night? It's imperative I find him."

Calvert was a good valet, and I read the struggle between loyalty to me, his true employer, and loyalty to the one he served most often, my grandson. After a moment's hesitation he averted his eyes. "If you'll allow me to walk you back to the suite, we could see if Mr. Charles is there. If he is not, I might be able to ascertain his whereabouts."

Despite my ill humor I felt a half-smile play at my lips. Faithful Earl had taught his son well. The valet had found a way to please me without betraying Charles.

When we arrived at the door, Louise greeted us without her usual reserve. "The engines are still silent, I'm sure of it."

Calvert stepped forward. "There has been no alarm. Perhaps you'd like to make our mistress comfortable. I will continue about the boat and return as soon as I have news."

Under normal circumstances Calvert wouldn't dare take charge, but as I looked into Louise's eyes, I realized a genuine fear, and a little introspection revealed my own upset—whether for Charles or the strange goings-on of the ship, I did not know. But Calvert was sensible enough to provide direction for us. It was the sort of leeway I'd allowed his father, my faithful chauffeur, during those difficult days after the death of my husband. A new respect for Calvert grew within me.

Louise set about fluffing a pillow for my lower back. Her fussing annoyed me, but it seemed she needed an occupation.

Where was Charles? Surely after the ugly circumstances in London he hadn't entangled himself with another woman. Still, it was just the kind of behavior I'd expected—another frenzied exploit to distract himself from reality.

I could only imagine what he must have felt when that floozy fell upon the corner of the brick fireplace. It was her own fault, of course. If she hadn't hung on him, tried to trap my wealthy grandson into a relationship with a star-crossed lover, he wouldn't have shoved her.

She'd be alive.

Chapter 22

Jeff reached up and stilled the motor before the cylinder was finished. "That was his secret. He murdered that woman."

"No, not murdered. It was an accident. Somehow in their arguing, he pushed her."

Jeff wasn't sure why this story affected him so much. Could he see a little of Charles in himself? Not willing to grow up. Arguing constantly with his father. Of course, he'd never slipped into philandering, but that was probably due to his mother's influence. If it had just been Dad and him, no brothers or sisters, would he be bent on destruction like Charles?

"I wonder if he'd have gotten onto the ship if she hadn't died." Jeff hoped there was some redeeming quality in Charles.

"I don't know." Ember tilted her head as she considered this. "I think Grandma Olive would have somehow stalled the departure from port to find him."

Jeff chuckled. "Yeah. She's a formidable woman, isn't she?"

"An unsinkable woman on the unsinkable *Titanic*. Do you think she eventually broke like the ship?"

"Well, let's find out."

Jeff lowered the needle onto the cylinder, and once again the self-proclaimed great Olive Stanford continued with her tale.

* * * *

Cylinder Four Continues
Olive

Louise poured me a cup of tea as I sat, waiting for Calvert's return. While I didn't desire refreshment, the distraction was helpful, and I must admit a long sip of the warm liquid emboldened me. A swift glance at the clock revealed that ten minutes had passed since Calvert left us. It felt an hour. I reached for a book to distract myself. I'd turned the first page when there was a pounding at our door. A voice called from the alleyway, "All passengers on deck with life belts on."

I glanced at Louise, nodding toward my favorite evening wrap. She helped me into the life belt then covered the whole ensemble with the woolen shawl heavily embroidered with birds and flowers. I typically loved the elegance of the beautiful, long, black fringe along the wrap's hem, but it seemed ridiculous tonight, covering a life belt.

Louise put her life belt on top of her coat. I considered wearing my fur but felt sure the drill wouldn't last long and didn't want the discomfort of wearing both the life belt and my thick coat.

There were a few people in the alleyway now, talking and greeting each other, speculating on the strange drill in which we were expected to take part. We followed the general movement toward the deck. When I stepped outside, bitter cold burned my cheeks and bit through my outer garments.

"Should I go back for your coat?" Louise asked.

I shook my head.

The air was frigid and the moisture in my nose hardened. Around us, sailors prepared lifeboats for launching. Louise and I paced the deck, scanning the growing crowd for Charles.

Half past midnight they began loading the lifeboats, calling for women and children. We were offered a seat, but I was in no mood to carry the exercise to that extreme—at least not until I knew the whereabouts of Charles Malcolm. Besides, the lifeboat hung out, a fair distance from the deck, suspended many feet above the black ocean below. Feeling quite sure I was safer where I was, I stepped away. Louise followed, but I saw honest trepidation in her expression.

"Go back and take a seat."

Her eyes widened. "I couldn't leave you, madam."

"You can and you will. If this nonsense continues I will follow in a later boat."

She hesitated.

"Louise!"

"Yes, ma'am."

Her fear was palpable, and I refused to breathe it in. "Just go."

Standing my ground I watched as the men practically threw her from the *Titanic* into the lifeboat. When they began to lower it, I noted how empty it looked. I learned later it was built to hold sixty-five people, but I'm sure it didn't have even half that number taking refuge. Perhaps others, like me, had no desire to risk disembarking the unsinkable *Titanic*. How easily we Americans trust in the advances of the age.

Louise lifted a gloved hand as the lifeboat dipped beyond my view, and I felt a sudden panic. Shocked that the absence of Louise would affect me so, I decided my poor nerves had taken quite a pounding from my conflicts with Charles Malcolm. I was simply worn-out, cold, and alone. What was I doing, roaming around in the bitter air after midnight?

The sailors began to load another boat. Again I pulled away from the scene, determined to find my grandson and just as determined not to be flung over the dark sea into such a small vessel while the strong *Titanic* floated beneath me. Again the lifeboat dropped to the water with scant passengers.

"Madam."

At the sound of Calvert's voice, I let out a pent-up breath. "There you are."

"I came back for you and Louise as soon as I heard the announcement, but you'd already vacated the cabin." He glanced around, a frown about his eyes.

"Louise has boarded a lifeboat. I'm waiting for Charles."

"Of course." He offered his arm, and I took it with great relief. "See the lights over there?" He pointed to the distance where there was a yellow glow. "I'm told the ship is to come and help us as we assess the damage of the iceberg." He stood young and strong beside me, and his calm presence offered reassurance.

"You've confirmed we've struck one, then."

He nodded.

I gazed toward the distant lights then brought my attention back to the urgent matter at hand. "Did you not find him?"

He hesitated. "When I heard the call for life belts, I believed the more immediate need was to attend to you and Louise."

"Take me to my grandson. You know his whereabouts."

The sound of ragtime drowned out his reply. Focused on our own endeavors, I hadn't noticed the *Titanic* band assembling on deck, but there they were, playing the lighthearted fare of parties. The talented Wallace Harvey stood directing them, resplendent as always in band uniform. Reality began to blur, everything surreal and nonsensical. It was surely nearing one a.m., well past my bedtime, yet here I walked in freezing cold air, seeing my breath in little cloud puffs, listening to music as lifeboats dropped into black waters.

But there was one thing I knew to be true. I had to find my grandson. "Take me to him, now."

Calvert nodded, and we worked our way through the gathering crowds. Suddenly there was a deafening roar, following by hissing. My fingers tightened on Calvert's arm, clawing my fear.

"I believe they are relieving pressure in the boilers, madam." Calvert placed his hand over mine. I didn't mind, and this very fact made me realize the strangeness of the situation.

Then the news began to be whispered that the bow was sinking and the stern rising. "Isn't she unsinkable?" was asked time and again. "She can't go down, not with all those locking compartments." All around me the safety of the *Titanic* was discussed, and all the while sailors continued their call for us to fill the lifeboats.

Now people pressed toward the tiny vessels. Instead of launching half-empty crafts, the sailors were left with the task of keeping the swarming crowds from overloading the boats. I began to wish for a seat upon a tiny boat, myself. But not without Charles.

I quickened my pace and Calvert matched my step. As we passed another boarding station, I recognized Mr. and Mrs. Straus. They had just loaded their maid onto a lifeboat, and the sailors encouraged Mrs. Straus to board, but she argued with them. I watched the exchange as Calvert led me around the edge of the crowd.

The sailor turned to Mr. Straus. "Perhaps you could go as well, in deference to your age, sir."

Mr. Straus looked appalled. "I wouldn't take a seat that could be given to a woman or a child!" He turned to his wife and said something. I couldn't hear his words, but I saw him gesture toward the lifeboat.

"We have lived together many years." Mrs. Straus's determined voice carried. "Where you go, I go."

I caught my breath. The woman's devotion jarred me to the bones. How must she have been loved to give up her chance of safety for the elderly man rising next to her? Stunned by such a display of affection, I evidently stopped walking for Calvert gently pulled on my arm. "We must hurry, madam."

Of course. We had to find Charles, the one I loved so desperately that, in search of him, I had passed three lifeboats. I glanced behind me as I walked.

The men stood helplessly about Mrs. Straus, staring at the determined woman. Finally, Mr. Straus took her hand and led her away from the crowd, their fingers clasped between them.

"This way, madam." Calvert led me to an enclosed part of the promenade, and I felt relieved to get out of the night air. We walked swiftly to wherever Calvert was leading. Suddenly, Mr. Astor was before me. A lifeboat hung outside the window of the enclosure, and he helped his wife onto it. His tenderness astonished me—a man of such worth and power, so solicitous of her care. Could the reports of their love have been true?

"Might I accompany her?" Mr. Astor pointed to his wife, white-faced next to him. "She is in a delicate condition."

"Women and children only, sir."

Mrs. Astor argued, but Mr. Astor saw she was seated safely. "The ladies have to go first." He tossed her his gloves. "Good-bye, dearie. I'll see you later."

As we walked away, the glint of a spark caught my eye. Mr. Astor calmly inhaled on a cigarette.

It was to be the last time I saw him.

As the swirl of people increased, my palms felt sweaty. "We're running out of time."

Calvert nodded. "I believe we'll find him on the second-class deck."

Life father, like son.

"Perhaps you should secure a place on the lifeboat with Mrs. Astor while I continue to look for him."

"No."

Calvert looked pained and quickened our pace.

"Mrs. Stanford!"

I turned to the familiar voice. Mr. Keaton stood before me, pale and determined. He thrust a satchel toward me. "It seems very likely there will be room only for the women on the lifeboats." His voice was low and serious. "Would you take these small tokens of affection to my wife and child?"

"Surely—"

"Mrs. Stanford, you can always return them to me, but in the chance I don't meet those dearest to me again in this life, it would bring me great comfort to have your word they will receive this."

"But of course." What could I say?

Calvert took the leather pouch. "God speed, Mr. Keaton."

We rushed from him with his expressions of thanks ringing in my ears. The last thing I heard him call to me was, "Tell her I love her, Mrs. Stanford. Tell her my love is eternal."

* * * *

Ember lifted the needle from the cylinder. "He didn't make it."

Jeff sat still at her side.

She slowly looked at him. "That's how Olive had his things in her possession."

Something cracked around her heart, and she clutched at the pain.

"It seems so." Jeff's words were barely above a whisper.

"No. No, that's not possible." She had held onto her belief for so long, the possibility that she and every woman in her lineage were wrong would not shake off. "They must have gotten separated after the rescue. She couldn't find him. He was hiding from her, then marked himself as a survivor and walked away. From Josephine. From baby Elizabeth. From her oppressive father."

"Ember—"

She looked at Jeff knowing she must seem like a madwoman. "No. He couldn't take the fact that he was less of a man, and he left it all. Just walked away."

"And maybe he died that night."

"Then why was he on the survivor's list?"

Jeff opened then closed his mouth. Finally, he said, "I don't know. I'm sure it was a mess when they got to New York. Maybe it was an error."

"Not likely."

They sat in silence for a few moments longer. Then Jeff set the needle once again.

* * * *

Cylinder Four Continues
Olive

I saw one last boat being loaded on this deck. We rushed past, trying to reach the second-class deck and Charles, but I couldn't help but note Edith and one of her aunts rushing forward. "You'd better come with us, Mrs. Stanford," the aunt called. "The boats are all lowered from the other first-class deck. They sent us here!"

The two women didn't wait for a response but continued to the crowd waiting to load. My steps faltered. Was it true they were running out of lifeboats?

Calvert slowed next to me. "Would you board, Madam?" His eye pleaded with me. "I will continue the search for Mr. Charles and do all within my power to deliver him to safety."

I looked into the resolute expression of our dedicated valet and knew he would be faithful to his word.

Nearby, Edith spoke to her aunt. "You go first. You are married and have children."

The aunt boarded the lifeboat, which was closer to the side of the *Titanic* than the others had been. One of the officers stood, a foot on the gunwale and another on the lifeboat, helping her into the craft.

Precious seconds ticked by, and for a brief moment I thought I might climb aboard after Edith. But then I knew. "I can't."

Calvert nodded, and we resumed our frantic path.

Behind me I heard Edith's voice. "Never mind! I will take a later boat!"

Calvert and I rushed toward the second-class deck. By this time I'd begun to work up a cold, clammy sweat, and my breathing was labored. It was obvious, even to me, the great *Titanic* was sinking and lifeboats were becoming scarce.

And then I saw him! "Charles!"

His frightened eyes met mine and as one we grabbed hands and headed to the nearest boat where a crowd had gathered.

I never thought I'd be relieved to climb into such a flimsy wooden vessel, but now we found a spot among several others, mostly women, but with a fair amount of men. I thought Calvert had boarded with us, but once we were situated, I looked for him and saw him still upon the *Titanic*.

"There is still room. You must board, Calvert!"

He shook his head. "I am sorry, Mrs. Stanford, but this is one time I am unable to fulfill your wishes. I hope to see you soon, but if by chance I do not, please give my regards to my father."

"Don't be a cad, Calvert!" Charles voice held a quiver. "Of course you must join us!"

I thought surely Calvert would reconsider, but all he did was drop down to me the bag he carried from Thomas Keaton and give a short bow. Then he disappeared into the crowd of men lining the deck.

The pain that played across Charles's features broke my heart. I reached for his hand.

"Women and children only!" A gruff voice cut the air as a pistol was fired above our heads. "All men disembark!"

Another shot rang out, and the men in the boat began working their way back to the deck of *Titanic*. Charles's stricken gaze met mine.

With a deft move of my fingers, my shawl came off, and I slipped it over Charles's head. His wide brown eyes peered at me.

"Keep quiet!" I hissed.

It was a mercy no one seemed to notice us in the scuffle to unload the others. I shivered, exposed to the cold, as the officer directed women from the *Titanic*'s deck onto our boat. As the drama unfolded around me, unfamiliar faces became people with stories, people torn from the company of those dearest to them.

Those on the lifeboat scooted toward the ends to make room for more travelers. A woman climbed in next to me, obviously grieved to be parted from a man on deck. "Don't be nervous, Annie." He called. "This will test our faith. I must stay and let the women go."

Tears glistened in her eyes, but she showed no other emotion. The energetic man calling to her must have been only ten years my junior, but he stood strong and robust before us. "If we never meet again on this earth, we will meet again in heaven."

Then a man rushed to the railing, holding two little boys. He yelled for help, holding the children aloft. Some of the sailors and the passengers reached for them. The older child—he looked to be about four—was thrown over the railing and safely caught. Arms were again raised, and the baby, a chunky little toddler, was also thus tossed into the boat and received into waiting hands.

"Lower away!" The call of the sailor caught my attention and the lines jerked.

"Annie!" The energetic, robust man stood close to the father. He pulled the tie from about his neck. "Put that around your throat."

The lines jerked again, and the lifeboat descended toward the icy water. The man threw the tie toward Annie. "You'll catch cold."

Our little boat hit the black sea with a splash. The father and the man stood side by side, staring after us. The father raised his hand, waving to his boys. The sailors on our lifeboat called to each other to get away from the *Titanic* before she went down. They pulled hard upon the oars, and our craft began to move, cutting through the calm, glassy water.

No one spoke.

Above me the stars flickered like festive lights at a celebration. From the sinking deck of the *Titanic* came strains of "Alexander's Ragtime Band," followed by a waltz. The scent of saltwater mingled with the smell of cold. The frigid air numbed my skin as the bizarre numbed my emotions.

I couldn't turn my gaze from the great ship, illuminated from stem to stern. A flood of humanity began to fill the boat deck. Steerage passengers, no doubt, had made their way from the bowels of the *Titanic* only to find no lifeboats available. Above them it looked as though some sailors were trying to cut loose a collapsible lifeboat.

And still my craft glided away, her engine the bulging muscles and hard breathing of those at the oars.

A movement where we'd last been upon the deck caught my attention. The man who'd thrown his tie waved his arms. I couldn't hear what he was saying, but men began to form a haphazard circle about him. I watched as he signaled to the band, then disappeared below the bodies surrounding him. The men lowered, like dominoes each following the person in front of him. It took a moment to realize they were all kneeling. A familiar form at the edge of the circle was the last to find his knees.

Mr. Thomas Keaton.

And then the party songs that had emitted ceaselessly from the band became a single hymn. I've never treasured church songs, but I have been exposed to them. Like it or not, the words climbed into my conscience, verse after verse, as the band played.

Nearer, my God, to thee, nearer to thee!
E'en though it be a cross that raiseth me,
Still all my song shall be, nearer, my God, to thee.
Nearer, my God, to thee, nearer to thee!

Though like the wanderer, the sun gone down,
Darkness be over me, my rest a stone;
Yet in my dreams I'd be nearer, my God, to thee.
Nearer, my God, to thee, nearer to thee!

There let the way appear, steps unto heaven;
All that thou sendest me, in mercy given;
Angels to beckon me nearer, my God, to thee.
Nearer, my God, to thee, nearer to thee!

Then, with my waking thoughts bright with thy praise,
Out of my stony griefs Bethel I'll raise;
So by my woes to be nearer, my God, to thee.
Nearer, my God, to thee, nearer to thee!

Or, if on joyful wing cleaving the sky,
Sun, moon, and stars forgot, upward I fly,
Still all my song shall be, nearer, my God, to thee;
Nearer, my God, to thee, nearer to thee!

Not a word was spoken as we rowed, rowed away, eyes trained upon the horror behind us. Most, like me, couldn't turn from the scene, but a few had faces buried in hands or upon nearby shoulders. Two people from me, the woman called Annie cried softly, whispering, "Oh, Robert."

The *Titanic* settled, her lights at an unnatural angle, going down rapidly until the last row of portholes was barely visible, the bow and bridge completely under water. A wave washed over the deck where the men kneeled, washing it clear as the ship continued to sink.

The sailors rowed harder.

The end was surely near.

Then the great RMS *Titanic* swung upward, the stern seeming to shoot out of the water. Her lights, which had shone so faithfully suddenly went black, flickered on again for a single flash, and then were gone forever. Suddenly there was a terrible noise. It was as though all the heavy things I could imagine were thrown downstairs from the top of a house, crashing, smashing everything in their path. When the noise was over, *Titanic* hung, vertical, suspended in dark shadow underneath the star-lit sky.

It seemed an eternity she stood on end, her mammoth propeller dangling from the stern, out of place in the night air. It was perchance five minutes—or some lesser amount. Then she slid slowly forward in the water as her haunches slipped slanting down . . . down . . .

And she was gone.

Nothing remained to prove she'd been there except the crushing chorus of a thousand or more voices moaning, crying, begging for salvation from icy death. They bobbed in the water in life belts, clung to the wreckage scattered upon the dark, bitter wet.

I hear them now. They haunt my every breath.

Chapter 23

Cylinder Five
Olive

For forty-five minutes the eerie, distressed cries reached across the frosty depths, tugging at our very souls. Their words were unintelligible at this distance but not their agony. They cried with decreasing volume as the mass of dying humanity became a crowd, a cluster, and finally a solitary whimper.

The quiet that followed, may the gods help me, brought great relief. At first my tortured ears strained without permission, listening for that one more sound of life, but I knew it would not come. Not from those frozen corpses shrouded in darkness. Not from that bitter grave.

It was finally—mercifully—silent.

We were bathed in deep black. The only light was the stars overhead. There was no wind, no wave. Just black night, black waters, blackened hearts. We feared the elements as we turned our thoughts to survival, imagining a hundred different rescue ships, fabricating the glow of their yellow lights as we shivered upon the icy depths. But each hopeful phantom disappeared into despair.

There was very little talk in our lifeboat. We huddled together, a miserable band of survivors, lost in our shock and grief, beyond shivering, cold to the core. The harder I tried to push away the travesty I'd just experienced, the more the bleak night gave way to bleak imaginings. My mind roamed from the horrific deaths of those who drowned, then circled back to Harriet Snow. I could see her in the picture of my mind, see the blood matting her blond curls and the cessation of movement in her ample bosom as her breathing was forever silenced. I could see Charles Malcolm's stricken eyes as he boarded the boat train, telling me there would be "no further encumbrance."

I knew nothing about the girl beyond Charles's stunning revelation that she was a kept woman. Did she have family?

The woman was obviously a tramp, looking for payroll. But she was so young. So beautiful. So much death.

Death.

What would this mean for Charles? Just because my grandson sat shivering and sniffling beside me didn't mean he was saved. If indeed a ship cut through the water even now to our rescue—if we climbed aboard her and were delivered to our own docks in New York City, it meant nothing if Charles Malcolm was found out.

Had anyone seen him leave the woman's home? Would there be an officer waiting for us in New York, ready to lock my boy away for her death? And even if we proved it an accident, what would happen to our social standing—to the golden future that could be his for the taking?

It was all lost still. We would survive the sinking of the famed RMS *Titanic* only to lose all that was important.

The satchel upon my lap called to me. I'd forgotten all about it as the drama of the night unfolded. But I had upon my lap tokens of Thomas Keaton's affection. I pulled open the bag. It was too dark to see into its depths, but I slipped my hand inside, exploring with fingertips. My hands brushed mohair, and I envisioned a toy. There was the crackle of paper. Money? Letters? Personal documents?

I closed the bag and stared back to where *Titanic* had gone down. It was likely Thomas Keaton's voice had been snuffed out with the others, but of course one couldn't be sure.

A bold idea began from this tiny thought. I nudged my grandson, who sat dazed beside me. "Address me as Mrs. Stanford from now on," I whispered.

"Why?"

"Do as I say." I kept my voice low but punctuated each word.

I could feel him acquiesce. He didn't understand, but he would obey. The trauma of the night had taken his fight.

But it had not stolen mine. If we were rescued, if there was indeed a ship even now just beyond the edge of the dark, I would find a way to save Charles Malcolm from a ruined life, just as I had saved him from being forced into courageous manhood, left to die on *Titanic*'s deck.

As the stars began to dim, a sliver of a moon rose in the sky, barely appearing before the streaks of light from the sunrise did. With light came the realization we were in a field of icebergs. There must have been close to fifty of them, some stretching high above us. From somewhere on our lifeboat came a young, high voice, ringing out to welcome the day, "Oh Muddie!" the child cried. "Look at the beautiful north pole with no Santa!"

Charles, next to me, gave a humorless chuckle at the innocent words. Then a titter of excitement went through our little craft, for just beyond the icy terrain bobbed a ship. At first we thought the boat moved toward us; then we realized she was waiting, unable to brave our treacherous winter wonderland. The sailors began rowing.

As the sunrise intensified it cloaked the icebergs in ornamental dress of peachy-pink, then with full light left them white once again, striking and dangerous against the cobalt sky. Numb as I was from shock and cold, our journey through the icebergs to the *Carpathia* waiting beyond felt, for a moment, like an expedition in a child's fairy book, so otherworldly the setting.

White was the vessel of rescue, whiter still those horribly beautiful icebergs, and as we drew nearer and nearer the good ship, we drew nearer and nearer to those mountains of ice. The floe glistened like a never-ending meadow covered with new fallen snow. As far as the eye could see they rose. Each one more fantastically chiseled than its neighbor. Those same white mountains, marvelous in their purity, had made of the just-ended night one of the blackest the sea has ever known.

My eyes scanned the horizon for other lifeboats. From what must have been a distance of a few miles, fanning across the Atlantic, they, too, made for the boat, tiny specks which grew larger with each heave of our oars and theirs. For a brief moment I wondered if Thomas Keaton might have found his way onto one of those lifeboats. If he had, the plan budding in my mind would not work.

But if Mr. Keaton was gone . . .

I took quick account of our craft's passengers. I knew not a soul. How fortuitous we had boarded by way of second class instead of first.

With the rising of the sun had come the rising of the wind— and with wind came the rising of the sea. As the minutes crawled by, our sailors hard at the oars, the Atlantic became more restless. I'm not sure what time we reached the *Carpathia*, but the disturbed waters made me all the more glad to see her massive hull towering above us.

Carpathia's flag flew at half-mast. All along the ship's rails waited quiet people, scanning the lifeboats. There were rope ladders along the ship's side for the few strong enough and brave enough to mount them from our lifeboat. A mailbag was lowered and the toddler was placed in. The bag was sealed then lifted quickly by strong sailors on the *Carpathia*, pulling at the ropes attached to it. His older brother went next, and the other children on our boat followed.

Then they began unloading the women. When it was my turn to leave the craft that had carried me to safety, I felt a momentary, nonsensical trepidation. Ignoring the strange emotion, I admonished Charles to come after me, calling him, "young sir," and acting very solicitous of his care. Then I leaned close and whispered to him. "You will find me and follow my lead once upon ship."

He offered a barely discernible nod in response.

I wrapped the strap of Thomas Keaton's leather satchel about my neck then was seated in the boatswain chair. Charles handed me my cane, and I gripped it and the rope that held the cradle I sat in, squeezing hard so as not to drop it. No conversation drifted to me from the Carpathia's passengers above, and only necessary words were spoken from my fellow travelers. All was very solemn. I suppose neither the *Titanic*'s survivors or the *Carpathia*'s passengers knew how to speak as the gravity of our experience hung over all of us.

The rope jerked, and my heart fluttered. I squeezed tighter, my curled fingers white in their desperate grip. Afraid to fall. Afraid to drop my cane. I'm sure the crude chair was quite safe, but a short, flat board swung from ropes didn't fit my notion of security. I snapped my eyes closed and didn't open them again, even when the crude chair bumped and scraped across the *Carpathia*'s side. I ascended rapidly then was met by strong arms, lifting me through the gangway and onto the ship.

Once upon the *Carpathia*, my hands began to tremble. They had remained steady all that awful night, but I suppose the reality of safety was too much for me. The sailors held me firm as I tried to place my cane upon the floor, legs and hands unstable and shaking. As I steadied, they took off my life belt.

A young purser asked my name and recorded it on a list. The others returned to their work as he continued to support me. "It is within my power to offer you a cabin, madam."

I looked to him, surprised.

"A generous passenger vacated it for use of one who might need it more than he. Considering your gender, and, if you'll excuse me, your age, I think you just the person for it."

I was astounded by my good fortune. The plan budding on the lifeboat now took root.

The purser suggested I allow him to find someone to assist me to my new quarters, but I said there was a young man on my boat in great need of motherly attention, a Mr. Keaton, who I wished to share the luxury of a cabin with. He helped me find Charles, and before they could speak I did. "This is Thomas Keaton." I nodded toward the purser's list of names.

As his head was bent over his paper, I shot Charles a warning look. Thankfully, my grandson said not a word. The purser handed another sailor a key. The sailor led Charles and me to the tiny cabin. It was in sharp contrast to the opulence of our rooms aboard the *Titanic,* but perfect provision for the course I'd mapped in my mind.

"There is hot coffee and soup available." The sailor paused, his hand upon our door. "Please let someone know if you have further needs. We've set up a hospital of sorts—and we can telegraph a message to shore of your safety."

"You've been most kind." I swallowed hard. "I am quite desirous of news about my grandson, Charles Malcolm Stanford III. If you—" I allowed my voice to crack and paused for dramatic effect. "If you hear news of him . . ." I should have been in theater, the way my voice trailed off with desperation. Of course desperation had been the emotion of the last many hours, so it was easy to make the ruse sound genuine.

The man's expression softened. "I surely will." He nodded toward me then shut the door behind him.

Charles turned on me then, his sunken, hollow eyes flickering with anger. "What was that about?"

It was good to see some life in him.

Instead of explaining, I pulled the satchel from around my neck and spread its contents upon the bed. There was a letter addressed to "My Dearest Josephine" and a white Steiff teddy bear, made of mohair as I'd suspected, and wearing a sailor shirt. Also enclosed was a small leather pouch. I opened it to find Thomas Keaton's passport and a few other papers.

"What is all this?" He reached for the passport. "How did you come to have it?" He paled as he looked upon Mr. Keaton's name.

Mr. Keaton had opted not to include his photo on it. I brightened. "Mr. Keaton gave it to me."

"When? For what purpose?"

Until that moment I'd had no prick of conscience, only determination to save my grandson. If I could keep Charles Malcolm hidden from society on the *Carpathia,* he could assume Thomas Keaton's identity and disappear to safety. Charles Malcolm Stanford III would be mourned with *Titanic*'s victims, never sent to trial for the death of the hussy.

However, as I sought to explain my plan to Charles Malcolm the ugly truth made my words halting and uncharacteristically unsure. I began to shiver again, my teeth chattering as I explained the plan. I told myself it was the aftermath of the trauma, the result of the hours in the icy Atlantic. And perhaps that was part of it.

But there was more.

I was asking my grandson to betray his new friend. I was breaking my word to the good Thomas Keaton.

"You don't even know he's perished." Charles's white face colored with heat, pink spots appearing on his cheeks. "He could be in another lifeboat—picked up by another ship!"

I fought hard against the physical reaction, the chattering teeth. "He . . . was . . ." I took a deep cleansing breath and tried to gain full control of my body. ". . . on the deck just before the end." I pressed upon my cane and stretched to my full height. "We must seize the opportunity!"

"But if he lives—"

"We will chart a different course. But . . . I think it unlikely he survived. I saw a huge wave sweep over the deck where he was."

Charles grabbed the letter and shook it in my face. "This no doubt holds sentiments of love. His wife and child need to know the truth!"

Forcing down the legitimacy in his words, I kept my voice steady. "She will recover, but without this plan you won't. Your life will be wasted in a dark London prison."

The color drained from Charles's features once again.

I raised an eyebrow. "The great Charles Malcolm III, cold, alone, closed in darkness for the remainder of his days." Leaning toward him, I stared at him. "Is that what you want?"

Charles fell upon the bed and began to weep.

I sat next to him and softened my tone. "You didn't mean to kill that woman, but who can prove it?"

If he refused this plan we would fight for his freedom, procuring the most powerful of lawyers. But Charles didn't need to know that. Whether convicted or acquitted, the scandal would ruin the Stanford name.

"Let me manage this, Charlie." I fingered his dark hair. "I'll take care of you." I rubbed a trembling hand over his back and let him cry. "Stay hidden in this cabin. Let the world believe Charles Malcolm Stanford III went down with the *Titanic*, and there will be no trial, no prison."

I could feel him giving in.

"You will be free."

I knew the moment he reached his decision, not because he told me, but because I knew his ways. There was one more great sob, then quiet whimpers.

I thought I'd won a great victory, but it was only the beginning of sorrows. I had entered a cell crafted by my own hands.

Chapter 24

Ember moved through her morning on autopilot. Olive Stanford's voice had echoed in her dreams and now in her thoughts all throughout teeth brushing, showering, coffee, and toast.

If I could keep Charles Malcolm hidden from society on the Carpathia, he could assume Thomas Keaton's identity and disappear to safety.

I was breaking my word to the good Thomas Keaton.

I think it unlikely he survived. I saw a wave sweep him away.

Could it have been possible? Or was the voice on the cylinders only that of a deranged woman writing fiction?

Ember's gaze sought out Bear in the living room, waiting patiently in his child's rocker. She stood in front of him, questioning him with her thoughts. Then it became clear.

Bear knew. And somehow his expression held the smallest quirk of a grin. He had been in Olive's possession, along with the letter and passport. Those were tangible items, not fiction.

She lowered herself in the leather armchair. As the burden of the century-old lie began to lift like a helium balloon to the ceiling, Ember found she couldn't release the string just yet. She'd been holding it too long.

Ember's gaze moved from Bear to Grammy's picture on the mantel. How she wished she could share this new revelation with her. Wherever she was right now, did she know? Was she sitting at a table with her Keaton female ancestors, sipping tea and discussing how an incredibly spoiled, wealthy woman had destroyed their lives with her betrayal? Were they now celebrating the fact that all was out in the open, and cheering Ember on to move into a new era, one free of this bondage?

What a responsibility! Ember squeezed her eyes shut. Regardless of what had happened in the limbs of her family tree, she still had men issues. Her grandfather had never loved her, and she didn't know if her own father knew she existed. She preferred to think he didn't.

The phone rang, startling her out of her reverie. She reached for the cordless near her chair and answered it.

"Hi, it's Frannie."

Ember popped out of the chair and ran to the kitchen, seeking out the clock on her microwave. She'd forgotten about the shopping invitation.

"Hi Frannie. Listen, about today—"

"That's why I'm calling. We never talked about how to meet up. Would you like to come here and leave your car? Washington Square Mall is in the other direction, so it would be more convenient that way. Unless, you'd rather we come get you."

"Actually . . ." Was she up to a shopping trip with three women she barely knew?

"Oh, I hope you're not considering cancelling. Claire would be so disappointed. She hoped that with your staging skills, you could do more than just throw a crib and dresser in a room. And I'm looking forward to getting to know you better."

A smile bloomed on Ember's face, the roots reaching into her heart. "And Jeff's other sister?"

Frannie chuckled. "Lacie? Ah, she's our little rebel. We rarely know what she's thinking. And when we do get a hint, it sometimes frightens us."

Ember laughed. What little she'd seen of Lacie, she could totally understand Frannie's comment.

Now that she'd been drawn away from thoughts of *Titanic*, lies, and generational curses, Ember performed a quick systems check: Heart eager for female companionship. Check. Midsection spreading a little from lack of exercise. Walking a mall is exercise, isn't it? Check. Feet eager to get out of her apartment. Check.

"I'll drive there and leave my car. Did you say ten o'clock the other day?"

"Yes, that's perfect. I'm really looking forward to this."

Ember hung up the phone. Suddenly, she was too.

* * * *

"I'm so happy you could join us, Ember." Claire reached across the table and squeezed Ember's hand. After wandering the mall and finally finding what they wanted at Pottery Barn Kids, they had all voted on The Cheesecake Factory for lunch. "Your practical ideas and fun sense of color are going to make Baby Girl's room special for years to come."

Ember preened at the compliment. She didn't know much about babies, but she did know style. "I think that white three-in-one crib will be a great focal point for the room. Drape a sheer canopy over it in pink or purple to match your garden theme, and your baby will think she's a princess."

"And I love that it will grow with her." Claire shook her head. "I've heard of cribs being turned into youth beds, but who would have thought to take the back panel of the crib and turn it into a headboard for a twin bed? Genius!"

Frannie sipped her iced tea. "I love that it has an antique look. Your father will be pleased with that."

"I hope so," Claire said. "I didn't want to offend him by not taking up his offer to find a real antique, but I just don't think they're safe."

"I still think a black crib with dark purple sheets and stuff would have been the best idea."

All eyes turned to Lacie.

"What?" Lacie continued. "How do we know she's going to like garden colors? Pinks. Blah. Greens. Blah. Blues. Blah." With each *Blah* she splayed her hands as if throwing the colors on a wall. "Maybe she'll be like her Auntie L and prefer to sink into a cool, dark abyss." She closed her eyes, breathed in deeply, pinched the air with both hands, and drew them down to her stomach while blowing the air out slowly through her mouth.

Claire tweaked her sister's dyed-black hair, eliciting a yelp of pain. "No dark abyss for my Baby Girl."

"Yeah, well. Wait until she's old enough to hang with Auntie L."

Claire sent her mother a look of mild terror.

Frannie ignored her daughters as she took another sip of tea. "I'm famished. Hope our food will be here soon."

Ember watched the exchange and suddenly longed for sisters of her own. Absentee parents, no siblings, and one grandmother—no matter how wonderful she was—shaped Ember's loneliness. She understood dark abyss, but it hadn't ever been cool or comforting.

Frannie sought out Ember's eyes as if trying to see what was going on in her head. "I hope my offspring aren't offending you. They really do love each other." She shot a warning look toward her daughters.

"Oh, not at all," Ember said. "I was just thinking how nice it would be to have sisters to squabble with."

"You're an only child? No brothers either?"

Ember shook her head. "Only my Grammy, and now she's gone."

"Your parents?" Frannie's eyes held her concern.

How much should Ember tell? She tested the waters carefully. "My mother . . . travels extensively. I was pretty much raised by my grandmother. My father . . ." Oh, how should she put it without horrifying this moral family?

"You needn't say anything else, dear." Frannie stroked her arm. "I didn't mean to pry."

Frannie's smile became a beacon of light for Ember's soul. She could choose to embrace it, or turn back toward the darkness. "My father," she continued, "was never in the picture." She had averted her gaze so as not to see Frannie's reaction.

"You, too?"

Ember's head jerked up. "What do you mean?"

"I never knew my dad. It seems my teenage mother got into a bit of trouble and put me up for adoption. It wasn't until recently that I found her. We have a good relationship now. But my father rejected me. Didn't want to meet me." She shrugged as if this wasn't the most devastating thing in the world for her. "I can understand. He's married with kids and grandkids. Why upset their world?"

Ember glanced at Claire and Lacie. Apparently they already knew this about their mother.

"The family who adopted me were distant, and I often wondered why they bothered to adopt. They had two natural children, a boy and a girl, who also suffered from parents who weren't hands-on. They cliqued together but had little patience for me. I was always the outsider."

"Oh, Frannie. Who did you talk to?" Ember thought of Grammy. Had it not been for her, she would have gone insane.

"Just imaginary friends." Her peaceful smile was in sharp contrast to her devastating story. "But then I met Ron. He wanted a big family. At first that scared me to death. But as each one came along, I couldn't remember what it was like to be lonely. My family has become my life and breath." She reached out to her daughters and pulled both of their hands in for a kiss on their knuckles.

Their food orders came and soon they were digging in. Throughout the rest of the conversation, Ember reflected on what she had just learned.

Frannie climbed out of her abyss. Why couldn't Ember?

* * * *

Ember sat in the backseat next to Lacie, who bickered with Claire in the front. Both women were in their thirties, but apparently the child-like rivalries never changed.

Frannie made the final turn into their neighborhood and pulled into her driveway. It was still early afternoon, but their shopping excursion was cut short due to Claire's swollen ankles.

Frannie invited them all in for some hot tea, but both Claire and Lacie declined.

"I'd like to go home and lie down," Claire said as she eased her way out of the car. She grabbed her back and waddled to her minivan. At eight months, she looked about to pop.

"Me too, Mom." Lacie shut the car door.

"You have to go home and lie down?" Frannie's eyebrow rose.

"No. Pete is taking me to a Massacre concert tonight."

Her sister frowned. "You know your husband doesn't like that kind of music."

"Yeah, but we compromise. I saw Kenny Chesney with him last month." She kissed her two fingers and tapped her heart. "Peacin' Momz! Siz! Had a great time, Embz. We should do it again."

Embz? She had a nickname!

As Lacie drove away in her little hybrid, Claire said to Ember, "Apparently *peacin'* means good-bye." She shook her head. "Pete's a little bit country, and she's a little bit . . . I'm not sure what she is."

"Oh, Mom!" Claire opened her back passenger door. "I've got this box of clothes that Marcus has outgrown. Can you find a good home for them?"

Frannie pulled out the box and began looking through it. "I hate to see our little guy grow up, but I'm sure someone can use this in my church's Single Parent Attic." She turned to Ember. "We have all kinds of things there to give away. It's not a real attic, but we like the way it sounds. When someone needs something, they can say they're going to the 'spa.' Makes them feel better about their situation."

"I like that. Practical and sensitive." Ember lifted the hatchback of the SUV. "I'll carry your bags inside, Frannie."

"Thanks. I'll be right there."

Ember slid the handles of Frannie's Nordstrom's and Macy's bags through her left hand, and picked up her own small one from Bath & Body Works. She had found a lovely eucalyptus and spearmint sugar scrub, guaranteed to relieve stress, and tangerine scented hand soap for her kitchen.

She deposited her bag into her car then walked into the Dawson house. As she entered, she heard voices coming from outside on the deck—one male and one female, his halting in his speech.

Normally, she would have minded her own business, but snatches of sentences reached out and grabbed her, insisting she investigate.

Ember dropped the bags on the couch and peered out the window, not believing her eyes. A middle-aged woman, showing way too much skin in tight capris and a tighter blouse, was leaning over Ron in his wheelchair. She was shoving cash into her cleavage, and then she kissed him on his forehead.

"You need to . . . leave," Ron said. "Frannie will be here . . . soon."

"Is she suspicious?" The woman's husky voice reminded her of Beverly's, ruined by too many cigarettes and illegal substances.

He nodded.

"I'll be discreet."

Panic clawed up Ember's throat. Backing away before she could be seen, she left by way of the kitchen, through the garage. She didn't want to have to explain her hasty retreat to Frannie, who was entering through the front.

Ember ran to her car, backed out of the driveway, and pulled onto the street. As she waited for traffic at the stop sign a few houses down, she looked in her rearview mirror. The woman she had just seen with Ron scurried around the side of the Dawson house and hustled up the street to a gold Mercedes. The suburbs must pay well in her profession.

How could Ron associate with such a woman? Then again, what did she really know about him? Before his stroke, he had only been the nice man who wanted to help find a phonograph for her.

What about Jeff? Was he just like his father? Sweet because of his job, but in reality a totally different person?

The "Men Are Scum" record began playing again in her head. After exonerating Thomas Keaton, the tune had faded somewhat.

She shouldn't have let her guard down.

* * * *

Jeff locked the shop door and flipped the sign over. He peered out of the window, once again wondering why he hadn't heard from Ember. She had gone shopping with his mom and sisters earlier, and he was eager to hear what they had talked about. In particular, if they had talked about him.

He called Ember's cell phone, the third time within the last couple of hours. It went to her voicemail. This was in addition to the two times he'd called her house.

"Hey, it's me again." He rubbed the back of his neck. "I was wondering if you were coming over tonight to listen to another cylinder. If you aren't here in a half hour, I'll go ahead and leave." He stopped, wanting to say something more, but not sure what.

As soon as he hung up, his phone rang. "Ember?"

"No, it's Claire."

"Oh, sorry. I didn't look at the caller I.D."

"That's okay. Is something wrong?"

Jeff leaned on the glass counter and stared at an early 1900s era necklace he had procured from a vintage jewelry store going out of business. The pendant was an Art Nouveau piece with leaves in pink and yellow-green shaded enamel with freshwater pearl droplets underneath. After some research, he knew he could get $1200 for it. He had considered keeping it to give to Ember, but he found something more meaningful for her.

"No, nothing's wrong. At least, I don't think so. How did shopping go today?"

"Eventful. Ember is a whiz at decorating. Can't wait to show you what we bought. It'll be delivered in a few days."

"How did she seem when you got home?" He tried to ask this tentatively, so as not to cause alarm.

"Something *is* wrong." Leave it to Sis to pick up on his mood.

Jeff wandered to the front of the shop and looked out the window. A light rain had started. "She usually comes here just before we close so we can listen to the cylinders. But I haven't heard from her all day."

"She may have been tired after all that shopping. I know I was."

Jeff chuckled. "You have several pounds worth of baby to drag around, too."

"Good thing you added the 'baby' part, little brother." She sighed. "But you're right. As fun as it was, I couldn't wait to get home and put up my feet. The sitter stayed to keep Marcus away so I could get a nap. But then the two screamer monkeys hit the front door after school and it was all over."

"Hey, you called me. Do you need something?"

"Cameron is working late. Could you stop somewhere on your way home and bring us dinner? We're starved."

"Pizza?"

"Perfect."

He hung up, wishing his Call Waiting had kicked in while talking with Claire. Ember wouldn't have been so tired she would have forgotten about the next cylinder. Maybe she just needed to think more about what she'd learned about Thomas Keaton. Still, she would have called him to say she wasn't coming.

How he wished he could go to her apartment and check on her, make sure she was okay. But he had a very pregnant sister, a four-year-old Marcus, and two screamer monkeys waiting for pizza.

Chapter 25

By six o'clock the next day, Jeff was seriously beginning to worry. He'd made up his mind that if he couldn't get Ember on the phone, he would go break down her door.

But when he called, for the fifth time that day, she answered.

"Ember? Where are you? Are you okay?" He hadn't meant to grill her, but then again, how could he not?

"I'm fine." Her voice sounded weak. "I'm sorry I haven't returned your calls. I had some . . . thinking to do."

"Where are you?" he asked again.

"I'm on the coast."

He looked at the shop window where rivulets of rain made it nearly impossible to see out. He knew the coast was socked in. "What are you doing there? Something to do with work?"

"Not exactly." She paused. "Actually, I just needed to think."

"About?" *I'm here, Ember. Please talk to me.*

"I don't think I should discuss it with you." Her voice went cold.

"Did I do something to upset you?" He wracked his brain trying to remember their conversation the last time he'd seen her. They had just finished listening to the fifth cylinder. She had just found out that Olive Stanford had betrayed Thomas Keaton's trust and stolen his identity. Keaton was last seen being swept away into the icy waters. If anything, she should be angry with old lady Stanford, not Jeff.

When she didn't answer, he pressed. "Ember? Talk to me."

"It's your father."

"W-what?" Jeff's brain twisted like a pretzel trying to remember every encounter she'd had with his dad.

"I've said too much."

"Ember? Don't hang up." But it was too late.

He pressed his forehead against the cool glass of the window. What had happened?

* * * *

Jeff somehow made it home. He couldn't believe how much his heart hurt. He was going to swing by his parents' place, but then remembered they had gone out for their anniversary. He was so grateful Dad felt well enough—not to mention that he was alive—to celebrate their forty-second.

The minute he walked in the door of his sister's house, the nephews tackled him.

"Wanna play Lego Star Wars Ace Assault, Uncle Jeff?"

"No video games tonight, Bob."

"Come look at my fish, Uncle Jeff. I think he's dead."

"Not tonight, Ty."

"Do you want a hug, Unca Jeff?"

Jeff looked down at Marcus. How could someone so young be so astute? "Yeah, that would be nice."

He scooped Marcus up and the two squeezed until Jeff had no feeling from the neck up and Marcus squealed, "Can't. Breathe. Unca. Jeff."

"Oh, sorry, buddy." He released his hold and Marcus staggered away, a little too overdramatically.

He entered the kitchen where Claire was scooping chili into bowls from her large Crock-Pot. "Did you hear from Ember?"

"Yeah. She finally answered."

Claire raised her brows. "Well?"

"I don't know what happened." Jeff pulled out a chair and sat. He could hear the boys upstairs and was grateful they hadn't followed him. "All I got from her was that she was upset with Dad."

"Dad? Whatever for?"

"I don't know. She was on the coast, or I would have gone to her apartment to confront her." He grabbed a toothpick from the lazy Susan in the middle of the table and snapped it into four tiny pieces.

"Oh, I don't think confrontation is a good idea." Claire lowered herself slowly into a chair next to Jeff. "Sounds like she's trying to work through something."

"But how could she be mad at Dad? He's done nothing but try to help her. He welcomed her into his home." He cursed. "He practically made her a daughter."

Claire removed the second toothpick from his hand before he splintered it. "We don't know what happened. Just wait until you get her side of the story. I'm sure all will become clear."

All throughout dinner and halfway through the night, Jeff wrestled with the possibility that Dad had done something to offend Ember. But, knowing his father, the one the family called the World's Oldest Boy Scout, he knew it must have been a misunderstanding. But how could he defend Dad when Ember wouldn't give Jeff a chance to talk?

Around two o'clock in the morning, he finally decided he'd do as Claire suggested and let Ember work through whatever stupid thing she imagined. He didn't like it, but he realized forcing her might make things worse.

And this was why he was single. Women just weren't worth it.

The next day he barely made it through work. Dad hadn't been in since his first time back, but for some reason, today he decided to give it another go.

So, on top of already being irritable from lack of sleep and anger at Ember, he had to temper his words with Dad.

It hadn't even been a week since he'd promised to computerize the shop. But here was Dad, the original antiprogressive, pestering him.

"When do we get the . . . new database? How about the . . . website? Can you show . . . me how to search online?"

All Jeff wanted was quiet. But he answered as best he could, and finally, Dad retreated into the office. By late afternoon, Jeff looked in on him. He was asleep in his wheelchair with a ledger in his lap. Jeff saw that the drawer marked 1999 was open.

His cell phone rang, and Jeff fumbled in his pants pocket, scampering to answer it before it woke Dad.

"Hello?"

"Hi, it's Ember."

Jeff scooted out of the office and pulled the door shut. "Ember," he hissed, trying to be quiet. But then, he couldn't think of anything to say. *How are you?* or *Are you still mad at my innocent father?* seemed inappropriate at the moment.

"Are you alone?" she asked. "No customers?"

He glanced around. "Nope. The rain has kept everyone away today." He took a deep breath. "Are you back from the coast?"

"Yes, I stayed in a hotel, but I came home this morning."

Jeff heeded Claire's advice not to be confrontational, but he had to bite his tongue to do it. He waited for Ember to continue.

"Jeff?"

"I'm here."

"I just wanted to explain something."

It was about time.

"I thought about not saying anything, but now I think you should know."

"Know what?" The hair on the back of his neck prickled.

"I think your father is seeing someone."

"What?" Jeff bellowed, then glanced at the closed office door. He stepped outside and huddled under the canopy of the business next door. He decided the first thing he would do when—crud, did he really think that?—if he took over the business would be to put up an awning. Cold rain drizzled off the canvas overhead and splashed on his shoes.

He'd missed part of Ember's conversation during the exodus out the door. "I'm sorry. What was that?"

"You're going to make me repeat it? It was hard enough the first time."

"No, I really didn't hear you." He gripped the phone so tight he feared the batteries would pop out.

"I said, I caught your dad with another woman."

"When?"

"After shopping with your mom and sisters."

Jeff squeezed his brain to make sense of what she was saying. "That was . . . when? Two days ago?"

"Yes. I'm really sorry Jeff."

"Wait. Was she wearing skin-tight clothes? Looked like a streetwalker? Voice of a trucker?"

"Yes, how did you know? Oh! You must have seen her, too. I'm so sorry, Jeff. I wish I hadn't seen what I did. There is help out there for your dad. With a little counsel—"

"Wait just a minute. Why would you assume that my dad would do anything inappropriate?"

"Because I saw—"

"No, that's not an excuse." Jeff heard Claire in his head telling him to stop the assault, but all of the tension he'd felt since the previous evening came out in a rush of words. "My dad is a good man. He would never cheat on my mom. He loves her."

"But I heard them."

"What? What could you possibly have heard?"

"He gave her money and told her she needed to leave before his wife saw her. She told him she would be discreet."

Jeff leaned against the building. "Oh, Ember. That was my dad's sister." He waited for Ember to react. When she didn't, he assumed she was stunned. He continued. "My parents just celebrated their anniversary. Dad told me yesterday that Aunt Jan came over to deliver the diamond necklace and earrings he'd bought before his stroke. Her husband is a jeweler." He waited. "Ember, are you there?"

"I'm here."

"Mom was already suspicious." A car drove by, sending a wave of muddy water up his pant leg. Shaking the water off, he continued. "If Mom had seen Aunt Jan that day, the jig would have been up. They all had a good laugh about it."

"I'm so sorry, Jeff."

"Yeah, well, an apology doesn't make up for the fact that you attacked my father's character."

"It was an honest mistake."

"Was it? Really?" Prickles of adrenaline shot up his spine and over his scalp. "Or maybe you got tired of comparing all men to your sorry life and decided to start in on mine." Crap. He shouldn't have said it that way.

"How dare you!"

"Hey." Jeff took a deep breath, trying to calm himself. He tried to sound apologetic. "I know that wasn't fair."

"Yet, you must believe it, or you wouldn't have said it."

Jeff heard knocking and glanced toward the shop window. Dad was there, trying to get his attention. By his hand movements, it seemed someone was on the shop phone wanting to speak with Jeff.

"I have to go. Can we talk about this in person?"

"There's nothing to discuss."

"Then you're not coming over so we can listen to the rest of the cylinders?"

"I will send someone over to collect the phonograph."

"That's it? You're going to sever our friendship over a lousy misunderstanding?"

"I called it a misunderstanding. You called it an attack."

Touché.

She sighed. "I'm sincerely sorry about what I thought about your father. Please thank him for all of his help."

What about Jeff's help? Hadn't he done all the legwork, the repair, staying late so she could hear the cylinders?

"Ember?"

Silence. She'd hung up.

He shook the phone and roared at it. This woman was so frustrating. Good riddance.

As he walked his soggy self back into the shop, he resolved more than ever to fix his life. Move on and never look back.

* * * *

The rain fell in a mist, finally clearing up after days of downpour. This would probably be the last of it until June. Sunshine filtered through the thinning clouds enough to brighten Ember's kitchen without turning on a light as she drank her morning coffee.

Her laptop open, she scanned the Internet, browsing properties and local companies who might be ready to take on another Realtor. She had planned on taking three weeks before jumping back into work, but her argument with Jeff the day before had fueled something inside of her. She was tired of being the victim.

Today, she was going to take charge of her life.

As her whole-wheat toast popped up, there was a knock at the door. She looked at the microwave clock. It was seven thirty. Who could it be at that hour of the morning?

"Ember? I know you're in there." The familiar voice on the other side of the door threatened to send her newfound bravado scurrying to a dark corner.

But Ember reminded herself this was a new day. She grabbed the door handle and ripped it open. "What do you want, *Mother*?"

"Wow." Beverly swept into the room uninvited. "Is that any way to greet your grieving mom?"

"What could you possibly be grieving?" Ember hated the edge to her words but loved the power behind them.

"You really have to ask? I come to town not even a month ago to find my own mother dead, and you gone. Couldn't you have called to let me know she was sick?" Huge tears hung dramatically in the corners of Beverly's eyes. She blinked, and they dropped onto her cheeks in perfect synchronization, as if they'd been choreographed.

"I tried." Ember gritted the words through her teeth. "You don't make it easy, you know."

Beverly moved through the living room, her eyes scanning every wall, every knick-knack, every photo, finally settling upon Bear. "What is this?" She scooped him up by one arm and dangled him, treating him like a bag of smelly garbage. "Really, Ember. Aren't you too old to play with dolls? Where did you get this?"

Ember rushed to rescue Bear from Beverly's clutches and set him back into his chair. "Why are you here?"

Beverly sank onto the couch. She pulled a tissue from her gaudy purse, bright orange with brass studs and big enough to steal a lamp from the table of a fine restaurant. Ember had seen her do that once. She was so ashamed.

"I received an interesting communiqué while abroad."

By abroad, Ember knew that meant she'd shacked up with some guy with an accent.

"Apparently," Beverly continued, "someone had been looking for me for quite some time."

Ember hoped it was the authorities but knew better. Beverly wouldn't be on her doorstep over that kind of trouble.

"Get to the point, Mother."

"A lawyer, a Mr. James Williams, seemed very interested in contacting me."

Ember's mouth went dry. Her throat constricted, a good thing since she wanted to scream.

"His note was several weeks old, but he said he needed to speak with me about an urgent matter. Something to do with someone named Olive Stanford." She pinned Ember with snake eyes, patient and ready to strike. "Do you know what that was all about?"

"Yes, I do." Ember pulled herself to her full height, reminding herself she had a backbone. Now was the time to use it.

Beverly rose from the couch and continued her search throughout the house, more obvious now. "Yes. You know exactly what I'm talking about. Because you went to New York in my place. I called, Ember. I spoke with the lawyer. He was very vague, said he 'wasn't at liberty' to discuss it." She mocked James's voice, and Ember wanted to slap her. "But he did say the matter was resolved, and that you now have the items in your possession."

Beverly moved to Ember's bedroom, where the cylinders were sitting on the floor in her bag. "What items, Ember? What do you have that is rightfully mine?"

Ember snapped. "What right do you have to ask me that? After you rampaged through Grammy's house like a rhino? You took everything that was precious to me."

Beverly turned steely eyes on Ember. "As. Did. You." Each word slapped Ember in the face.

She shrank from her mother's venom. "What are you saying?"

"You stole my mother."

Ember, the fire gone from her now, finally grasped how much hatred her own flesh and blood held against her.

Beverly moved to another room, and Ember weakly opened her bedroom closet door and toed the bag inside, out of her mother's radar.

With leaded feet, Ember somehow made her way into the kitchen. Let Beverly tear the place apart. If she didn't find something of monetary value, she wouldn't be interested. Ember poured herself a cup of tea and sat at the table, bobbing the teabag up and down, enjoying the weightlessness of it. When she looked up, Beverly was standing in the doorway, seething with rage.

"I'm watching your bank account, babycakes. If it suddenly has a windfall, I'll sue you for everything you've got."

"You know that's not possible. Lies, Mother. That's all you have."

Beverly turned abruptly and left the apartment, slamming the door behind her.

A few minutes later, there was another knock. Ember ignored it. She wasn't going to tolerate Beverly's false apology. Her pattern was to implode, sucking Ember and everyone in close proximity into her vortex, then request forgiveness. It astounded Ember to think of how often she had fallen into that trap.

Well, no more.

A new flame surged within Ember as she realized she had just stood up to Beverly. She didn't give in. She didn't confess what she'd found in New York. And she called her out, speaking the truth to Beverly's warped sense of reality. Whether it had been Grammy's influence or something Ember had within her all along, she didn't know. But she liked this new strength.

Another knock, more insistent, followed by a male voice. "Ember? It's Jeff. If you're there, open up. I mean, well, if you're not there, I guess you can't, but—"

Ember swung the door open. If she could stand up to Beverly, she could take on the world. "What do you want? You want me to apologize again? You want me to forgive you for your nasty remark? What?"

Jeff hugged a cardboard box to his chest and blinked as if she'd just singed his eyelashes.

"Here." He shoved the box, about eighteen inches tall, into her hands. Then he turned and bounded down the stairs. "Have a nice life."

She stood there, wondering if it were a time bomb.

Finally, after trying to make sense of what had just happened—including her own behavior—she shut the door and took the package into the kitchen. She slit the packing tape with scissors and flipped open the flaps on top. Green Styrofoam packing peanuts lay inside. She dug in underneath the top layer, and her fingers felt something cool, glass-like.

She pulled the porcelain vase out of its container and brushed aside the Styrofoam, no small feat since they were statically committed to protecting their object.

"Oh, how sweet." Her heart melted. Jeff must have called the antique shop in Everett and bought her that vase.

Okay, she was now officially unmad at Jeff. After thinking about it, she was probably done with her anger hours ago. She took the vase to the sink, deciding to fill it with the flowers she had brought back from the coast. When she set it on the counter it rocked a little. Part of the packing was stuck on the bottom. She turned the vase over to remove it then nearly dropped it when she read the words, "For Ember" on the bottom.

She hugged the vase to her heart, then read the words again. Had Jeff written them there? No, not only was her name written in Grammy's beautiful calligraphy, the date was also there, marking the day she decided to bequeath the vase. She hadn't told Jeff that part, because, quite frankly, she'd forgotten the date was there.

She inspected the rest of the vase, simply because it was still unreal to her. A note had been placed inside.

Dear Ember,

I know how much it affected you to lose something so closely tied to your grandmother. After our trip to Everett, I got online and searched, hoping your mother had sold it. Sure enough, after several tries, I found your vase.

On another note, please forgive me for my tactless remark. I would not have hurt you for anything in the world.

Please continue to be my friend. You're the bright spot in my dank and dusty world.

Love,

Jeff.

Ember let the tears fall onto the vase. Generations be hanged, she liked this guy. He wouldn't cheat or sweep something precious, like the sale of a house, out from under her. He wouldn't disappear into the great unknown like her father. And if their relationship should progress and they married, she knew he would be as hands-on with their children as he was with his nephews.

Still hugging the vase, she walked into the living room and called Jeff from the cordless. She couldn't go another minute without resolving everything. She heard the ringing on her end, but she also heard the *Star Wars* theme on the other side of her door. When she opened it, he was standing there, that boyish grin on his face, the phone to his ear, saying hello.

Chapter 26

Ember could think of no more comforting company after the encounter with her mother. She poured the whole story out to Jeff, beginning with her lonely childhood. They chatted in the kitchen while he made his "special eggs" because he said he was starved. They lingered over coffee at the table. They progressed to the living room, where he shared his fears of the future.

By evening, they had slid the coffee table aside and were camped out on the tapestry rug leaning back against the sofa, the colorful throw over their laps, and their bare feet toward a cozy fire. Strauss played softly in the background. They finished the pizza they had delivered, and now sipped hot cocoa— Grammy's recipe.

"I have an idea," Ember said. "Let's take all of the cylinders to your parents' house and let the family listen."

"We still have the last three. Are you ready to hear them with others around?"

"Yes." She didn't even need to think about it.

Jeff set his cocoa aside and took Ember's from her hands, placing it with his. "Come here." He opened his arms, and she scooted to snuggle under the blanket with him. "You know, I didn't like you very much when I first saw you."

She pulled away enough to look into his eyes. "This is how you begin a romantic evening?"

"I thought you were stuffy." He ignored her but pulled her even closer, brushing her forehead with his cheek. "But there was something about you I just couldn't shake."

"Better. You may go on." He smelled of chocolate, pepperoni, and century-old furniture.

"It wasn't the fact that you needed my help. It wasn't because you were vulnerable after losing your grandmother and your job. It wasn't the hell you had to go through listening to those cylinders." He lifted her chin. "It was the strength I saw inside you."

She wanted to laugh. Ember? Strength? Those two words were never synonymous in her mind.

"The more I got to know you, the more I wanted to be a part of your journey. I needed some of that strength. Thank you for allowing me in."

She rose to meet his kiss—soft, warm, and safe. She was home . . . in his arms.

* * * *

"Thank you, all, for taking an interest." Ember addressed the adult members of Jeff's family. The phonograph had been set up in the middle of the Dawson living room, and every sibling, spouse, and parent were clustered in small groups, their faces showing anticipation.

Now, she perused the room, seeking out Claire and her husband, Cameron. "And thank you, Claire, for suggesting a sitter and providing your home for the young ones."

Claire laughed. "Well, we wanted to hear the cylinders, didn't we?"

Ember was glad that all the parents agreed what they were about to hear might be too intense for children.

Once everyone settled down, Ember cranked the machine and set the needle onto the first cylinder. Olive Stanford's voice filled the room, and they were all transported back in time.

Ember sat on the couch in the protective circle of Jeff's arms. She wasn't sure how hearing the story again would affect her, but she was stronger and thought she could handle it. Was it because of her acceptance into Jeff's family? His support? Or perhaps her new strength that now fanned the weaker Ember into a flame? She didn't know or care.

Bring it on, Mrs. Olive Stanford.

* * * *

Ember's teary gaze followed Jeff as he removed the fifth cylinder. Even though she'd already heard the account of the sinking, her heart still mourned the loss of so many. Everyone else sat quiet, as well. Even Lacie allowed Pete to rock her as she wept in his lap.

Jeff glanced at Ember. "Should we give everyone a moment to collect themselves before listening to the rest of the cylinders?"

She looked around the room. Everyone, even some of the men, was a mess. "Yes. I could use some air."

They moved to the backyard where the afternoon sun played in the tops of the trees, sending dappled beams to the moist lawn. The spring rains had finally ended, and Frannie's flower bed burst with color. Azaleas, rhododendrons, hyacinth, and clematis.

They all defied the past winter.

After snuggling in the double glider quietly for several minutes, Jeff kissed Ember, his lips tenderly brushing hers. With his eyes, he motioned toward the house. She nodded a silent assent, and they stood to face the last cylinders.

Chapter 27

Cylinder Six
Olive

As I rubbed Charles's back his breathing became deep and even. As he slept the occasional whimper escaped. I found a blanket in the tiny closet and covered him. Slipping into the alleyway, I locked the door behind me.

If only I could lock it from the outside.

My weary, trembling body almost betrayed me, but I had to persevere a little longer to ascertain whether or not my ruse had a chance of success. I first visited the dispensary where a purser handed me a cup of steaming coffee. The hot, aromatic liquid warmed me and most of the shaking subsided. Surveying the area, I found few faces I recognized among the strangely clad people, certainly not Mr. Keaton.

From there I went to the deck above. In the dining saloon more people in various stages of dress met my eyes. If it were not so tragic, it would have been comical to see such a plethora of grown women parading about in night dresses, dressing gowns, cloaks, and shawls. One woman kept her fur coat tightly about her. I suspected she had little underneath. Few had taken the time, as I had, to fully dress. Of course they had not been awake, traipsing after a rogue grandson.

In every corner of the room there were people, some resting under rugs or blankets. I heard tell that wet clothing could be dried in the baking oven and wondered about the state of dress of those under the cocoon-like wrappings.

Again, I didn't see Mr. Keaton. Not all the lifeboats had landed. Perhaps he was still to arrive. I made a point to ask several people if they'd seen my grandson. Dull expressions met my inquiries. Shakes of heads. Sometimes a whisper of encouragement.

A steward came in with a bundle of telegraph forms. I took two, filling in one stating my safe arrival upon the *Carpathia* and the report that I knew not if Charles and Calvert had been rescued. A similar message I signed with the name Thomas Keaton. I slipped both into the pile of completed missives. I then went to the top deck to hang over the rails with the other spectators, scanning the lifeboats.

As one boat emptied, Louise was placed in a boatswain chair. Immediately a pang cut through my chest, seeing in my memory Calvert's last bow, remembering his brave words. I'd passed up many lifeboats on the *Titanic*, refusing to board. I couldn't imagine Calvert had found another. The craft I finally climbed upon seemed to be the last. Indeed, many people had gathered on the deck before us, eyes hungry, but voices quiet, when no more room was to be found.

Grief was followed by relief. Louise was alive! Just as swiftly came the thought that Louise and Charles must not see each other.

It was not long after eight o'clock when the last lifeboat emptied of her passengers that morning. Captain Rostron called for a service to be held in the saloon. *Carpathia*'s passengers joined those of us from *Titanic*, crowding into the room. As the *Carpathia* searched for survivors, steaming over the spot where the great *Titanic* was thought to have gone under, thanks was given for the lives of those who filled the room, quiet respect to honor those lost.

Held to my spot by the necessity of searching the gathering for the face of Mr. Keaton, my stomach revolted. As we stood, my heart in mockery of Divine Providence, the *Carpathia* circling the area, it seemed a cruel joke, this belief in a God who not only created the world but cared about it.

No more survivors were found.

A roll call was taken in that same saloon. Each time information was gathered I gave my name. Once or twice I mentioned having seen Mr. Keaton. Always I asked if my grandson had been seen. Eventually the group disbanded, scattered about the cluttered spaces of the boat.

When the *Carpathia* left those frigid waters she carried away just over seven hundred survivors, and the *California* took up the job of searching. Many believed the *California* had picked up other survivors, and that they would be united with their loved one in New York. I held no such illusions. I'd seen the water sweep over the deck. I'd heard the mass of humanity crying out for salvation.

And I'd heard their pleas go silent when no savior arrived.

Exhaustion overcame me. All around little groups of survivors found rest upon the floor or dining room tables. I was surprised to see Margaret Brown moving among the women of all classes, passing out blankets and clothing the passengers of the *Carpathia* had donated. Her command of multiple languages amazed me, and she offered great comfort in utterances I couldn't understand. But I could perceive the gratitude in the faces, the gentle responses, even when I didn't know the words. I told her a young man I knew was in need of clothing, and she handed me worn trousers and a mismatched shirt.

It would be perfect. If Charles were to pass onto American soil without being recognized, he certainly couldn't dress like himself.

I had no more energy. Making for the cabin, it was not lost upon me how lucky I was to have a bed. Once there I slipped beneath the blanket shrouding my still sleeping grandson and joined him in his repose.

When I awoke, Charles stood above me, pacing about, straining to get out of the room. I talked until he calmed, helped him sneak down the hall to relieve himself—there were no private lavatories, here—did everything within my power to keep him focused on anonymity.

Later that evening I brought him food. When I could take no more of his moods I issued strict instruction for him to stay put and escaped to the deck above, draped in my woolen shawl. I couldn't bear the saloons. People were everywhere, sleeping, staring straight ahead. I had to escape the crowd and clear my head. I needed to plan how to keep Charles hidden, how to get him off the ship and to safety without being recognized.

I paced upon the deck, cold and confused. Suddenly, two violent flashes of lightning tore across the sky, followed by two booming thunderclaps, so ferocious they shook the boat. As I rushed for cover, many of the other survivors clambered onto the deck, wondering if calamity had again struck. The lot of us were a ravaged bundle of nerves.

Of course, it was simply the beginning of a storm. The fog rolled in, and for some reason I was comforted. It seemed appropriate that we continued our journey shrouded under this dismal cloud.

I hunted the various dining saloons until I found Louise. She rushed to me, and I believe she almost hugged me before I lifted my chin and stayed such a display.

"You look well enough." I was glad she'd had her coat that cold night upon the ocean.

She nodded. "Yes, madam. And you are a sight for sore eyes."

A hint of tears glistened in her expression, and I almost loved her in that moment. "I've been given a cabin, very small quarters, but I'm grateful for a bed when so many have none."

Louise nodded, then hesitated. "Do you have information about Mr. Stanford or Calvert?"

Calvert's brave stance upon the *Titanic* swept over me. "Calvert and I searched for Charles until the last possible moment." The crack in my voice was natural and real. Calvert had served me faithfully. "We never found Charles. I was loaded upon what I believe was the last lifeboat to leave the ship. It carried only women and children and a few sailors."

"Perhaps they were picked up by another ship."

"Yes." I spoke a bit sharply.

Allowing an uncomfortable silence to lengthen between us, I looked away from her. Finally, I turned back to her, my heart pierced by the ache in her expression. "I'd like you to do something for me, Louise."

"Of course."

"Instead of tending me upon the rest of this voyage, offer your services to others. I heard Mrs. Brown is gathering thread and sheets to make clothing for the little ones without proper attire. You're quite good with a needle."

Louise looked at me, a quizzical arch to her brow.

"There is nothing to necessitate your service to me right now." I shrugged. "I have a comfortable cabin, food, and only one dress to wear. There are many who could do with your assistance. I plan to spend the remainder of the voyage resting."

"Yes, madam. It will be an honor to serve where there is so much need."

My heart softened despite myself. I gave a gentle squeeze to her arm. "You're a good person, Louise."

Surprise flashed across her face, and she sputtered a response. We were both uncomfortable with such intimacy, and I stepped away, intent upon retiring.

On the way back to my room I procured a book and a dominoes game from the library. They might go a small way in entertaining Charles Malcolm until we made port in New York City. It would not be an easy task to keep my restless grandson in check.

The next morning, Tuesday, April sixteenth, I brought Charles his breakfast, placing it on the tiny table between the bed and the single hard-backed chair.

Lines crinkled about his eyes as he glared at me. "I don't feel like eating." He raised a hand.

"Charles!" I felt sure he was about to send the food and dishes crashing to the floor. "Don't be ungrateful when so many have lost everything!"

He crumbled at this and slumped into the chair. He didn't do anything destructive, but he didn't touch his food. I picked up the novel I'd brought to him the night before. Of course, it was also untouched. I opened it with a creak of its binding and began to read to him. After two chapters, I sensed he was engaged in the tale. Placing the book on the table near him, I left the room. No words were exchanged between us, but my understanding of Charles's constitution was astute. He would pick the book up and read. Eventually hunger would drive him to eat the food I'd brought.

That afternoon, I attended the meeting of those survivors who were uninjured. Mr. Samuel Goldenberg presided. He appointed a committee, which included Mrs. Margaret Brown, to care for the unfortunate aboard who were left without resources. A collection was taken to ensure the steerage passengers who'd been saved would have enough income for hotel and travel to their destinations.

The vivacious Mrs. Brown stood above Mrs. Astor and me as she wrote out a generous check, and I a promissory note. The Captain graciously cashed both so the steerage survivors, mostly immigrants, would have money in hand once we arrived in America.

Mrs. Brown singled me out. "My dear Mrs. Stanford, your efforts toward the misfortunate have been indeed generous, but I'm sure you agree that money alone doesn't solve everything. Won't you accompany me as I care for the suffering?" She sought to make me an example for the others to follow, I'm sure.

Margaret Brown was at least twenty years my junior. I perceived it took much self-control for her to slow her pace to mine, but she seemed intent on directing those of us from her social circle to become the benefactors of the needy on the *Carpathia*, and my financial assistance was not all she required.

As I followed her, I used the opportunity to ask if anyone had information on my beloved grandson. I played the concerned grandmother with expertise. After all those years seeking to hide my worry about Charles and his poor choices, I now had reason to be public in display of anxious discourse.

It was rather relieving.

Mrs. Brown led me to the sewing circle where Louise and several other ladies fashioned crude clothing from sheets for the children who needed it. They sewed with thread and needle procured from the *Carpathia*'s passengers.

In the sewing circle sat a young woman with a little girl, about five or six years of age, clinging to her. The child's eyes seemed ancient in her drawn face. Though I'd seen many children looking confused or scared, their pain never ceased to reach to me, and I felt a stab of sorrow for the lost-looking girl.

I think Mrs. Brown first thought to encourage me to join the sewing circle, as it would be productive work that didn't require much physical exertion, but I'm no longer able to do needlework and let it be known. As we exited the library, the little girl peered at me from behind her companion's skirts. "Her father is John Harper, a widowed preacher from London," Mrs. Brown whispered. "He wasn't in any of the lifeboats."

I glanced back at the child, offering a smile. She ducked her head.

From there Mrs. Brown led me to a makeshift hospital. She sat me next to a young Swedish man recovering from hypothermia and insisted I serve him tea. Inwardly I cowered. It was quite unconventional to break the social code, as the man was obviously traveling steerage.

"This is Mr. August Wennerstrom." Mrs. Brown spoke as if the introduction settled it. She lingered, her bright eyes upon me.

I poured the tea.

Mr. Wennerstrom looked to be only a few years older than Charles Malcolm, and I sensed if we'd met under better circumstances he would've had those same winsome ways about him. This day, however, his face was drawn.

I coaxed him to sip a bit of the liquid. After a couple of slow drinks, he began to speak broken English mixed with Swedish. His limited command of my language made it impossible for me to decipher the story he seemed determined to tell. Finally, a young man on my other side repeated Wennerstrom's discourse in English.

"The steward told us to come up deck. Said it was just a precaution." The young translator paused after the phrase, then looked at Wennerstrom, who continued. After a moment the man translated again. "It'd been such a merry trip my friend thought perhaps there'd be more drinks, but the bar was closed. We entertained ourselves by starting a ring dance."

Wennerstrom emitted a humorless laugh then continued, his words once again smoothed out by the other stranger. "The lifeboats filled, and we didn't think much of it. We helped some of the girls aboard, smoked a cigar, and watched everything. It felt like we were the audience for some drama, not like it was happening to us. We felt no sorrow or fright. After the last lifeboat pulled away from the ship, the band played a hymn instead of party music. Suddenly, all became real to us. We began to believe the unsinkable boat was going down."

The translator paused as Wennerstrom collected himself; then Wennerstrom choked out the words in English, "Cry, cry everywhere. Prayer and more prayer."

His words became mixed again with his native tongue. The translator looked at me with sad eyes, "He says 'God has not often been remembered or called upon as He was that night.'"

A tremor went through me.

The flow of words continued. "My friends and I searched for life belts. The boilers exploded. The second explosion threw me into the air. As the ship tilted, my friends and I held hands and tried to climb, but the angle was too steep. We held onto each other then and slid down, bumping into a collapsible lifeboat that had been left behind. It was not entirely intact, but we cut it loose, and it floated."

Wennerstrom became quiet, and I thought perhaps he'd shared all he intended. Then he grasped my arm and a flow of mumbled, painful words were whispered. His piercing blue eyes clouded as he spoke though his intent gaze never moved from my face. He spoke continuously, giving no time for translation. As the words poured forth, raw pain flowed from him like thick lava from a volcano that had suddenly erupted. I didn't have to understand his words to know the heat of his pain.

When he finished, his clasp on my arm tightened. I glanced down where his hand met my sleeve, then back to his face. He shook his head back and forth, back and forth—tiny, stuttering movements. It was as if he tried to shake away the very speech he'd just articulated.

Then he turned from me, rolling on his side, covering his face with his arm.

I knew he would not again receive tea from my hand, and I placed the teacup on the tiny table between his bed and the translator's.

Our session was over, but I had no idea what story I'd just heard. After a moment, I turned to the other man.

The translator was solemn. "There was a Swedish woman with four children. Her name was Alma Pålsson." Now that he spoke, his voice was reverent. "She had a mouth organ and tried to keep her little ones from fear by playing upon it. When the end drew near, she thrust baby Gösta into Mr. Wennerstrom's arms and sought to comfort the older children. Mr. Wennerstrom tried to hold onto the baby, but the child was swept away when he hit the water. The woman and all her children were lost."

The translator heaved a sigh.

I thought perhaps he was done, but his deep, quiet voice began again. "He was only fifty feet from the spot where the great ship went down, and there were many people where it had disappeared. Some died quickly. Others fought hard but could not overcome the cold.

"Mr. Wennerstrom found himself floating atop three dead bodies. The same blast that had thrown him into the sea took the bottom from the lifeboat he'd found, but it was made of cork and continued to float. He was able to get onto the bottomless lifeboat, and helped his friends, Edvard and Gerta. He held tight to Gerta's hand for as long as he could but had to watch her float away when his grasp would hold no longer. He realized then that Edvard was already dead."

The young linguist paused, stared at the ceiling for a moment, then continued without looking back at me. "For six hours he clung to the little boat. Of the dozens that first held fast with him, only thirteen live. Mr. Wennerstrom's last words were, 'When a man has lost his hope, no life preserver in the world can hold him up. No one is going to help you but yourself. You must do your duty.'"

The silence between us was heavy, but neither of us cared to speak. I glanced again toward Mr. Wennerstrom. His back shook with silent sobs. The translator turned away as well.

Without speaking, I rose to my feet to seek out Charles, my child who lived.

* * * *

Ember cried for Alma Pålsson and her children. Her sweet baby swept away before her eyes. The rest perishing with her. It had been Alma's boarding pass that Ember had received when she'd gone through the Titanic Museum in New York. All she knew of the woman at that time was that she traveled with her four children, apparently no male companion.

And now, to hear the awful truth, her heart grieved.

Jeff pulled her closer and whispered, "Are you okay? You're taking this one especially hard."

She nodded, but her voice only allowed her to squeak out, "Later."

* * * *

Cylinder Six continues
Olive

It is not my habit to dwell on the misfortunes of others, but as I leaned upon my cane, even more tired than before, I couldn't put Alma Pålsson's little ones from my mind. Charles and his father before him had been such delightful babies. Both were full faced, plump, and endowed with great energy. They kept their nanny busy chasing after them, even clothed with long baby dresses to impede their movement. How I adored simply watching them crawl with all their might, then sit up suddenly on their fleshy little bottoms.

A prick of tears surprised me, and I put away such unwelcome emotion. Who knew how long a bout of tears would last if I gave way to such expression? Stanfords didn't cry in public.

Mrs. Pålsson's loss increased my determination to see my one living relative to safety. I would do all within my powers to ensure the life that now stretched before my grandson would be lived outside the doors of a dank prison cell.

The plan for Charles Malcolm's escape took greater shape. I found a purser and asked for baking soda to cleanse my teeth. When I'd slipped the bundle inside my sleeve, I found a different purser. "I'm sorry to bother you, sir, but I've detected some mildew in my cabin."

A faint flicker of irritation passed over his features, and I suppressed a smile. His reaction was just what I'd hoped for, knowing how overworked the crew was, how ridiculous it was to complain when people slept on tables.

He gave a stiff bow. "Under normal circumstances I would offer to investigate immediately. But . . ." He spread his hands and allowed his voice to trail off.

"Oh, my!" I touched my heart. "Surely you don't think I expect you to take care of it when you have so much of greater import to attend to!"

His expression softened.

"I wouldn't even bother you at all if it weren't for an allergy that affects my breathing at night. I've discovered in my own home that cleaning with a little hydrogen peroxide clears things up for me. I only meant to inquire where I might be able to find some. I intend to take care of the issue myself."

As I hoped he immediately dispatched another crew member to retrieve a bottle for me. I took it eagerly.

When I reached the cabin I scanned the alleyway to ensure I was alone before slipping as quickly as I could into our room. I pulled the door closed behind me and clicked the lock. Charles and I had work to do.

Chapter 28

Cylinder Seven
Olive

Congratulate me on my cleverness."

Charles frowned at me. I set the bottle of hydrogen peroxide on the table and then pulled the baking soda from my sleeve.

He wrinkled his brows together. "What are you talking about?"

"Your disguise of course." I pointed to the worn clothes I'd placed in the small closet earlier. "We must do everything possible to ensure you look as little like Charles Malcolm Stanford III as possible. The clothes will help, but they aren't enough."

"And what does that have to do with those?" He pointed to my treasures on the table.

"A few years ago it was all the rage to bleach straw boaters with hydrogen peroxide, remember? It turned the brown straw more yellow."

"And?"

I grinned at him. "And, when that was all the rage, I heard a very funny story at a tea. One of the women had a daughter who wished for lighter hair. The girl made a paste of these two substances and took color from her hair."

"Surely you don't—"

"Oh but I do!" I pulled Charles Malcolm to sit next to me on the bed. "We have to get you off this ship and out of New York City without your being recognized. The press would notice the handsome Charles Malcolm Stanford III with his rich brown hair, immaculate clothing, and clean-shaven face. I stood and took the shaving bowl provided with the room. "By the time we reach New York, your face will be full of stubble—

light brown, maybe even blond. And that stubble will match your hair."

I made a paste while Charles buried his head in his hands. The man was vainer than I ever was, but he saw the wisdom in my plan.

I rubbed the paste on the shadow already beginning on his face and into his thick, dark hair. "I'm sorry, Charles." Perhaps I was the one who had made him vain for I could barely stand the thought of tampering with his beautiful hair. We let the concoction set for a long while before washing it out with the pitcher and basin in our room. We waited until it was very late, then I watched the alleyway to make sure it and the lavatory were clear. Charles carried the basin and I the empty pitcher. We dumped the basin and refilled the pitcher for use the next day, then returned to our cabin and fell into exhausted sleep.

Morning dawned too early. I was sad to see the rich, dark brown gone from Charles's hair, but it was still too close to his normal color. We would do another application in the night.

I brought us breakfast and made small talk with a subdued Charles. Perhaps hurting his vanity was a good way to reduce his desire to leave the room.

My focus was on rest and caring for Charles. I was used to Calvert and Louise waiting at my elbow to meet our every need, but now not only did I take care of my own requirements, I was fully responsible for Charles. Thankfully, my needs were less than I thought possible. Accustomed to changing clothes four or more times a day, I was amazed at the time and energy spared me when I had only one dress. Here on this ship, all of us stunned by real tragedy, social custom had fallen away. Rebuilding our strength and surviving the trauma was the bulk of our task.

I slept a good deal on that morning, then ate lunch and sneaked food back to Charles. After he ate, we slept again for a while, but he startled me from my slumber, crying out from a dream. I patted his back, and after a time his breathing deepened once again. I couldn't work past the images that had filled my head when he woke me. His cries brought memories of those I did not want to hear ever again, and sleep did not return to me.

It was not yet time for the evening meal, but I slipped from the cabin to find a distraction. After the emotional strain of caring for Mr. Wennerstrom the day before, I did my best to avoid Mrs. Brown and the makeshift hospital room where she had taken me. I sought the company of Louise, who had found a place to sleep on the floor of the library where many other women also claimed a place. Beyond her a woman spoke French to the two little boys who'd shared my lifeboat. I assumed their father had not been found.

"Oh, good! There you are, Mrs. Stanford!"

I raised my eyes from the children to the source of the voice calling for me. Lady luck does not play fair. Margaret Brown's eyes brightened. "I was just looking for help feeding some of the more unfortunate men. We have just enough time to care for their needs before we take the evening meal ourselves."

I opened my mouth to protest, but she continued talking, praising the Stanford name, the good stock we came from, and our ability to rise above the unpleasant and serve others. Rarely does someone better me in getting her way, but embodied in the character of Mrs. Brown was a steel that rivaled my own. I suppose I had little energy to fight the woman. Saving Charles required all my reserves, and—I can admit such things now— serving the unfortunate soothed my aching conscience.

Louise came with me as we followed Margaret Brown to our duties. Mrs. Brown led us through the alleyway and to the hospital, where she placed each of us with a patient. Seated next to a young man whose legs and feet were wrapped, I scorned myself for avoiding such service earlier. It was a small thing to ladle soup. The man sat up in his bed, propped against pillows, his hair dirty and unkempt. No complaint came from his mouth as I settled next to him and offered nourishment, but pain was clearly marked on his stoic face. He took the bowl upon his lap, and its fragrance made my stomach rumble.

The young man ate very little, and for a long while I simply sat next to him, handing him the cloth napkin, or his cup of coffee as he reached for them. He didn't actually require my help, but I suspect he'd not eaten much since the sinking. It was as though he forced down each tiny spoonful of soup, each minuscule sip of coffee. I came to understand my presence wasn't required for physical assistance as much as for the hope I could coax him to receive more nourishment.

I stayed faithful to my task, hoping he wouldn't try to make conversation. The view of the *Titanic* sinking, the echo of all those voices crying for help, was trauma enough. When Mr. Wennerstrom had given me his close up account of the sinking, he gave birth to further violent imaginings. Extended speculation about the tragedy, the horror all those poor souls faced, was unwelcome, but harder to resist after that conversation. I loathed the thought of another.

"They hauled me from the water, you know."

Here it came, the story I didn't want to hear. Maybe if I didn't encourage him, he wouldn't keep talking.

"I dove into the Atlantic just before the great ship went down." His voice was husky for one so young. The half-empty soup bowl lay forgotten upon his lap, the salty scent dying away as the nourishment cooled.

"I found a piece of debris and grabbed hold of it." He didn't even look at me, didn't seem to need my affirmation to continue. "Here I am floating, that frigid water like a million pointed icicles stabbing my skin. I'm hanging on tight, growing numb. Then I seen him. This crazy fool is swimmin' from person to person. 'Are you saved?' he calls out in a Scottish brogue."

The young man looks at me then, and I note his smooth skin, surmise that he can't be over twenty-five.

"Can you imagine it?" His eyes widen. "People are crying, screaming for help, pushing their way through the living and the dead, fighting for life. And the crazy man is preaching."

My hand grabbed my cane, and my body prepared for flight. I placed pressure upon that cane but not enough to stand.

For some reason I stayed. I listened for what was coming.

The man stared far away, the look of one in deep remembrance. "Then he sees me. He swims right over and says, 'Are you saved?' My body's fighting not to go into shock, and my brain is all fuzzy-like. I pull myself from the numbness and tell him 'no.' Then he does the darndest thing." The young man paused then looked down. "Pardon my language, ma'am. I didn't mean to slip before a lady."

I just stared at him.

"But it's plain old crazy what he does next." His voice rose. "The man treads that freezing water and begins loosening his life belt. He takes it off. Takes it off! Then he tosses it to me and says, 'You need this more than I do.'

"Just like that, he gives me his life belt. All because I'm not saved!" The young man looked away then. He shifted his legs, and the spoon in his half-empty soup bowl clattered against the side. "I'm no fool. I grab that floater with one hand, keep hanging onto the debris with the other. The buoyancy helps me get a little farther out of the water.

"The man moves on, keeps swimming, keeps talking to dying folks about the state of their heart. I recognized him then. He was that preacher, John Harper."

My thoughts flickered back to the little girl I'd seen the day before.

The young man sighed. "I suppose watching him gave me something to think about other than how I was freezing to death. I follow his progress a good while, then suddenly he swims back to me." The young man's voice deepened. "'Are you saved now?' the preached asked me. His words were slowing, becoming more slurred with the cold. I couldn't answer him. Then he said it again—what he'd been saying to all the others. 'Believe on the Lord Jesus Christ and you shall be saved.' It was the last thing anyone on this earth heard him say, and he said it to me."

My heart thudded in my chest, the sweet little girl's innocent eyes haunting my recollection.

Her father was dead.

I glanced away and cleared my throat. When I looked back toward the young man, this young person whose feet and legs might never recover, who'd floated in the Atlantic watching all around him die, I fought even harder for composure.

"Just when I knew I couldn't hold on any longer, a lifeboat pulls up next to me and strong arms lift me inside. They looked for more people to rescue out of the deep, but weren't many who hadn't already froze."

It was rather abrupt, how quickly I stood. Offering the young man a curt nod, I walked away.

In the dining saloon I barely forced my food down. Then I took a portion for Charles and made for the cabin. After I served his evening meal we applied another baking soda and peroxide paste. His hair faded a little more.

Thursday morning I stayed close to the cabin. We were expected to make New York City that night, and there was much to discuss with Charles. He sat in the hard chair, reading the novel I'd brought to him on Tuesday night. His eyes were lowered, and I admired the full, dark lashes that almost brushed his cheeks. He'd lost his polish with the horrible whiskers beginning to claim his face, and hair that now was light brown, instead of the rich, dark color I so loved.

But he was still Charles.

I stroked his arm. "We need to talk."

He closed the book and laid it aside. "I know."

"This won't be easy for either of us. You can never come home. You can never again live as a Stanford."

"What will I do?" His voice was barely a whisper.

I reached for his hand, so smooth in my own. Rubbing it against my cheek, I thought of how chubby it once was, of how it knew no labor, of how I would never hold it again. "You'll follow my instructions to get off the ship without being recognized. Then you'll go to this address." I handed him the paper I'd already prepared. "You must stay hidden there. After a few days I'll come to you with enough money to start afresh. Then you must board the train and start a new life in the west, far from New York City. St. Louis, first. Then Denver or San Francisco."

His eyes widened. Maybe he hadn't yet realized the extremes of his situation.

"In New York City, you'll leave a trail behind you, using Mr. Keaton's name. You'll board the train under that name, but once you're in St. Louis, you'll abandon anything connected with him. Burn his papers and his passport. Shave if you like. Darken your hair. Buy new clothes. Assume a new name. What one would you like?" I tried to make it game, this giving up of the Stanford name, this abandoning of everything he'd known.

"How would I know, Grandmother? I never thought to name myself."

The bitter edge in Charles's voice dug at my heart. "I wish there were another way. If you know of one, tell me now."

He straightened. "I could face the charges and the consequences."

"Could you?"

He slumped.

"Don't tell me the name you pick, but plan it out, Charles. Become someone new."

He stood and paced the room. "I have no trade. No training. Without the Stanford name I will have no connections."

"You are not without intelligence. You'll find a way to make a new life—and I'll send you with ample funds."

He knelt in front of me and fell upon my lap. I fingered that tough, light brown hair, loved him with such fervency my heart broke into pieces. Until that moment all my planning for his safety was distant. In my rush to save him and the Stanford name, I'd neglected to acknowledge that I would lose him forever.

Chapter 29

Cylinder Eight
Olive

When the *Carpathia* finally docked at Cunard pier that dreary night, Thursday, April nineteenth, we were a solemn crowd. Immigrants were passed quickly through the legal proceedings. There was to be no Ellis Island for *Titanic*'s survivors. The rest of us gave our names as we left the ship, one final tally of the fortunate who'd braved the Atlantic and won. I held back, separated from Charles Malcolm. I'd given him careful instruction to flash Mr. Keaton's passport as he disembarked. It would add credibility to our story if it were ever questioned. I also instructed Charles about how to avoid being ushered to Keaton's waiting family, and prompted him to time his departure in conjunction with Mrs. Brown's. All eyes, all cameras would be upon her, affording him less attention.

I could not hover. He would have to navigate by himself.

When my turn came, I walked with Louise, moving slowly down the gangplank, stoic in my resolve not to give way to emotion. I could have kissed the earth, so relieved I was to be upon solid ground, but for the ache in my heart, and the watching crowds. The sky dripped tears, crying for the hundreds lost at sea, crying for my Charles.

Reporters rushed forward, snapping pictures of the *Carpathia* and her strange stock. Seven hundred and five of us, along with two little dogs, navigated the crowd. There was the occasional quiet weeper, but most of us were resolute. We had braved the ravenous waters, and we would brave this hungry, swirling mass of humanity.

Earl had the automobile waiting to whisk us away, of course. I avoided looking into the grief in his eyes, but his hands trembled as he helped me into the backseat, and they trembled as he drove Louise and me home.

Earl had lost his Calvert, and I my Charles. It was easy to play the grieving grandmother.

I summoned my courage. "I will tell you of Calvert, Earl. Then we must never speak of this again."

"Yes, madam." His eyes flickered to the mirror, catching mine for a brief moment.

"Your son chose the road of courage." My voice broke, surprising all three of us. "I called for Calvert to accompany me into the lifeboat, but he bowed and gently refused. He gave his spot to save the women and children. Your son died a hero. The last time I saw him he stood resolute upon *Titanic's* deck."

"Thank you." Earl's voice was a shadow of itself.

When we reached home, I went immediately to my quarters, locked the doors, and cried all night. I spent the next two days alternately grieving and making preparation. After darkness fell on Saturday night, I called a cab. I took it downtown to the theater then stepped out of sight until it moved on and claimed another. I switched cabs one more time, pulling my big hat low over my face the whole time I rode in the third. Then I went to my Charles.

He opened the door at my first rap. I slipped inside, unnerved by the alcohol on his breath, unnerved by the stringy, straw-colored hair.

"I made another application of the peroxide. I'm practically blond now." His words were steady enough, as was his gait. He hadn't been drinking long.

The whiskey bottle sat upon the night table in the little room. I smashed it upon the bricks of the dark fireplace. "You have to keep your wits about you, Charles."

"I know."

His easy assent surprised me. He sat on the bed, his head in his hands, looking just like he had upon the *Carpathia* when he'd realized his course. My cane heavy within my hand, I made my way to his side. I sat next to him, not daring to touch him but seeking the warmth of his body close to mine. I would never again smell his scent or be angered by the spirits upon his breath. I reached for his hand, and he allowed me to take it. I surrounded that fine young hand with my two, blue-veined ones and smothered it. Then I lifted it to my lips. Releasing it, I reached into my reticule and pulled out a vast number of large bills.

Charles lifted astonished eyes to mine.

"I told you there would be enough for a fresh start. Hide it well. Spend little until you reach your destination, and then spend well, but not all in one place. Avoid attracting attention."

His hand shook as he reached for the money.

"Remember your instructions. You are to board tomorrow as Thomas Keaton, but once you disembark, you will darken your hair and change into the clothes I brought you. Then—"

"I know the plan."

I stood, fighting hard against the quivering of my chin.

Charles stretched to his full height, then pulled me into those young, firm arms. "It's okay to cry, Grandmother," he whispered into my hair.

I shook then, fighting back the sobs, refusing to give voice to my agony, but unable to control the tears. He held me until I calmed. Then Charles pulled his handkerchief from his pocket and gently dabbed my eyes, my swollen checks, the wet paths upon my neck. Not once did he cry out. Not once did the emotion in his dark eyes spill out to his cheeks. For this moment he was the man, I the simpering child.

When I regained composure he walked me to the door, lifted my gnarled hand to his sweet lips, and planted a gentle kiss.

I never saw him again.

The bulk of the next week was spent locked away in my room. No one questioned it, of course. I had lost my grandson upon the *Titanic*. Over time, the papers reported the strange disappearance of Thomas Keaton, how he'd stepped from the *Carpathia* and shown his passport, never to be seen again. At first the family feared foul play, but none was reported. A private investigator had been hired who found evidence

Thomas Keaton boarded a train to St. Louis, but he was never discovered beyond.

It was difficult maintaining my composure when the gossip began at the next ladies tea. It was widely believed Thomas Keaton abandoned his wife and child because Josephine's father had disinherited her. People assumed Mr. Keaton had married for money and found an excuse to escape the marriage and seek his fortunes in the west. It pained me to see the good man's reputation thus scarred, but what could I do?

Then there came a day that brought Josephine Keaton into my house. Louise ushered her to the parlor. Before stepping into the room, I steeled myself for whatever was coming, and collected myself with the Stanford reserve.

She rose and offered a gloved hand. "Thank you for receiving me."

"Of course. Please make yourself comfortable."

"I have no energy for small talk, Mrs. Stanford. I'll come right to the point."

My heart skipped a beat, but I maintained. I was a Stanford after all. "I like forthright women."

Her smile was small. "No doubt you've heard the rumors of my husband's abandonment."

I inclined my head.

"The detective I hired was told that someone aboard the *Carpathia* heard you mention seeing my husband. That—I'm afraid this sounds outlandish—he stayed in your cabin."

"Yes. Mr. Keaton was on the lifeboat with me." I had practiced my story for just this moment, and it flowed from me like truth. "I knew him because he was friends with an old pal of my son's, Samuel Jacobs."

At the mention of Samuel's name, Mrs. Keaton sucked in a quick breath. As I'd hoped, the addition of that detail substantiated my tale. "Mr. Keaton sustained a minor injury when boarding the lifeboat, and I offered to treat it. He was too healthy for the makeshift hospitals, but I thought he needed a recovery period before sleeping upon the floor with the other men. I suggested he rest awhile in my cabin. He slept there most of the day but didn't stay through the night, of course."

"So he was indeed upon the *Carpathia*." Her voice was a whisper. "He lived only to leave us."

Not trusting my voice to respond, I sat quiet. I hoped she thought I was being respectful.

After a time, I rose and placed a hand upon her shoulder. "Perhaps you should return to your father's home, Mrs. Keaton. Surely this unfortunate episode can be put behind you. With your father's resources you can marry again and establish your life."

The devastation in her countenance when she lifted her gaze to mine still haunts me as much as the cries of the unfortunate in the Atlantic.

"It seems my decision to marry Thomas is unforgivable, Mrs. Stanford. My father thinks it best for me to live with the consequences of my actions. There is no place for me, or my daughter, in his home."

It took all of the Stanford training for me to remain passive. My stomach roiled and bile bit the back of my throat.

Mrs. Keaton stood. "I've taken enough of your time."

"I'll escort you to the door." I walked a pace behind her as she left my parlor.

When she reached the front hall, she turned toward me. "Did he . . . speak of me?"

"No."

She nodded, heaviness wrapped around her like a garment. I closed the door behind her as she descended the steps. Then I rushed to the lavatory, where I retched. But no matter how much came from the pit of my stomach, the bitter bile of my deception could not be dislodged.

As guilt consumed my days, I thought to send her a check, to provide support one way or another for her and her daughter, but I feared solicitous actions would arouse suspicion. A few months later I happened upon a solution I thought would ease her life and mine. In conversation with a wealthy old acquaintance of mine, Weatherford Banks, I intimated that Josephine was beautiful, well-bred, in need of help, and had the sympathy of society. He took the hint. They eventually married, and Josephine and Elizabeth were given the comforts of wealth. Rumors say Elizabeth is growing quite handsome and that she will marry well. That's good, because they won't inherit, of course. The money will go to Mr. Banks's son from his first marriage.

I hoped my part in encouraging provision for Josephine would settle some of my remorse, and for a while it did. But I saw her at a party a few years after her marriage. Whispers of Mr. Banks's unfaithfulness marred the air, and indeed Josephine's eyes held the dull emptiness of an unhappy, bitter woman, twice mistreated in love. It pains me to this day. But perhaps, like the rest of us, she has learned to face the realities of this loveless world.

Authorities from London did eventually find their way to my door, but with Charles Malcolm having perished upon the *Titanic* it didn't take much of a bribe for the official to agree that there was no reason to tarnish the Stanford name. The matter was laid to rest. Had I not received this visit, I would have been tempted to seek out my grandson, for each day grew more lonely than the one before. I had assumed I would adjust to my solitude, but I did not. But the knowledge that the deed in London was known and traced to my door kept me determined to protect Charles.

There is one more piece of the story I am compelled to confess, for perhaps through it Charles will be understood as a better man than previously believed through this narrative. My own reputation I can no longer protect.

About five years after that awful night on the *Titanic*, I received a missive from my grandson. The return address was omitted, but the postmark said Denver, Colorado. I broke through the seal with trembles coursing through each finger. He wrote that remorse was tearing him apart and requested that I hand-deliver a letter to Mrs. Keaton, which he had enclosed. He asked also that I write to an address he'd given me to inform him of her response. The address was for a friend named Billings, and if I would place a second letter inside the first, addressed to David, the friend could be trusted to deliver the letter without reading it.

Of course I could do no such deeds. There is no way Josephine Keaton could be told the truth.

I read his heart-felt apology in which he spilled out the whole miserable story and assured Mrs. Keaton of her husband's affection. Immediately, I composed a reply to the address he'd given. In it I told him Mrs. Keaton had been very angry at first, but that after a period of a month she'd visited to offer her forgiveness. I said she was happy and well cared for in her new marriage, but that his words had allowed her to forgive Thomas, and she once again held him in high esteem. After I wrote the reply I addressed the two envelopes, the inner to David, the outer to Billings.

Then I put Charles Malcolm's original letters into the fireplace and watched the flair of the flame as it engulfed them. I added wood to the blaze, making sure it burned hot until the remnants of the letters were nothing but ash.

I hid my respond to Charles and mailed it a month later. It was truly the only recourse. I didn't want Charles Malcolm returning to unburden his soul and put everything I'd so carefully ordered into upheaval. I offered my grandson what I could not give myself: forgiveness. The lies I wrote would free him to live his young life beyond the reach of a dark prison cell. I believed he would find full freedom, once his conscience was allayed.

I am the only one left in chains.

Now I face the end of my days. The barest thought of recompense for the deeds I've done upon this earth leaves me quaking to the bone if I allow it. For most of my years, I have lived ignoring religion and supposition. What good would such speculation on the unknown do me, but to incite fear of judgment or remorse for my life? Nothing can be done now to redeem the past. I cannot change my choices; there is no recourse for reckless decisions.

Perhaps you judge me, son or daughter of the future, for my mistreatment of the good Thomas Keaton. But I can't imagine my pain any less than that of Josephine Keaton or her daughter, Elizabeth. For I, too, was left bereft of anyone to love or be loved by me. If I'd known the pain of being forever separated from my dear Charles Malcolm, I don't know if I could have stayed true to the course I set for us. I know not where Charles is today. The Stanford name was saved, but what of it? It will die with me.

As I close my affairs I've laid aside a stipend for faithful Earl and gentle Louise and given the rest to a fund for the orphans of the *Titanic*. Soon my beautiful old home will be gone. It will not be passed to the two men I have loved, for Charles II died an untimely death, and Charles III was cast away forever by my own hand.

I often find myself quite restless at night, and the month of April is the worst. I've lived almost thirteen years since that fateful trip upon *Titanic*, and it is thirteen years too long. As the anniversary nears each year, I become more and more agitated, more and more sleepless.

The tenth anniversary was the worst. I went to bed on April 14, 1922, determined to sleep, but was awakened by the worst nightmare I'd had since the sinking. I shook in my bed, fighting to catch my breath. I couldn't come to my senses enough to embrace reality. I just lay there, the chill biting into my very bones, reliving every horror. Images of that elegant ship hanging midair, her lights blinking on and off, twisted in and out of memories of Josephine Keaton and the look upon her face as I lied to her.

Shaking my head, trying to force away the pictures lodged forever in my remembrances, I tried to call out for Louise. On the third try I finally made myself heard. Louise rushed to my room in her nightcap and turned on my lamp. Then she helped me from the bed.

Together we went to the tiny sitting room attached to my bedroom. She flicked on the light there as well and covered me with a wrap. She left to make a soothing tea, which I knew she would lace with heavy spirits so I could sleep. The light from the beautiful rose-colored lamp penetrated the darkness of the sitting room, but it could not dispel my memories and regrets.

On the wall across from me was Charles's portrait. In it he stood tall next to one of our cherrywood chairs, ornate with carvings and tasteful design. His rich brown mane had not a hair out of place and was combed back in the style of the day. He had one hand in his pocket, and the dark suit was offset by a bright white vest and stiff white collar. A speck of white peeked also from the handkerchief in his pocket and the sleeves at the bottom of the arms of his dark jacket. How handsome he was! I gazed upon that youthful face, stood and walked to the wall. I raised a longing finger to brush across his smooth, white cheeks.

Louise found me there, tears trailing my face. She helped me back to my chair. "Shall I read from the *Ladies Home Journal?*"

Anything was better than my mournful musings.

First she began an account of how to take stains from a white blouse, which offered no interest at all, so I interrupted. She thumbed through the magazine, tried another story, and was interrupted again.

It seemed nothing would soothe me this night.

Finally she lifted cautious eyes to mine. "There is a story of the *Titanic.*"

"After all these years?" My words were almost a groan.

She shrugged. "It seems the author has interviewed several family members of various people who were lost, in honor of the tenth anniversary."

I hesitated.

"You never talk of it," Louise spoke with evident trepidation. "Perhaps the nightmares would lessen if you did."

"Read on."

The story talked of the little French boys' happy reunion with their mother, of Archibald Gracie's untimely death and how his wife had been awakened to pray for him at the time of his near drowning. It continued to expound upon the various memorials raised to honor *Titanic*'s heroes.

Louise paused. "The last section is about Robert Bateman. It says he traveled with his sister-in-law, a woman named Annie. Did you know them?"

In my mind I saw the man pulling off his necktie and throwing it to Annie. "A little," I whispered.

"It says here Mr. Bateman sent letters to both his wife and his nephew from Ireland, when *Titanic* docked to take on more passengers."

"The coast was so beautiful there."

Louise nodded and began to read, "To his wife, Mr. Bateman wrote of a revival he'd held in London. He called the event, 'glorious,' and 'the time of my life.' The letter written to his nephew, Tom, was more revealing. He told Tom that if the *Titanic* went to the bottom of the ocean he would not be upon it, but would be 'up yonder!'"

Louise paused as we both digested this information. Then she began to read again, the flow of her words so focused, so engaged, that I wondered if she had forgotten that I listened. "When the family pried open his locked rolltop desk, they were met with an unexpected treasure they will long cherish. Mr. Bateman had placed all his affairs in order. On top of the neat pile of legal papers was a card, trimmed with a black border. Penned in his own hand was a poem." Louise paused, lifted her eyes to mine.

"Well go on, then!"

She began to recite, her voice velvet soft, full of wonderment.

"Do you shudder as you picture
All the horrors of that hour?
Ah! But Jesus was beside me
To sustain me by His power.
And He came Himself to meet me
In that way so hard to tread
And with Jesus' arm to cling to
Could I have one doubt or dread?"

Her voice caught on the last stanza, and she covered her mouth with her hand.

I could see she was overcome with emotion. "Go! Collect yourself!"

When she left, I pulled the magazine close to me, read the words of the poem, analyzed every phrase.

And I saved it.

Thoughts of that night came to me as I began to dictate this final cylinder. In fact, they hung so close I stopped the cylinder, pulled the magazine from its hiding place, and read the poem again and again before recording it here. Never before has the question of what comes next invaded my musings in this way.

Is there an afterlife?

If there is, maybe confession in this world will ease my entry into the next. A lonely and forgotten woman, I face death this day, hoping it will come soon, begging the stars I won't have live through another anniversary of the sinking of RMS *Titanic*.

* * * *

The room was silent as the cylinder stopped. Ember snuggled into Jeff's shoulder. With gentle hands he wiped the tears from her face. She looked first at him then around the room at the people she had grown to love. She searched for a tissue in the pocket of her windbreaker lying next to her on the couch. Her fingers closed around something chalky, and she drew out the sand dollar. Still nicked. Still whole. Ember smiled.

Still whole.

Questions for Book Clubs and/or personal reflection:

1. Ember had to choose between understanding her past and moving into her future. Have you ever had to do that? What are some life-altering decisions you've made?
2. Ember found an unexpected friend in Cynthia. What made Ember trust Cynthia? Tell about a time you found friendship in an unexpected place.
3. Why did Jeff struggle with feeling his dad's approval?
4. Have you ever been torn between pleasing your dad and following your dreams? What's your opinion of how Jeff handled this dilemma?
5. Ember believes the Keaton women's bad luck in marriage began with Thomas Keaton. Do you think things like that can be passed from generation to generation?
6. Jeff told Ember he would break her family's curse. Do you think it's possible for one man to break the bondage begun by another?
7. Do you believe in generational curses? If so, what do you think it takes to break them?
8. Is there a generational curse you think you're dealing with right now?
9. Ember found the chipped, but whole sand dollar, and it made her think about herself. Why do you think she viewed herself as chipped but whole? How do you view yourself?
10. Jeff told Ember she had a strength he needed. Do you see that? If so, where?
11. Olive's primary two goals in this story were to protect her family name and her grandson. How do you feel about her goals? How about her methods in achieving those goals?
12. Olive judged the Harriet Snow by her clothes and demeanor. Do you think that is fair? Why or why not?

13. How did you feel about Calvert, Louise, and Earl? Do you think they were sincere in their service or playing a role? Why?

14. Many true accounts of the tragedy of the *Titanic* were woven into Olive's story. Which did you find the most impactful and why?

15. How do you feel about Mrs. Straus's decision to stay on *Titanic* with her husband?

16. Do you agree with the women and children only rule on the lifeboats?

17. Why did John Harper spend his last minutes "preaching"? Is there anything you are that passionate about?

18. Do you believe in an afterlife?

19. How do you feel about Olive's approach to the possibility of an afterlife?

20. Olive felt her deeds were done and there was no recourse for her. Do you think she understood the big picture? Why or why not?

21. Is there forgiveness for a person like Olive? Why or why not?

22. What was Charles's biggest fault?

23. Were there any redeeming characteristics in Olive and Charles? If so, what?

24. Why was the book called "Legacy of Betrayal?"

25. What negative legacy would you like to overcome? What positive legacy would you like to pass down?

Historical Notes from Paula

Much of my understanding of what transpired on the RMS *Titanic* was taken from two wonderful books, now available for free on the Internet. These books are, *Loss of the S. S. Titanic*, by Lawrence Beesley: and, *The Truth about the Titanic: A Survivor's Story*, by Colonel Archibald Gracie.

I found I couldn't begin writing until I'd read both, cover to cover. As I was writing, I often turned to them for historical accuracy. An astute historian will hear overtones of Beesley's thoughts at two poignant moments in the story—when the *New York* almost hits *Titanic* early in the voyage, and when *Titanic* sinks. For the noise as *Titanic* hung in the air I relied heavily upon a description found in Colonel Gracies' book. I went back and forth between the two texts as I crafted that scene and tried to give honor to both of them, their words, and the words of those they quoted. While I tried to place their historical accuracy and tone into my own words and story line, readers will notice much similarity.

Descriptions of the rooms of *Titanic* were built upon several sources, including but not limited to: http://www.titanicandco.com/inside.html, http://titanicarchive-online.com/index.php4?page=175, and http://titanic-model.com/articles/nigelbryant/interior.shtml. Lots of great pictures can be found by Googling "Images for rooms of the Titanic." It is interesting to note that most of the pictures taken on *Titanic* went with her to the bottom of the Atlantic, so much of what we know about her grandeur is built upon documentation of her sister ship, RMS *Olympic*.

The mustached Mr. McCawley of the *Titanic*'s gymnasium was well-thought of from all accounts and said to have been instructing people in the gymnasium to the very end, doing his duty (http://www.titanic-titanic.com/titanic_gymnasium.shtml). Some sites also say Mr. and Mrs. Astor passed the early harrowing moments before the sinking chatting with Mr. McCrawley in the gymnasium. This seems strange to me since separation of the sexes was strongly enforced in the gymnasium, swimming pool, etc. Of course who knows what delicacies were ignored as tragedy drew near.

Lawrence Beesley tells the story of the card players seeing an iceberg go by their window and joking about running on deck to get ice for their whiskey in chapter three of his book. Similar, but not identical, accounts of this incident appear all over the Internet. Beesley mentions how he has no doubt but that these fine young men played their game until the ship went down, and they were lost to the sea.

The stories of the Strausses, the Astors, and Edith Corse Evans are told in many *Titanic* collections and can be found in multiple accounts. Most of the sources differ in some little detail, so I picked my favorite way to quote these larger than life historic heroes and held onto whatever telling of their story best fit my needs. My favorite details on Miss Evans came from a blog: http://www.myspace.com/das_64/blog/537390231.

While there is evidence that directs the historian to the specific lifeboat each *Titanic* survivor rode in, where the lifeboat was on the *Titanic*, and what approximate time the lifeboat was sent to sea, I had to abandon trying to get the right people on the right lifeboats from the right location at the right time to tell my story. For more accurate information as to the loading of the lifeboats and who was saved on which boat, visit: http://www.titanic-titanic.com/lifeboat_lowering_times.shtml. If you want to really study this process, you'll need to do it with a map in hand to pinpoint the location of the lifeboats, familiarizing yourself with terms like boat deck, starboard, port, stern, and bow. Initially, I attempted this, determined to be historically accurate, then I realized if the novel was ever to be written I had to abandon such a studious endeavor and just tell my story, flawed though it would be in this area.

The band really was led by Wallace Hartley. Before the tragic night, the full band had probably never played together. Hartley was part of a quintet, and there was another group who formed a trio. The two groups played in different parts of the ship for different events. The eight of them did play together that night as the *Titanic* sank, playing ragtime, waltzes, and favorites of the day. Wallace Hartley's body was found two weeks after the ship went down. He still had on his band uniform and his music box was strapped to his body. All eight band members perished (http://www.titanic-titanic.com/titanic_band.shtml).

There is much debate about the last song the band played on the *Titanic*. Part of the trouble may be that the great ship was over 882 feet long and made of nine decks, so those few who survived and were still upon the *Titanic* at the end (or near it) would not only have been in various locations, but in various states of emotional turmoil. Also, those surviving in lifeboats fanned away from the *Titanic* where they had rowed to safety, giving survivors different vantage points.

Colonel Archibald Gracie is one who greatly disputes the band playing "Nearer My God to Thee." His work is one of the most respected firsthand accounts. Still, as the *Titanic* was going under, Gracie was aboard her, fighting for his life. He actually went under with the ship, but was shot up to safety on a rush of water. It's possible he didn't hear the music, because there are many survivors in lifeboats who said they did. Obviously, I chose to go with the treasured idea that the band played a hymn at the end.

Whether family lore about a beloved man, or historical fact, I don't know. But the man who threw Annie his necktie was Robert Bateman, known as Uncle Bob to the hungry children he served on the streets of London and as "the man who distributed more human sunshine than any man in Jacksonville," to those who loved him in Jacksonville, Florida, where he emigrated, became mayor, and built a mission to serve the city's down and out. Family lore has it that it was he who asked the band to play "Nearer My God to Thee" as the last song before the ship sank. There are also survivors who say they saw the "fiery evangelist" gathering men together and kneeling to pray as the ship went down. Much of my information came from these links:

http://cowart.info/Monthly%20Features/Titanic%204%20we b/Bateman%204%20web.htm, http://www.flickr.com/photos/brizzlebornandbred/20946823 89/, and http://www.encyclopedia-titanica.org/titanic-victim/robert-james-bateman.html. I didn't read Walter Lord's, *A Night to Remember*, but this book is often referenced in regard to Bateman's story.

I put the story of Bateman's rolltop desk in an account in the magazine, *Ladies Home Journal*. The *Ladies Home Journal* did exist in 1925, but to my knowledge Bateman's story was never told there. It came from this account, which quoted the poem I included: http://cowart.info/Monthly%20Features/Titanic%204%20we b/Bateman%204%20web.htm. The poem is said to have come from the book STRANGERS ON THE EARTH (BLUEFISH BOOKS, 2006) and was previously published in PEOPLE WHOSE FAITH GOT THEM INTO TROUBLE (IVP, 1990) c. 2005 by John W. Cowart.

The two little French boys have quite a story. Their father and mother were estranged, and the father took them under an assumed name onto the *Titanic*. After some time their mother was finally found, and she rushed to America for her boys. She'd no idea they'd been upon the fated ship.

When I read Archibald Gracie's book, I was overcome by the power of the description of the ice floe, written by Elizabeth Shutes, and included on page 259 of Gracie's book. I knew I had to include it in my story, and so it is quoted, word-for-word, in Olive's voice in the scene where the Carpathia is sighted. However, I can only take credit for placing her words in my story, not for writing them. The quote about the North Pole with no Santa was also taken from Gracie's book, page 250.

Charles takes Thomas Keaton's passport when he assumes his identity. There were passports in 1912. Some had photos on them, some didn't, and they were not always required for travel as they are today.

The story about August Wennerstrom (also known as August Edvard Andersson) was difficult for me to piece together. According to the information at http://home.mchsi.com/~dutcherp3/TITANIC.HTM (from the *South Bend Tribune* dated Sunday, April 19, 1998), Wennerstrom traveled under an assumed name because he was a political activist. The account is said to contain direct quotes from a little book where Wennerstrom had typed his story of the *Titanic* many years later, before his death.

Interestingly, the site which quotes his recollections does not include the Pålsson baby being pulled from his arms, but several other sites do. To create my character, I pieced together several accounts, never completely sure which was the most accurate. I composed or paraphrased what I found except for the following quote: "Cry, cry everywhere. Prayer and more prayer," which is said to have been typed by Wennerstrom in his personal account, which he gave to his family before his death.

The last discourse I gave to Wennerstrom, the one about no man helping you but yourself, was also said to have been a direct quote from Wennerstrom's typed account. I paraphrased it for the purpose of this story. What is particularly interesting to me relating to these thoughts, penned later in his life, is that some of the accounts say Wennerstrom was on the *Titanic* because he was fleeing his troubles as a political activist with socialist sympathies.

http://connections.smsd.org/titanic/andersson.htm;
http://home.mchsi.com/~dutcherp3/TITANIC.HTM
(from *The South Bend Tribune* dated Sunday, April 19, 1998)
http://books.google.com/books?id=ojBQ4QCU_SwC&pg
=PA54&lpg=PA54&dq=August+Edward+Wennerstrom&sou
rce=bl&ots=ME5R4F4j1m&sig=wm-
idVZhSiNUByH9FbsDlpTbe3M&hl=en&sa=X&ei=qmJmT9
DOMdClsAKJx9i2Dw&ved=0CD8Q6AEwBA#v=onepage&
q=August%20Edward%20Wennerstrom&f=false

I must also note that there are several accounts of how Alma Pålsson's husband was overcome with grief when the *Carpathia* docked, bringing with it the full realization that he'd lost all dear to him. It was said he grieved more loudly and publicly than anyone else.

John Harper was a preacher from London who traveled to speak at Moody Church Chicago. A widower, he traveled with his six-year-old daughter. You can read several newspaper articles and other historical documents about this here: http://www2.wheaton.edu/bgc/archives/docs/titanic.htm. In 1997 Moody Press released a book about him called, *The Titanic's Last Hero*. Several online sites tell the story I shared here. One is on YouTube: http://www.youtube.com/watch?v=uIMpXn1Q54U.

I really wanted to tell more of the experiences of steerage passengers, but found I couldn't do it and remain true to my story. One story I found particularly interesting was written about Margaret Murphey by her granddaughter and found on Jim's Titanic Website: http://www.keyflux.com/titanic/passdata.htm. There are several accounts, so if you want to know more, scroll down to her name.

If you'd like to hear more about *Titanic* history, you can visit Titanic Tuesdays on my blog at www.paulamoldenhauer.com.

Acknowledgements

From Paula:

This novel was birthed by two of us—filled with the joy and passion of creating with a best friend. Thank you, Kathy, for going for it! I laugh thinking about the times I said, "This is a great idea. I love this story!"

And how you rolled your eyes and replied, "How many times am I going to have to listen to you say that?"

Then there are all those hours you were lovin' the spreadsheet and getting the duckies in a row while I moaned, "Can we write *now?*" But the introduction of this seat-of-the-pantster into the world of those more organized was a good learning venture, and I believe my stories from here on out will have better form and structure because of it.

The best part, of course, was the hours we spent together doing two of the things we love best, hanging out with each other and creating. Your sweet, calm spirit and steady faith brings out the best in me, and my soul craves your playfulness. I'll sing show tunes with you any time. Thank you, my friend. Let's do it again.

Special thanks to the JOY Writers (Holly Armstrong, Deborah Besaw, Jill Hups, Kathy Kovach, Jeanne Leach, Donna Robinson, and Margie Vawter) for your invaluable critiques and insights. Learning together and stepping into publication together over the past many years has been quite a ride. I'm forever grateful.

This is my first published novel. Deep gratitude goes to Marlene Bagnull, director of the Colorado Christian Writers Conference and to my agent, Rachelle Gardner. Marlene, my Elsa, for ten years you called me into the new world of writing. Your passionate belief in me and your practical help kept me going through the fears, disappointments, and successes of this journey. Thank you for training me, loving me, and never letting me slip off the radar. Deep gratitude also goes to my agent and friend, Rachelle Gardner. You took me on five years ago when I struggled with discouragement and needed to know I could succeed. Thank you for keeping me as your client even when I took a break from seeking book publication. I am humbled by your steadfast loyalty and belief in me. Your sage advice (including input on this book), your ability to help me process the journey, and your joy in aiding in my success propel me forward. Here's to a long and productive relationship!

My dear Council of Kings (Deb Besaw, Jill Hups, Kathy Kovach, and Margie Vawter), we could have never done it without all the prayer and support. When the Lord called us together to pray, we had no idea the path we'd stepped upon. I love you always. May the way continue to part by His hand.

K. Rose, Kathleen Schaffer, and Megan DiMaria, you're cheerleaders and prayer partners, as well as beloved friends. Niki Nowell, you helped keep our table stocked in this season. We're forever grateful. Thanks also to all the gang on the ACFW prayer loop. You've held me together by your sacrifice of prayer for many years now. And to the other friends who offered love, prayers, blog posts, and Facebook statuses, each and every one of you are a part of this book. Many specific names come to mind, but I can't say them all here. You know who you are.

Lynnette Horner, I was sad when you moved on to a different critique group, missing the regular interaction of your friendship and valuable insight, but you're true blue to the end and your content reviews made this a better book. Thanks also, Margie Vawter, for lending your expertise to us through line edits and proofreading. Your skills and friendship are treasured. I'm still asking the Lord why you had to move away. It's wonderful when professionals are also friends. It makes the work so much sweeter.

Kim Liddiard—how many years has it been? Your friendship is precious, and it has been way cool how the Lord has interfaced your talents and mine as we both step further into our passions. The cover art is fantastic. And speaking of covers, where would it be without Mary Davis taking the shirt off her back (literally) and sharing it with our model? I couldn't think of more fitting models for the cover than my beloved neighbor, Bernice Garrett, whose generous care and faithful love has made her more like family than neighbor, and my own daughter, Sarah Moldenhauer, who not only has beautiful hands, but a beautiful heart. Love to all of you.

To the family: Thank you for cheering me on. Curtis and Anne—you always believe in me. Ken and Bonnie—countless meals came our way this last year as you offered not only loving relationship but tangible relief from my heavy schedule. Sarah, Seth, Stephen, and Sam, you've been on a demanding ride with a writer-mom. I know my hours grow long at the computer, and when I'm especially buried they grow too short in the kitchen, but you guys are awesome. You never stop supporting, praying, and cheering me on. You are the joy of life.

Jesus and Jerry ~ The two of you hold me together, believe in me when I can't believe for myself, and call forth from within me more than I knew was there. The best decision of my life was saying yes to Jesus as my Lord and Savior; the second best was saying yes to Jerry as my husband. I'm eternally grateful to both of you. Your love turns me upside down and inside out. I am undeserving, but You and you give unconditionally anyway. I pray I will love you both better every day.

I bow my heart before the God of the Universe and place it all in His hands.

From Kathleen:

My writing partner has already covered everyone I would have thanked except these:

Jesus ~ Thank you for helping me fulfill the desire of my heart in 2002 at the Colorado Christian Writers Conference. Your sheer joy over my accomplishment there is what gave me the courage to continue. I will always remember the words You joyfully spoke into my heart that day: "What are we going to write next?"

Paula ~ When we met almost a decade ago, I had no idea our souls would meld as they have. You're my prayer partner, my writing partner, and my partner in crime. Thank you for your beautiful grace that has taught me to always see the other side. When I'm with you, I often feel as if I'm in a prayer bubble.

ACFW ~ To American Christian Fiction Writers, and all the authors within this organization who have helped me hone my craft. I would not have attempted this project had it not been for the confidence I've received under your care.

Google ~ You don't often see an entity in the acknowledgements, but I had to express my thanks to you. Had it not been for your search engine, the contemporary portion of this story would not have been told with accuracy. I knew nothing of antiquities when I began my portion of this book. But you, my friend, were always there to lead me to the right site, urging me to open page after page of interesting material. You will never read this outpouring of my heart, but please know that I am very grateful to you.

Jim ~ For every book I publish, I always have a short, sweet dedication for you. This is largely due to the space allowed by the publisher. But here, I can pour my heart out as you so deserve. From the time we were nineteen-year-old kids standing at the altar, you pledged then to always believe in me. Thank you for your continued support in all of my serious, and not so serious, ventures. Never have you wavered, although you may have questioned my commitment a time or two when I broke down declaring that writing was too hard. But, because of your support, your love, and your patience, you have helped me fulfill my heart's desire to become an author. After this long dedication to you, I continue my tradition of the short, sweet dedication:

To Jim, who floats my boat.

Meet the Authors

Award-winning author Kathleen E. Kovach lives in northeast Colorado where she leads a critique group and is a member of American Christian Fiction Writers, serving as Rocky Mountain Zone Director. An award winning author of Christian romance, she presents spiritual truths with a giggle, proving herself as one of God's peculiar people.

Online presence:
www.KathleenEKovach.com
www.KathleenEKovach.blogspot.com
www.CraftCinema.blogspot.com
www.facebook.com/pages/Kathleen-E-Kovach/74835695268
Twitter: @KathleenEKovach

Author, speaker, and mom of four, Paula Moldenhauer has published over 300 times. Her first two novels release in 2012. She serves as the Colorado Coordinator for the American Christian Fiction Writers and homeschools. Paula loves peppermint ice cream and walking barefoot. Her greatest desire is to be close enough to Jesus to breathe His fragrance.

Online presence:
www.paulamoldenhauer.com
www.gracereign.blogspot.com
www.facebook.com/SoulScentsBreatheHisFragrance
www.facebook.com/PaulaMoldenhauerAuthor

Coming Fall 2012
Postmark: Christmas

Four Couples are Stamped with Love in Christmas, Florida

People from all around the country send their mail to Christmas, Florida, to receive a special Christmas postmark. Four couples linked by the post office find their Christmas holidays stamped for romance when wreath postmarks and manufactured snow turn the sultry southern town into a festive paradise.

Barbour Publishing, Inc.

Barbourbooks.com

You might also enjoy this Titanic story.

Titanic: Voyage of Intent
Mary Davis

Will trying to save her brother's life cost Brenna her own?

Brenna Kelly's brother has been accused of a murder he didn't commit and sentenced to die. Brenna follows the real murderer aboard the luxury liner Titanic to find the proof to save her brother from the gallows. Little does she know that her fate is as tenuous as her brother's.

Cliffton Statham is charmed by Brenna and sets out to help her and win her affections. But his flimsy relationship with his uncle puts his future in jeopardy, and he must decide between Brenna and saving himself. Can Brenna find the proof she needs in time? Will love be a help or a hindrance?

Will the icy waters of the Atlantic be the end of them all?

Available April 2012
http://marydavisbooks.com

CPSIA information can be obtained at www.ICGtesting.com
Printed in the USA
LVOW10s1541160915

454436LV00015B/814/P